"Jordan, stop being an interviewer for five minutes and just watch the northern lights."

He made mental notes, trying not to think of Nicole standing there in the close, intimate darkness, or the heated imprint of her body against his. A cool breeze across the park did little to dispel it.

Focus, he ordered silently. For example, he should ask why she and her partners had chosen Seattle when there was such an active fashion industry in Southern California. Hollywood was there, too. Since Moonlight Ventures was obviously interested in areas beyond modeling, they were a significant distance from some of the most lucrative markets to place their clients.

"You can't do it, can you?" Nicole asked. "I can practically feel the tension emanating from your body, as if the questions are charging through every cell."

Actually, it was hormones charging through his system. The questions as a journalist were the only things keeping him sane.

Dear Reader,

If you've read my book *At Wild Rose Cottage*, you may remember that the heroine had a sister, supermodel Nicole George. In the beginning I didn't plan to tell Nicole's story, but then she decided to take a big risk in changing her career to become a talent agent in partnership with her friends.

As the idea grew, Nicole's story became more and more irresistible to me. Besides, I moved her to Seattle, a beautiful city in which to spend time, whether for real or in a book. In Nicole's new home she soon runs into someone from her past, Jordan Masters, who isn't exactly a childhood friend—more a thorn in her side. I enjoyed spending time with Nicole and Jordan in Seattle, and hope you will, too.

I love hearing from readers and can be contacted at: c/o Harlequin Books, 225 Duncan Mill Road, Don Mills, ON M3B 3K9, Canada. Please also check out my Facebook page at Facebook.com/callie.endicott.author.

Best wishes,

Callie Endicott

CALLIE ENDICOTT

—

Moonlight Over Seattle

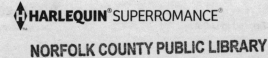

HARLEQUIN® SUPERROMANCE®

ISBN-13: 978-1-335-44909-2

Moonlight Over Seattle

Printed in U.S.A.

www.Harlequin.com

As a kid **Callie Endicott** had her nose stuck in a book so often it frequently got her in trouble. The trouble hasn't stopped—she keeps having to buy new bookshelves. Luckily ebooks don't take much space. Writing has been another help, since she's usually on the computer creating stories instead of buying them. Callie loves bringing characters to life and never knows what will prompt an idea. So she still travels, hikes, explores and pursues her other passions, knowing a novel may be just around the corner.

Books by Callie Endicott

HARLEQUIN SUPERROMANCE

Montana Skies

Kayla's Cowboy
At Wild Rose Cottage
The Rancher's Prospect

That Summer at the Shore
Until She Met Daniel

Other titles by this author available in ebook format.

For all the people who pursue their dreams, even when someone else calls those dreams impossible. The grandest things have happened when the impossible is turned into possible.

PROLOGUE

NICOLE GEORGE TURNED and lifted her arms, pushing up against the beach ball hanging from the boom. She tried to project the same energy she would have if she was actually playing a game in the sand rather than modeling a swimsuit.

A sense of déjà vu came over her.

How often had she done this? How often had a photographer's camera captured her image for a magazine or billboard? A pang hit her at the thought that this was one of her last days as a model. After all, she'd been modeling for thirty years. It was what she knew best.

Although there were a few tedious moments, inevitable in any career, she enjoyed her work. All the same, for the past six months she'd been turning down contracts and only had a few more commitments left. It was time to get started on the other things she wanted to do in her life. Besides, sooner or later, modeling jobs would become less plentiful and she liked the thought of leaving the business while she was at the top.

"Rachel, there's a shine on her collarbone," Logan called, and Nicole's friend, Rachel Clarion, stepped forward with a powder puff to dab it away.

Because she put so much energy into her job, Nicole always perspired when working, even when it was cold. Logan winked and she grinned at him. Another close friend, Logan Kensington was a great fashion photographer—one of the best in the business—and had his own way of keeping things light on the set.

"So," he said, "why did the chicken cross the road? Because she wanted to show the possum it could be done," he answered before Nicole could open her mouth. "Why did the punk rocker cross the road? Because he was stapled to a chicken."

Nicole groaned. "Those jokes weren't funny the first time someone told them, at least two generations ago."

"There you go again, suggesting I'm using dated material."

"Suggesting? I'm saying it outright."

Unfazed, Logan continued shooting. They hoped to finish photographing the summer clothing line that afternoon.

"It's time for you, Adam," Logan called finally. "I want to finish with the romantic shots."

Adam Wilding came over, dressed in what the designer hoped would be the hottest men's swimsuit of the coming year. With dark wavy hair, blue eyes and a firm chin, he looked like a dashing Irish buccaneer…or he would have if not for the swimsuit.

Trying to hurry, but not *look* as if they were hurrying, she and Adam posed together in different positions. Rain was predicted and summer wear didn't advertise well with storm clouds in the background.

"Okay," Logan finally called. "That ought to do it."

A family had stopped to watch and their adolescent son was staring at Nicole with wide eyes. His sister, on the other hand, seemed entranced by Adam, though she ran over to Nicole after he'd headed for the dressing trailer on the parking lot.

"Aren't you Nicole George?" the girl asked.

Nicole smiled and put on a terry robe. "Yes."

"Jeez. I've seen your picture, like, a gazillion times. Can I have your autograph?"

"I'd be happy to sign something for you." Nicole took the pen and postcard being held out. "What's your name?" she asked.

"Tamara."

To Tamara, Nicole wrote on the back. *Hope you have an amazing life! Nicole George.*

The teenager stared at the message in delight. "Awesome. Uh, I was, uh, wondering, is it hard to become a model?"

It was a common question from kids Tamara's age.

In the past two years, Nicole and three of her

friends had grown interested in becoming talent agents. So she studied Tamara the way she would a prospective client. The girl was pretty, had nice bone structure and her face was surrounded by a cloud of shiny brown hair.

"Some of being a model happens through persistence, but I'd say quite a bit of it is luck and timing," she said honestly.

Being an agent wasn't going to be easy—there were plenty of pretty girls with good bone structure and high hopes. You had to have the right look, at the right time, with the right people to make it happen. The question was whether *she* would be the right person to aid clients in reaching their potential. Sometimes she felt nervous about it; she took influencing people's lives seriously.

Tamara bit her lip. "How did you start?"

"I had parents in the fashion industry, which helped. I've been modeling since before I can remember."

"But do I have a chance? I could diet and color my hair. I could even get my nose fixed or do anything else that's needed."

This was an area in which Nicole had particularly strong opinions, something she planned to act on as an agent.

"You're healthy and attractive the way you

are," she answered firmly, but she had a feeling the kid wasn't listening.

"I'd do *anything* to look like you," Tamara breathed.

"Don't turn into a clone of someone else. Be yourself. There's nothing better than that."

"But I bet guys just look at you and fall in love."

Sure, Nicole thought to herself, *they look at me and fall in love, but they just want the surface.* Through bitter experience she'd learned that too many men saw only the image on the magazine cover…the fantasy. Either that, or they couldn't handle the notoriety that came from being involved with a supermodel. She'd believed her ex-fiancé, Paulo, was different. Instead, he'd wanted perfection—the ultimate trophy wife. Paulo was a nice person and had loved her in his own way, but that hadn't been enough for her.

Adam's voice intruded. "Nicole, are you coming?"

"On my way," she called back. "Bye, Tamara. I hope this helps. Sorry I have to go now, but I'm freezing. Good luck with whatever career you choose." Turning, she swiftly walked to the dressing trailer.

She was shivering harder now, despite the terry robe, and it was a relief to put on jeans, a T-shirt and jacket.

"See you later," she called to Rachel as she ran to her car. They were all having dinner together and she wanted a hot shower first.

The warm water felt wonderful after a cold day in skimpy swimsuits and shorts, yet a part of her mind was preoccupied with what Tamara had said, *I bet guys just look at you and fall in love.* Nicole hadn't wanted to get into a discussion about the difference between love and lust with a teenager, but it was something she'd learned the hard way.

It might be different if she'd ever gotten involved with Logan or Adam—they were terrific guys—but they'd remained friends, not lovers. And after multiple broken hearts and betrayals from men more interested in hitching a ride with a well-known face than genuine love, she'd decided friendship was far more satisfying.

Nicole dressed quickly and in less than an hour, rang Rachel's bell.

"Hey," Rachel greeted her at the door. "Adam and Logan are already here. Hope you're hungry."

"I'm starved. I know you said not to bring anything, but I ordered a super-sized pizza to be delivered."

Rachel staggered backward and clasped a hand over her heart. "Pizza? That's treason." She laughed.

"Just call me Benedict Pepperoni."

"You never gain weight, anyhow. But what

about the healthy glow that fruits and vegetables are supposed to provide? 'The camera can tell you eat crap,'" she said haughtily, quoting one of the fussier photographers they'd worked with.

Nicole shook her head. "I've only got a few more jobs left, so I'm not worried about it."

"Then you're serious about quitting."

"If I'm going to make a change, I have to actually do it."

Rachel whistled. "The press will claim it's a play for more money."

"They'll print whatever they want, no matter what I tell them." Nicole knew she sounded cynical, but didn't care. She'd run out of patience with reporters a long time ago. When they didn't get the story they wanted, some of them just invented one they liked better.

"Don't I know it," Rachel muttered.

Nicole squeezed her arm in sympathy. Rachel had started in the modeling business in her early teens and become a star, only to have her career end after a terrible accident on a modeling set. The scars left from it weren't disfiguring, but they were enough to put her out of demand by advertisers who generally preferred their own version of flawless. Now she handled makeup on shoots and seemed happy enough, but once in a while the so-called journalists dug the story out again, usually when there was a scandal surrounding her ex-husband.

"How do your parents feel about your plans?"

Nicole rolled her eyes. "I haven't told them. They think I'm taking a vacation to find a husband."

"Seriously?"

"*Yes.* I tried to soften the news by saying I wanted a normal life. But I made a mistake in talking about it at my older sister Emily's wedding in Montana."

"At least you enjoyed meeting Emily's husband and his family."

"Very much. Trent is a good guy and the whole thing was beautiful and romantic. Em positively glowed. Anyhow, Mom and Dad assumed that's what I wanted when I talked about having a more normal life. I didn't tell them I'd been turning down contracts *before* that. They feel if I must get married, it's easier to find someone suitable while I'm working. And by 'suitable,' they mean a husband who won't interfere with my career."

"I suppose you could have chosen a better moment than the wedding to make your announcement. Especially since you'd just broken things off with Paulo."

"That's for sure." With a not-so-humorous laugh, Nicole followed Rachel out to the balcony where Logan and Adam were kicking back in chaises.

"Nicole just confirmed she's taking an extremely *long* vacation from modeling," Rachel announced.

"I have only two more contracts left to fulfill."

Logan sat forward, his eyes intent. "That makes my announcement even more interesting." There was a pause while he waited for everyone to focus on him. "I've been putting out feelers and got a call yesterday—Moonlight Ventures in the Seattle area is going up for sale. Kevin McClaskey will give us first crack at buying the agency."

Nicole caught her breath. They'd talked about finding a small talent agency to purchase and develop. All of them had benefited from people who'd helped them and they wanted to do the same for others.

And Moonlight Ventures? The agency had a great reputation. They were especially familiar with it because Kevin had once managed Rachel's career, and Logan had worked with the McClaskeys several times while arranging photo shoots. Moonlight Ventures was small since Kevin and his late wife had wanted to keep it that way, but with four of them, they could expand.

"Is it in the same building?" Rachel asked.

"Yep and the building goes with the purchase. There are solid renters in the space the agency doesn't use, so that will provide some maintenance income."

"But increases the price."

"Not outrageously, and I think it's worth the investment. But there's a wrinkle," Logan said. "With the loss of his wife last year, Kevin has decided he wants to sell almost immediately and retire." He looked at Nicole intently. "You're the only one who'd be free to run it until the rest of us can join you."

Nerves sent Nicole's stomach roiling. It was one thing to talk of buying a talent agency and working on it together, and another to know everything would depend on her, at least temporarily. Sure, she'd researched and knew the job in theory, but there was a gap between knowledge and reality.

"What do you think?" Adam asked. "Could you grab the ball and run with it until we can get up there?"

Nicole took a deep breath and nodded. She'd always thought she loved a challenge; now she would find out if she'd been lying to herself.

CHAPTER ONE

NICOLE GLARED AT her living room wall and let out a shriek of frustration.

Toby, a young beagle recently adopted from a rescue center, yipped in concern. Since the front door stood open to let in fresh air, she'd tied his long leash to one of the few chairs in the room.

"Don't worry, boy," she said soothingly.

But she made a face at the wall that *still* glowed green through the two coats of paint. She couldn't understand why the brilliant shade hadn't been eradicated by now.

"Is everything all right?" a voice called. A man stood at the open door. He wore faded jeans and a sweatshirt with Harvard printed on the front. A scruffy beard and mustache covered the lower half of his face. *Harvard Guy*, she mentally tagged him.

"What do you mean?"

Toby trotted over to lean against her leg, straining at the leash. He'd already grown quite attached and affectionate and even let out a small growl of warning.

"I heard someone yelling," said the man, "but maybe it was somebody else."

Nicole winced. "It was me, releasing my frustration. I didn't know anyone else was around."

The concern faded from Harvard Guy's face. He seemed vaguely familiar, but she couldn't place him at the moment.

"What's wrong?" he asked.

"Nothing serious, but I've painted twice and can still see the original green."

"Oh." He gazed at the wall. "That's strange. A primer usually takes care of color bleed-through."

"Primer?"

His eyes widened and Nicole got the impression he thought she was dense. "Yeah. It's a special first coat used as a sealant."

"I'm using what the clerk at the store recommended." She gestured to a stack of paint cans.

Harvard Guy went over and picked up one of the cans and studied it. "Some paint has primer included, but not this one."

Nicole sighed. Maybe the clerk had assumed she already knew about primer. He *had* been busy, with a long line of customers.

"I didn't know—I've never tried this before." Painting was hard work and the remaining green glow meant she had to start all over again. Maybe that was why her parents had always hired someone to do painting at their house, which had left her completely ignorant about the process.

"Really?"

What looked like condescension showed on Harvard Guy's face, and the sense of familiarity increased.

"The condo I used to own came freshly painted, so it never came up. Anyhow, it was nice of you to check that I was okay."

"Happy to help, or at least try to."

"Obviously I'm new here, but from what I've seen, that's what this neighborhood is like," Nicole said. "Lots of vintage architecture and friendly residents." She'd met the elementary school teacher who lived next door, and he'd told her about a neighborhood barbecue coming up in a couple of months. A businesswoman two houses over had brought a casserole, and a nurse further down the street had delivered a bouquet of flowers from her own garden.

"You like old homes?"

She nodded. "The Arts and Crafts era is my favorite. This house only mimics the style, but it's just as well. While I love American Craftsman architecture, I prefer modern kitchens and bathrooms."

Harvard Guy's eyebrows rose and the sensation that she knew him hit her again. Maybe if he wasn't backlighted by the sun coming through the door and windows, it would be easier to say for certain. The "have we ever met before" or "you seem really familiar" comment felt like a cliché… Just as she decided to ask anyway, he spoke again.

"Some critics think Arts and Crafts architecture is passé."

Nicole narrowed her eyes; he hadn't insulted her tastes, but was treading close to it. "I'm not bound by the opinions of other people," she returned calmly.

"Fair enough." His cell phone rang. "Sorry, I'm expecting a family call." He hurried outside.

After releasing Toby from his leash so he was free to use his dog door into the fenced yard, Nicole grabbed her purse and an empty can of paint, then headed out herself. Harvard Guy was on the front walkway, talking urgently on his phone. It looked as if it might be a long conversation.

She'd parked on the driveway and he looked at her as she walked to the car. She pointed at the paint can, figuring he'd realize she was going to the store.

"Thanks," she mouthed. He seemed distracted, but made a gesture of acknowledgment.

When she glanced in the rearview mirror, Harvard Guy was still on his phone and the face above his beard was carved in tense, sharp lines. She realized she hadn't even gotten his name. But if he lived in the area, she would probably run across him again.

Nostalgia had played a big part in her decision to purchase the house. The Seattle-area neighborhood reminded her of the one where she'd grown up in Southern California—friendly for the most part, with everyone looking out for each other. Not that her family had been home much, particularly after her modeling career had really taken off.

The thought led to remembering again how upset her mother and father had been that she'd quit modeling. You would have thought she was betraying them in some hideous, underhanded way. *We handed you a fabulous career and you're turning your back on it*, her mother had wailed.

Jeez, why couldn't they just want grandchildren like other people? She supposed they were counting on her older sister for that. As a matter of fact, Emily was already pregnant and expecting her first baby.

Patience, Nicole reminded herself. She didn't have any reason to feel guilty and her parents were starting to come around, anyhow. They were even making recommendations for the agency, though mostly she'd thanked them and ignored their advice. They simply didn't understand how she and her friends wanted to run Moonlight Ventures. Nicole just hoped she *was* doing it right. She had regular conference calls with her three partners, and they flew in to help out whenever possible—like Adam had the past few days—but implementation was mostly up to her. And that included working with a reporter over the next several weeks for some magazine articles.

Her phone rang; it was Ashley Vanders, one of the agency's longtime clients.

"Hi, Ashley," she said, pulling over to the side of the road. She could have talked while driving, but preferred to focus on what she was discussing. Still, she wasn't concentrating as much as she would have liked, because Harvard Guy's face kept intruding.

Was it the strange sense of familiarity, or the tingle of awareness he'd evoked?

JORDAN MASTERS RETURNED to his condo. It was an ironic twist that he lived relatively close to Nicole's new home. In fact, he commonly used the nearby fitness trail. The area was popular with new residents in the Seattle area. An old high school pal had moved there, even before Jordan had.

If only he could have managed a more productive first encounter with Nicole. He'd driven over to make a casual contact, to get reacquainted… and lay the groundwork for the articles he was writing for *PostModern* magazine. He wasn't sure how Nicole was going to react since Sydnie Winslow had arranged the interviews with Nicole *before* asking him to do them.

Jordan cursed mentally.

As editor in chief, Syd had turned *PostMod-*

ern into one of the trendiest publications on the market. They were old friends and she'd begged him to do the articles, saying it was ideal since he also lived in Seattle. She'd figured he would have an "in" with Nicole because they'd grown up on the same block in Southern California. Syd was wrong, but after everything they'd been through together in the early days of his career, he hadn't tried too hard to get out of it.

But that didn't stop him from wishing he could forget the whole thing and head down to his boat. A sail on Lake Washington would be wonderful. Having the boat was a luxury, but his columns were syndicated in over twelve hundred publications around the world, so he could afford it. Other than traveling and his condo in Hawaii, it was his only serious indulgence.

His notebook was full of subjects he wanted to write about. He commented on everything from food to politics, religion, relationships and animals. Nothing was out-of-bounds. He'd worked his way up through various newspapers and magazines to become a columnist, but he still felt fortunate to have reached the level where he had the freedom to write about what interested him.

Jordan stared at his computer as if it was the source of his problems. He didn't *care* if a supermodel dropped out of the fashion scene for a while. Nicole had done it before, whether as a ploy for more money or a publicity stunt, he didn't know. Either way, he hadn't paid attention—in fact, he wouldn't have been aware of her absence or reappearance at all if his mother hadn't gone on and on about how you couldn't expect anything better from Paula George's daughter.

His mouth tightened.

Too bad Mom hadn't decided she disliked the George family when he was a small kid, instead of later. Then he wouldn't have gotten hog-tied into doing stuff for "precious" Nicole so often. Lord, everyone had been expected to pamper the little princess as if she was made of spun glass. When she was home, that is. Luckily she'd been gone half the time on modeling assignments.

Still, the past was the past.

Restless, Jordan dropped to the floor and did a dozen pushups, unable to stop thinking about Nicole now that his past was colliding with his present.

After a lazy month in Fiji he was sporting a beard, and they hadn't seen each other since they were teens, so it wasn't any wonder she hadn't recognized him. Syd had suggested he refrain from shaving and see how Nicole responded to a stranger in a casual encounter—would she be pleasant or off-putting? He'd been curious as well, which had kept him from introducing himself immediately, though he hadn't planned to take it very far.

His cell phone rang again and he pulled it out,

hoping it was from his sister, Chelsea. She'd been in her boyfriend's car when it got broadsided. Her injuries weren't severe, but he was still concerned.

The number on the display belonged to his editor. He answered, figuring he'd get off quickly if another call came in.

"Hey, Syd," he said in a dry tone. "What a surprise, you're checking on my progress."

"Don't be a paranoid drama queen."

Jordan chuckled. Syd was a beautiful woman who'd stormed her way to the top of the magazine publishing world. She was tough as nails and more than one man had mentioned being hot for her in one breath and wishing he "had her balls" with the next.

"All right, but don't try to micromanage me. It won't work," he advised. "What do you want?"

"Have you seen Nicole George yet?"

"Yes, briefly. She was screaming, so I rushed in to see if there was an emergency."

And practically got knocked on my ass by how gorgeous she is, he added silently. It didn't make sense that he'd reacted to Nicole that way. She'd been a thorn in his side when they were kids, and he had rarely thought about her since, even when seeing her photo on various advertisements.

"Screaming?" Syd repeated.

Jordan shook himself. "At her living room wall. She didn't know that primer is necessary to keep paint colors from coming through. What kind of person doesn't know about using a primer?"

"The kind you're talking to right now," Syd returned crisply. "Apparently my husband doesn't know, either, which must be why we can't get rid of the spectral purple in our bedroom. He's on a DIY kick that's driving me crazy. Listen, you promised to do this with an open mind, Jordan."

Clearly his diplomatic skills were rusty. "Of course I'll be open-minded."

She snorted. "Maybe I should have listened when you told me you might not be the best choice, but having you in the area was too great an opportunity. Did Nicole recognize you?"

"Uh, no. But even without the beard, it's been almost fourteen years since the last time we met," he said. "Until I shave, my own sisters could probably pass me on the street without realizing I'm their brother, and Nicole sure didn't expect to see me at her front door."

"Okay. What did Ms. George say when you explained who you are beneath the Grizzly Adams impersonation?"

"I didn't have a chance to introduce myself," Jordan admitted. "I got a phone call and she hurried out, presumably to get more paint. I'll shave before my appointment with her on Monday. It was great to let it go in Fiji, but not here."

"Actually, I think it's an improvement. Sexy,

in a beach bum sort of way. Be sure to have fun with your childhood pal."

"Hardly a pal," Jordan growled. "And, by the way, don't keep calling me. It messes with my tempo."

"You don't *have* a tempo. Sometimes I'm not even sure you have a pulse. But don't worry, I've got better things to do than yank your chain."

Typically, Syd hung up without a goodbye.

Jordan picked up his laptop and tried to focus on his writing. But his mind kept returning to the rush of attraction he'd felt when seeing Nicole that afternoon… something he was determined to ignore.

NICOLE'S CONVERSATION WITH Ashley Vanders finally ended. Ashley always wanted to talk longer, but Nicole was trying to wean the young woman from needing to be coddled by the agency. That had been how Kevin McClaskey had treated his clients when he'd owned Moonlight Ventures.

Rachel had warned them about Kevin's management style before they bought the agency. She'd loved him and his wife dearly, but had wondered if their constant handholding kept her from being as independent as she should have been.

With a sigh, Nicole started her car again and drove on, reminding herself that every job had its drawbacks. And while Ashley was a challenge, she'd just gotten a contract as the "face" of a huge car dealership chain. It was a three-year deal and maybe she wouldn't want as much attention once she settled down and started seeing herself on TV.

For her first two months in Seattle Nicole had worked closely with Kevin McClaskey, and he still came around a lot. It was okay. His old clients missed him and he had volumes of knowledge about the talent business. She sometimes wondered if he regretted selling, but suspected his visits to the agency and other tenants in the building were primarily because he needed company with his wife gone.

Nicole turned into the hardware store parking lot. There was a woman at the paint counter with "Jo Beth" on her name tag. "Can I help you?" she asked, gazing at Nicole attentively.

"I'm told primer is an excellent idea when you're covering bold colors," Nicole said. "I suppose I didn't ask the right questions when I was here before." She held up the paint can. "I also need more of this to go over the primer."

The clerk efficiently put together what was needed, gave her a discount and loaded everything into Nicole's trunk.

"Ask for me whenever you come in." Jo Beth handed her a business card.

Nicole drove home and trotted the cans of paint and primer into the living room. She looked at Toby who'd dashed in to see her. "Okay," she announced, "we're trying this again."

The beagle seemed to whine a protest.

She reached down and petted the dog. "I know, buddy, you're bored watching me paint. Maybe we could work in the garden for a while instead."

Toby loved the backyard, but preferred having her out there with him. Perhaps it was from being a rescue dog—the trauma of having been abandoned on the Seattle docks must linger.

Grabbing a shovel, she went out to where a fence divided the yard. Before moving in she'd had the deck installed and the front section landscaped, leaving space for fruit trees and a vegetable plot in the undeveloped area at the end of the double lot. She'd discovered that digging was therapeutic.

Her original plan had been to buy a loft in downtown Seattle. In the interim she'd sold her condo down south, furniture included, and rented a studio while she searched for something permanent. But after deciding to adopt a dog she'd known having a yard would be best, and the whole thing had escalated. As soon as she'd walked into this place, it had felt like home.

Toby lay nearby, drowsing in the sunshine. Nicole figured he liked the outdoors so much because of having been cooped up for months waiting for adoption. He was a sweet animal, barely out of the puppy stage, and loved being able to go in and out through the doggy door whenever he wanted to sniff around the huge fenced yard, or needed to do his business.

The purchase of the talent agency had gone as smoothly as her house purchase. With four of them sharing the investment, no one would be in trouble, financially at least, if Moonlight Ventures fell apart. But they were anxious to make it a success for other reasons, which was why she'd agreed to work with a reporter from *PostModern* magazine. They all respected the publication, and the editor had told her the articles would be an unbiased look at how a supermodel was transitioning into a serious businesswoman.

Nicole sighed. She didn't want to be the story, and she was no crazier about reporters now than she'd ever been, but the publicity would be good for the agency.

AFTER AN HOUR of yard work, Nicole went back inside, Toby at her heels, and contemplated the living room.

She wasn't ready to start painting again.

"Want to go for a run?" she asked Toby encouragingly.

He'd promptly curled up on the floor for another nap. At the sound of her voice he opened his eyes briefly, then closed them again. So far running wasn't his thing; he needed time to build his stamina after living in a kennel. A brisk walk was okay—brisk for his short legs, that is—but right now she needed to stretch her muscles in a way that working in the yard hadn't accomplished.

After rubbing Toby's soft ears she donned her running clothes and headed for the park. Then she saw Harvard Guy again. She instantly turned onto a side path.

Strange how familiar he seemed. There was something about his eyes that reminded her of…

Holy Cow.

Nicole stumbled and righted herself before she went down. Harvard Guy was Jordie Masters.

Jordan, she reminded herself. As a bratty neighborhood kid he'd been known as Jordie, then in high school he'd insisted on being called Jordan. Now he was a popular newspaper columnist. He'd changed *a lot*. She'd had no idea he lived in the Seattle area and knew there wasn't any way he could have been at her house by accident. Nicole got a sinking feeling that he was the reporter doing the articles for *PostModern*.

Though she'd avoided Jordan whenever possible as a kid, she had a few vivid memories, such as when she was seven and wanted to learn how to skate. She'd put on her sister's roller blades and started down the block, doing pretty well until Jordie had run into her. Nicole had always suspected it was deliberate. At the very least, he'd thought it was hilarious.

The resulting black eye had caused panic because she was supposed to model fancy dresses at a fashion show that weekend. They'd switched her to active wear and everyone had thought the black eye was makeup. The buyers had loved it. But after that, she wasn't allowed to skate or bike or do anything active besides working out. Her parents had only agreed to let her take up running because it was good for her figure.

Fuming, Nicole continued her run. A black eye twenty-three years ago was unimportant, as were the other clashes they'd had as kids.

What concerned her were the articles.

Once friends, their mothers now hated each other, and except for one evening when they were in high school, Jordan had always acted as if he despised her. Obviously that was a long time ago and he might have put her out of his mind the way she'd done with him. But his columns were based on his observations and opinions and loaded with his dry wit, so the question was whether he'd changed enough to be impartial.

She shook her head, not wanting to think about it. At the moment she needed to release her tension, and she wasn't going to let his presence in the park keep her from doing so.

Drat. There he was again, heading toward her. Determined not to let him put her on the defensive, she stepped onto a wide part of the path to let him pass. He stopped as well.

"Hi, Jordan," she said coolly. "Cute trick, but the beard only fooled me for a while."

"I wasn't trying to trick you."

"If you say so."

He shrugged. "I'd come over to say hello since I'm doing the articles for *PostModern*."

"I figured you were the one when I recognized you, but I thought you were a newspaper columnist, not a magazine writer."

"The editor is a friend. She knows we grew up together and since I live up here, too, she asked me to do it."

Nicole tried to remember if she'd ever heard where Jordan was living. She'd periodically read his columns and recalled that one of them had raved about tropical climes. If there had been any other indication about his home base, the information hadn't stuck.

"Why didn't you introduce yourself earlier, when it was obvious that I didn't recognize you right off?" she asked.

"I planned to, but I got that phone call and you left for the hardware store."

"Hmm." Nicole narrowed her eyes.

It was possible it had been a simple slip-up in communication. She'd been distracted by the paint and hadn't wanted to delay getting what she needed. Since Adam was in town helping with the agency for only a few days, she'd have less free time to work on the house after he was gone.

"Okay," she said, deciding not to get into an argument…at the moment.

Nicole cocked her head and studied Jordan. It was hard to say how much he looked like the boy she remembered. In high school he'd had a military-style haircut, but now his dark brown hair was longish. The beard he wore was scruffy, rather than neat and trimmed. His Harvard sweatshirt was gone, and except for high-quality athletic shoes, his running clothes were on the worn side. For the most part he'd fit in with the guys who stood on a street corner with a sign, asking for money.

Or maybe not.

His muscled physique nicely filled out the faded black T-shirt he wore, reminding her of a night in high school she'd rather forget.

"Why the starving artist imitation?" she asked, brushing her own cheek instead of pointing to his beard. "You look like Leonardo DiCaprio in that movie, *The Revenant*."

"I just got back from a month in Fiji."

"What was the story down there?"

"None. I can write my column from anywhere in the world. For the last month, it was Fiji."

"Nice work if you can get it," she quipped. Jordan's eyes were the same brooding brown they'd always been. Darn it.

"I've been lucky, same as you."

"Well, I didn't get to choose which countries I visited. I mostly worked hard once I got there, before moving on to the next location."

His wry, almost patronizing smile revealed his true feelings. Okay, maybe she was over-reading, but he probably agreed with the people who thought modeling was a breeze and life for a model was one long air-brushed idyll. The general belief seemed to be that someone with her level of modeling success couldn't have any problems; therefore, they should just keep quiet, forgo their privacy, live the way the world thought they should live, and remember they were the lucky ones.

She *was* lucky, but life wasn't always that simple. Someone smiling from an airbrushed photograph could be concealing a broken heart or other problems. Money and fame weren't guarantees of happiness.

Curiously, she was disappointed to discover Jordan was the same as so many other people with gross misconceptions about her "ideal" life. But then, his childhood had been turbulent—the epic battles between his parents had been legendary in the neighborhood. Maybe he needed to believe there was a world where everything was as perfect as the way it looked on a magazine cover.

"How about dinner tonight?" Jordan suggested.

"Sorry, but I need to get on with my painting project." Nicole kept her tone polite and impersonal, the way she always tried to sound with the press.

Still, she needed to remember that Jordan

wasn't one of the paparazzi-enemies of earlier years, the ones who'd invented a wild, party-girl history for her. Nor was he a friend. For the time being, he was simply a man writing about her and Moonlight Ventures. That it probably wouldn't be the open-minded piece she and her partners had been promised was a concern, but there was no need to start out with knee-jerk reactions.

"How about tomorrow night?" he asked.

"I've got plans."

"In that case I'll try another time," he told her smoothly and started up the path.

Refusing to watch him leave, Nicole continued her run. She hadn't seen Jordan since high school and had thought little about him through the years. But if anyone had asked, she would have said he *must* have improved—after all, being a jackass wasn't an incurable condition, was it? It appeared the jury was still out on that question.

One thing was for sure, he was as good-looking as ever, even with the beard. It was embarrassing to recall her brief crush on him when she was sixteen. The whole thing had started at a party when he'd kissed her on a moonlit patio. At first she'd been curious—as a senior he'd had *quite* a reputation with girls and she wanted to understand what all the fuss was about—then she'd realized how great his lips felt. Snuggling closer, she'd kissed him back wholeheartedly.

No one inside the house had known, probably

because most of the kids had been drinking. Her folks had shown up soon after, terrified she was going to spoil the "clean teen" image that had helped make her so popular. Besides, her mother had declared angrily, alcohol was fattening.

For the next several weeks, while on location in Hawaii for a modeling gig, Nicole had lived that kiss over and over again in her imagination. The days had crawled by as she'd anxiously waited to see Jordan again. But when she got home, he'd treated her with the same scorn as always.

Her crush had abruptly ended with the realization that he'd probably been too drunk to know which girl he had kissed. Nicole hadn't blamed him; *she'd* been the idiot with no better sense than to let a single kiss make her forget the way he had always behaved toward her.

Still, that was the past. The question was... what was he like as a reporter today?

CHAPTER TWO

JORDAN RETURNED TO his condo and showered, scrubbing off the sweat from his run. He'd gone several extra miles, trying to tire himself so that he could sleep on West Coast time, instead of Fiji's clock. Changing time zones could be a challenge, especially for a chronic insomniac.

His encounters with Nicole wouldn't make sleep easier, especially if he couldn't erase the image of her on the fitness trail from his mind. Her heightened breathing had drawn attention to the spectacular figure beneath her close-fitting T-shirt. He'd been glad that his sweatpants were fairly loose, and annoyed that it had become an issue for him.

It wasn't as if he'd been starved for feminine companionship. Most recently he'd enjoyed the company of an attractive and intelligent woman in Fiji, who had simply wanted a vacation fling.

Stepping out, he wiped the fog from the mirror and scrutinized his beard. In Fiji, he hadn't paid attention to his appearance. It was a great place to practice just being alive, and he had been tempted to stay another month. But it was just as well that he was home again. If he'd continued drifting in tropical-beach mode, his writing might have suffered. His readers didn't mind the occasional column about food or interesting parts of the world, but most of the time they expected a sharp edge to his writing.

Amazing how much hair could grow in a few weeks. It took a while to shave, then he showered again to wash away the last prickly bits.

After dressing he felt more like himself and sat down with his computer. Syd had sent him a ton of material. He didn't mind research, he just wasn't interested in the notes about Nicole. Still, he'd agreed to do the articles and would make good on his promise.

One of Nicole's last jobs had been modeling swimsuits and other sportswear, and she'd also done a top designer's wedding collection. Her absence from the modeling scene hadn't been immediately noticed because the fashion world tended to work ahead of itself, so after Nicole had dropped out a few months ago, magazine covers and ads with her image had continued to appear for a while. They still were, for that matter.

According to the research material, the Moonlight Ventures talent agency had been purchased around the time of Nicole's last job, and the buyers had been Nicole, Adam Wilding, Rachel Clarion and Logan Kensington. All were connected to the fashion world and were supposedly close friends. Though Nicole was the only one on the Seattle scene full time, there were reports that the others would eventually join her.

Jordan immediately started wondering if egos might get in the way of running the agency. It seemed possible.

There was an interesting entry from the researcher that Nicole's decision to "retire" had apparently come shortly after attending her sister's wedding to a Montana building contractor. Jordan had liked Emily George, who'd been in a number of his classes. She'd been nice, funny and smart. Even as a kid it hadn't seemed right to him the way her parents focused their energy and attention on Nicole, leaving Emily on the periphery.

In the notebook he kept for possible ideas to explore in his newspaper columns, he wrote a suggestion—*parental favoritism, long-term effects*?

After reading for an hour, he closed the computer, got up and stretched. His muscles were tense despite the run. It wasn't the articles ramping up the stress; he was worried about his sister. While Chelsea hadn't been seriously injured in the car accident, the whole thing was mixed up with her skunk of a boyfriend. The other driver had been at fault, but it had complicated her breakup with Ron.

His other sister, Terri, was trying to convince Chelsea to fly up to Seattle from Los Angeles for a visit. Jordan had already gotten her a ticket, hoping she'd decide to come.

In the meantime, he had a job to do. Jumping to his feet, he grinned. Maybe Nicole could use some help painting the interior of her house.

WHEN THE DOORBELL rang Nicole thought it was her pizza being delivered. And it was, except a clean-shaven Jordan was holding the box as the delivery guy walked back to his car.

He'd looked good with the beard, but without it he was strikingly handsome.

"Hello," she said, taking the box. "You probably cost that pizza joint any future business from me. A delivery person shouldn't just hand a pizza to a stranger on the street."

"Aren't you being harsh?" Jordan protested.

"No. You aren't a woman who needs to feel secure about food being delivered to her door. And the person making the delivery. Ask your sisters how they'd feel in the same situation."

He frowned. "I never thought of it that way. I offered the guy a good tip, but for all he knew, I was a stalker or something."

"Exactly."

"I apologize. Look, I didn't know you'd ordered a pizza, so I got takeout on the way over. How about a potluck dinner?"

"I told you I was painting."

"But you're obviously stopping to eat, and I

came set to help." He held up a new paint roller with one hand and a large bag with the other.

Nicole eyed him. Even as a kid, Jordan could always find an angle to work. The high school science teacher had thought he'd make an innovative researcher because of it. The soccer coach had proclaimed him the next star because he was so clever and agile. Everyone had liked Jordan, saying he'd be great, whatever he decided to do.

They hadn't said the same thing about her. The assumption had been that she would use her appearance to make money until she married rich or something. Perhaps she'd been too sensitive about it, but that was the impression everyone had given.

Lord. What was that line from the *Jane Austen Book Club* movie…about high school never being over? Nicole didn't believe it had to be that way, but it was a challenge not to remember adolescent growing pains when one of the ghosts of high school past was writing about her current life.

"How about it?" Jordan coaxed.

"For serious labor, okay," she agreed, deciding it was time to exorcise this *particular* ghost, once and for all.

"I'm here until it's done," he promised.

"Or until I throw you out," she corrected him.

"Okay."

Nicole led the way to her breakfast bar and Jordan glanced around. "You weren't kidding about liking modern kitchens. This one is top-notch. Are you interested in cooking?"

"I've never had much time for it, but I'll do more once my schedule isn't as crazy. You know kitchens?" she asked.

He put the take-out bag on the counter next to the pizza. "I enjoy cooking, especially the dishes I've encountered on my travels."

"That's right, I saw your column about the subtleties of Thai and Indian curry."

"You read my work?"

"Occasionally. I don't look for it, but I don't avoid it, either," she said truthfully. From what she'd read, she had concluded Jordan's columns were often cynical, yet could also be sharp observations on society and the world, and occasionally funny. At least his humor was no longer cruel.

"Hey." Jordan waved a hand in front of her. "Where did you go?"

"To the land of mean jokes."

"I didn't tell one."

"You used to, especially your senior year." She knew because she'd been one of his targets.

"I was a teenaged boy. That isn't an excuse, but..." Jordan stopped and a shadow seemed to crowd his eyes. "I was angry because of my parents' divorce and taking it out on every person available. I'm not proud of the memory. Now I dislike gags that laugh at people instead of with them."

He seemed sincere and Nicole decided to take him at his word. Lots of kids were rotten during high school, and, hopefully, most of them got over it.

She pulled out paper plates and found plastic silverware. "My apologies for the inelegant dinnerware. My kitchen stuff is still in boxes. I only moved in a few weeks ago."

The food he'd brought was from the local Chinese restaurant and Nicole ate quickly, enjoying the Szechuan dishes alongside the vegetarian pizza she'd ordered.

"I'll leave you to finish eating," she said. "I want to get going with the painting."

Jordan joined her in the living room a few minutes later and crouched briefly in front of Toby, ruffling his ears. "Hey, girl. How are you doing?"

"*He's* fine," Nicole corrected. "His name is Toby."

"Oh. I didn't mean to offend you, Toby."

With both of them working, the primer went on quickly, and it dried while they did the dining room. But once the top coat was on all the walls, Nicole stared in disgust. It was streaky and she wondered how the professionals got it to look good.

"I thought it would be better than this," she muttered, "but at least it isn't green any longer."

"It should be okay once it's dried overnight. What made you decide to do your own painting?" Jordan asked.

"Is there something wrong with wanting to handle it myself?"

"No, but it seems unusual. For you, that is."

"Why *me*?"

He snorted. "Come on, Nicole, don't pretend you don't understand what I mean."

"I'm not a model any longer. Can't I do normal things the same as any other person?"

His lips twisted. "Oh, that's right, poor Nicole couldn't live a real life because of her supermodel status. I've seen the pictures and I'm sure the whole world feels bad for you, going to all those parties and enjoying the international first-class travel."

THE MINUTE THE words left his mouth, Jordan knew he'd crossed the line.

Nicole straightened and sent him an icy stare. *"What?"*

"I shouldn't have said that," he told her hastily. "It was inappropriate."

She planted her hands on her hips and he couldn't help noticing how the movement drew attention to her slim waist.

"But you opened your big mouth, anyway," she

retorted. "So, you think it's ridiculous for me to want a regular life. Maybe you think I don't even have a right to normalcy. But, for your information, those parties were invented by the paparazzi, along with various photos that made it look as if I was in the middle of an orgy. I sued and it was proven that those pictures were faked."

There was a smudge of paint on her cheek and a few strands of her gold-spun hair were stiff with primer. She must have brushed against the wall at some point because the tight T-shirt she wore had a smear of paint over her right breast. Regardless, no one would mistake her as "normal." She looked like a supermodel in a paint company's commercial.

Jordan tried to keep his body from reacting. "I'd forgotten about the lawsuit. But you talk about wanting normalcy as if you've been deprived," he said carefully. "Yet you have fame, fortune and beauty."

"Are you suggesting I feel sorry for myself?" she returned sharply. "Nothing could be further from the truth. Frankly, it sounds as if you've already decided what you're going to write and how you're going to characterize me. If that's the case, just go home and write your articles. Save me the effort of dealing with you, because I'm too busy for pointless pursuits."

Jordan winced. It was true that he had preconceptions about Nicole. The irony was inescapable.

When Syd had asked him to do the articles, she had suggested it would be good for him because he'd be forced out of his "reflective reverie." He'd found her words annoying.

"I was out of order," he said quickly. "I genuinely want to listen to what you have to say. I can't promise not to have other biases, but I'll do my best not to let them influence what I write or my approach to the interviews."

For a long moment Nicole regarded him suspiciously, then she nodded. "Very well. I have my own prejudices about reporters."

"I'm not a reporter."

"Right," she drawled with patent disbelief.

"Okay, for the moment I'm sort of a reporter. I've been one in the past and might be again, on a limited basis."

"Acknowledging your problem is the first step on the road to recovery."

Jordan glared. "Very funny."

"I thought so, but I'm just the total idiot who didn't even know to use a primer when painting over bright colors, right?"

"I never said that."

"You didn't have to, your tone said it all. Not to mention the expression on your face."

He wanted to deny it, but he *had* been surprised she didn't know something that seemed basic to him. Yet even Syd—who was a very sharp lady—hadn't known about primer, nor her husband, who was a brilliant neurosurgeon. All at once Jordan was reminded of an editor he'd known when starting in the business. Fred had been fond of saying "intelligence and information are different beasts."

"In case it's too basic for you to understand, everybody has to start somewhere," Nicole continued. "The clerk was frantically busy at the hardware store when I bought the paint and somehow he didn't tell me about primer."

"Did you get better advice when you went in this time?" Jordan asked, wondering if the clerk had been distracted by Nicole's physical attributes. His own brain had short-circuited earlier that afternoon for the same reason, though he didn't think he'd been obvious about it.

"I hope so. This time a woman helped me. She was very professional. Tell me, is it possible for a woman to be as smart as a man about painting?" Nicole's voice dripped sarcasm.

Oh, Lord. Jordan felt a chasm opening at his feet. Not only had he opened himself to claims of journalistic bias, now she was challenging him about male chauvinism.

"Absolutely," he said. But a measure of self-honesty made him wonder if he still possessed caveman attitudes on some level. His sisters teased him about it now and then, but he'd figured it was just sisters being sisters. After all, if he was a total caveman he would have run Chelsea's latest boyfriend off with a bat and told him to stay away from her.

"I'd forgotten you were a runner," he said, pushing the thought aside. He wasn't crazy about doing emotional inventories at the best of times.

Nicole flashed a smile. "What's wrong, didn't the research department include my being a runner in their file on me?"

"What makes you think I have a file?"

"Jordan, no matter what some people assume about models, we have brains. A file comes with the territory. The *PostModern* research department must have worked overtime to get you all the available details."

"Does it bother you to think I have a file?"

"Being a reporter makes you bothersome, the rest just goes with the territory. I'll admit I wouldn't mind checking it for accuracy. Reporters have gotten things wrong so often it's laughable."

"I don't understand how you can complain about reporters when you've benefited from them making you even more famous. *PostModern* is also publishing these articles because of your fame, and your agency will profit by it."

"Fame isn't all it's cracked up to be," she returned. "I haven't sought out publicity and have always tried to have a private life, which the press seems to resent. Sure, I've modeled clothing, represented various products and said lines in television commercials—that's my job—but I've never been on reality TV and haven't cared if my name was known to anyone except photographers, agents and people wanting to hire me."

"Don't be a hypocrite. They wanted you in those ads because everyone knows who you are."

"Not everyone. My *face* is known in some circles, but my name wouldn't be familiar if it wasn't for the paparazzi following me around and trying to dig up saucy little fictions to titillate their readers. Which, by the way, the legitimate press has often repeated without an ounce of proof. I hope *PostModern* won't follow suit."

Jordan closed his eyes, partly to collect his thoughts, and partly to shut out the impact of Nicole's well-formed figure. For years—in the rare times he thought about her—he'd seen her as a face in a photograph. A face that reminded him of old annoyances. In person, she exuded a vibrant energy that sent his senses reeling.

"I'm doing a genuine interview," he said, looking at her again. "*PostModern* doesn't want sensationalistic stories. The editor demands in-depth material about real people. Right now she's interested in individuals who make radical changes in their lives, what their challenges are and how they find fulfillment."

Nicole's chin rose. "If that's really the story you're planning, then I'm in, but don't expect me to put up with any garbage. I'll give as good as I get."

Somehow, Jordan didn't doubt that for a second. She stood there, devoid of makeup or glamorous trappings, angry and full of life...and he was struck by her beauty in a way he'd never felt before today.

It annoyed him all over again.

Of course she was beautiful; she'd been the classic golden-haired tot and had grown into a sexy, gorgeous woman whose image was used to sell products around the world. He'd seen her on magazine covers and in television ads for most of his life. But he had never been personally attracted to her when looking at photos or watching ads, and hadn't expected to be on this assignment.

But his hormones had jumped to attention, the lousy traitors. He left as quickly as possible to go home and take another shower.

A cold one this time.

NICOLE RESISTED SLAMMING the door as Jordan left. She'd been foolish to let him into her house to either eat or paint. It would have been best to keep things formal, meeting at the office and doing standard interviews.

But at least he'd revealed his biases ahead of the game. And as she'd admitted, she had her own biases when it came to reporters, particularly the ones she classed as paparazzi. She shuddered, remembering the woman who'd gotten a job as a hotel maid and then gone through her letters, even sneaking a photo of her coming out of the bathroom wearing only a towel. *That* member of the "press" had worked for one of the sleaziest rags going.

But Jordan wasn't sleazy. However sardonic he sounded in his columns, they were also intelligent. Initially she'd expected to make fun of his writing and ideas; instead, he had mostly impressed her, tending to look at subjects from a different point of view and make his readers think about the ways things worked in the world. Maybe his articles weren't always as deep as they could be—with a breezy, entertaining tone—but how much depth was possible in such a short format?

He was also quite clear about where he was coming from. If he wrote about kids, he reiterated that he wasn't a parent himself and never expected to be. The same with marriage, saying he was happily single and intended remaining that way. Maybe he'd do something similar with the articles he planned to write for *Post-Modern*, being frank about their dislike for each other as kids and how that could affect what he was writing.

It might even be better this way. Another reporter would probably have preconceptions as well, but it would have been harder to get at them. With Jordan everything was out in the open from the get-go.

Still, Nicole wished he wasn't involved. It was an added stress she didn't need, especially while she was hunting for another office manager. Kevin McClaskey's wife had previously handled the job and he hadn't been able to face replacing Allison after her sudden death, just bringing in temps. It wasn't the best way to run the agency, so one of Nicole's first tasks after taking over had been to hire someone permanent.

It hadn't gone well.

Moonlight Ventures had now run through three different office managers and was back to using temps. It turned out that each of her hires had wanted to use the job as a backdoor to becoming a modeling client. One had even shown up at a photo shoot for a commercial, claiming the agency had sent her.

Nicole gritted her teeth. It had taken hours to resolve the mess. But she hadn't expected everything to be easy and would just have to fix each problem as it came, one way or another. With that thought, she went upstairs to shower and climb into bed. Fortunately the second floor of the house hadn't required as much work as the first. Mostly she'd just needed to buy a new bedroom set. No paint was needed, although most of the rooms remained unfurnished.

She closed her eyes, ready to drift off, but Jordan's annoyingly handsome face filled her mind. Nicole punched her pillow. She only had to put up with him for a while. Just because they lived in the same city again, that didn't mean they'd cross paths constantly.

Well, apparently he used the same fitness trail, but she'd only seen him there once… Sure, he'd been in Fiji for part of the time, but she'd been using the trail for months before moving to the house and hadn't seen him.

Hitting her pillow again, she tried to forget his lean, powerful body in running clothes. Disappointment in romance hadn't turned off her response to the opposite sex, but that didn't mean she had to pay attention to it.

THE FOLLOWING DAY Nicole was busy at her desk when she heard a tentative knock. A young woman stood in the doorway.

"Can I help you?" Nicole asked, thinking she'd seen her visitor before.

"I'm Chelsea Masters, one of Jordan's sisters."

The years peeled away and Nicole remembered the girl who'd always seemed unhappy and wistful. She didn't look much happier now. She was also wearing a heavy foundation that didn't entirely conceal dark bruises on her cheek and jaw.

"Chelsea, of course. How nice to see you again."

Nicole wondered how many of the Masters family would be coming to Seattle. Chelsea had been nice enough, but her siblings and their parents? Nicole shuddered. No wonder Chelsea had seemed unhappy while growing up.

Chelsea smiled uncertainly. "I thought Jordan might be here since he's doing those articles about you and the agency."

Standing, Nicole walked around the desk and gestured to a chair; Chelsea sank into it, her face pale. Nicole sat next to her. "I'm afraid he isn't here," she explained, "and I don't have his address."

"I do. I checked there first, but he wasn't around. He…he got me a ticket so I could, um, come and visit. I'm afraid I just jumped on a plane and came, so he didn't know when to expect me."

"Have you tried calling him?"

"I, uh, don't have a cell phone right now. It's lost, and I should have replaced it before leaving, but I didn't." Chelsea's lip trembled and she wiped a hand across her face, only to stare at the heavy smear of makeup on her palm. The bruise was now quite visible. It looked fresh.

"How did you get hurt?" Nicole asked, deciding it was best to mention it openly.

"Oh. I… I was in a traffic accident a couple days ago. It wasn't too bad."

Nicole wasn't sure she was telling the complete truth. Something difficult was going on in Chelsea's life.

"I'm glad it wasn't serious. Was anyone else involved?"

"There was the other driver and my boyfriend. That is, not anymore… I mean, we'd just broken up. It was his car. They say it wasn't his fault, but…you know."

The phone rang and Nicole sighed. "Sorry, I need to answer that. We don't have an office manager right now and the temp agency didn't have anyone to send today."

It turned out to be a photographer who'd seen their website and wanted a go-see with three of the agency's models. Nicole took down the details and swiftly texted the clients.

While she'd been on the phone, Chelsea had wandered away. When Nicole went looking, she found her visitor standing in the reception area, straightening files on the desk.

Chelsea turned and looked at Nicole. "I don't suppose you'd consider hiring *me* as your office manager."

"You're looking for a job?"

"I worked out my notice on my last position and haven't started looking, but I'm getting my résumé together."

"You don't live here."

"On the flight up I was thinking it might be a

good idea to move away from Los Angeles. I've really liked Seattle whenever I visited Jordan." Her face fell. "But…but I guess you wouldn't want to hire me. I mean because he's writing the articles and the way our moms… I mean, I'd never say anything to Jordan about anything here at the agency, but it wasn't fair to ask."

Nicole couldn't deny that privacy was a concern. On the other hand, she had nothing to hide. She wouldn't hire Jordan's little sister just to prove that, but it would be a side benefit should Chelsea prove to be suitable.

"What sort of work experience do you have?" she asked, playing for time to think.

"At the company where I used to work I started out as an office manager, though I've been in HR for the last three years."

Chelsea had experience a talent agency could use, yet the last thing they needed was a scared rabbit in the office. Nicole hesitated, but Moonlight Ventures was supposed to be about encouraging people to become their best. Why couldn't that apply to an office manager, as well as other clients?

She took an application from a file drawer. "Fill this out if you're really interested."

Chelsea's expression brightened. "I'll do it right now."

"One of my business partners should do the official interview. He's just here until the end of the week, so he'll probably want to see you this afternoon."

"So soon? I don't, that is, I…" Chelsea looked alarmed and gestured nervously toward her face.

"Don't worry, it's fine. We've all been there in one way or another."

Still looking apprehensive, Chelsea sat down to work on the application. The fact that she didn't cut and run seemed a point in her favor.

Nicole walked down the hallway and, with a brief knock, slipped into Adam's office. He was intently watching a video. Prospective clients had begun inundating them with portfolios and DVDs of amateur performances. Reviewing them was at least half of how he'd spent his time since arriving.

He glanced at her. "This one is painfully awful. It's from the stage mama of all stage mamas. She's in the video more than her child."

Nicole had already known that parents who pushed their kids unbearably would be one of the less palatable aspects of working as an agent. Over the years she'd come to the conclusion that parents were often trying to fulfill their own dreams through their children.

"I have someone interested in the office manager's position. She's filling out the application right now and I wondered if you had time to interview her."

"That's fine," Adam said. "Beats watching this

and we have to get somebody hired. You can't do everything alone and I won't be here full-time for another two months, give or take. Not that you haven't been doing a terrific job. Agency revenues are already higher than when Kevin owned Moonlight Ventures."

Nicole was glad she didn't need to explain the circumstances, just let Chelsea make her own impression. Hopefully, letting her interview was the right thing to do.

CHAPTER THREE

JORDAN STARED AT his sister in stunned surprise. "You did what?"

"I got a job. When I went looking for you at Nicole's agency, it turned out they needed an office manager. So I applied and interviewed with Adam Wilding, who's even more delicious in person than in his pictures. I start tomorrow."

Her words were fast and nervous, her hands twisting together. Jordan hated seeing her that way. For a while she'd come out of the shell she'd forged to protect herself from the constant tension in the house between their battling parents, then a string of cheating boyfriends had damaged her newfound confidence. The latest, Ron, hadn't been physically abusive, but he'd done his best to convince her that she was lucky to have him, and any issues between them were all her imagination.

Jordan sighed. His sister's new job would complicate doing the articles for *PostModern*. He'd need to have a discussion with Nicole about her motives in hiring a relative of the journalist writing about her and the agency.

"Congratulations," he said. "Shall we look for an apartment over the weekend, or would you rather stay at my condo while you get the lay of the land first?"

"I don't need to do either, at least not right away. Nicole has a guesthouse over her garage, and she says I can rent it while I get used to the Seattle area and figure out where I want to live permanently. Your place only has one bedroom, so this is much better than sleeping on the couch and crowding you. I know Terri usually stays on your boat when she's here, but this, uh…is best for me, I think."

Jordan wasn't sure whether to be annoyed or grateful. For months he and Terri had been encouraging their baby sister to break things off with Ron. Chelsea had struggled with the idea— hardly a surprise with the less-than-blissful example of domestic life in which they'd been raised. She probably believed that was how relationships worked. Now, after one visit to Nicole George's talent agency, she had a job that was twelve hundred miles from Ron Swanson.

Jordan decided it was something to celebrate, no matter how it had come about, or how many complications might ensue.

"Could we, um…go over to Nicole's right now?" Chelsea asked. "That way you could see the guesthouse with me."

"Sounds like a plan."

In his small two-seater sports car, he noticed Chelsea gulping and turning pale.

"Are you all right?" he asked. "Does being in a car make you nervous because of the accident?"

"Not exactly." She frowned at the dashboard. "I feel guilty, I guess. I'd just told Ron I wanted to split up. He got angry, and the next thing I knew we were broadsided." She pushed a hand through her hair. "I don't remember getting hit, just Ron swearing a blue streak afterward about the damage to his SUV."

"The police told Terri that the other vehicle ran a stoplight. It had nothing to do with you or Ron's driving."

"I know, it's just hard not to keep thinking about it."

Jordan winked at her, the way he'd done when they were kids. "Come on, Cheesy, you aren't to blame. The accident had nothing to do with you."

She grinned at the old nickname. "I guess not. Anyway, getting the job up here feels right."

It was harder for *him* to be certain of the same thing, but at least she was making decisions about her life.

CHELSEA HOPED SHE didn't look too anxious. She'd never lived anywhere except the Los Angeles area and the thought of moving to a different city in another state was scary, though her brother lived there, too. But this was the time to do it, while she was between jobs. She was even excited to think Seattle could be a whole new start.

She had quietly given notice for her old position two weeks earlier, asking her boss to keep it confidential. Since Ron worked for the same company, she'd figured it was best to cut all ties. The day before yesterday, she had finished working out her notice so it had seemed the right moment to break up with him. As soon as she'd told him they were over, she had felt a huge conviction that she'd done the right thing, but then the accident had happened and uncertainty had flooded her again.

In retrospect, telling him while they were driving might not have been the best choice. But she'd been afraid he'd yell or make a scene and had figured no one would hear if they were in his SUV.

It might take a while before she felt as if the world wasn't going to fall apart around her at any moment.

Jordan parked on a quiet residential street and she looked at the house, which wasn't what she'd expected. It was built in a homey style and there were hanging baskets of flowers on the front porch. She wasn't sure where she'd thought a supermodel would live, but it wasn't something so...so cheery and normal.

The door opened as they came up the walk and Nicole stepped out. "Hi, Jordan. Hi, Chelsea. Let's see if the guesthouse suits your needs."

Following Nicole toward the garage, Chelsea sighed with relief. The way things had happened seemed almost too good to be true; deep down it had been difficult not to wonder if Nicole would change her mind about both the job *and* the apartment.

Exterior stairs climbed up the far side of the three-car garage into an apartment that was even nicer than Chelsea had hoped.

"It's furnished, but the house isn't?" Jordan asked, glancing around.

"The guest apartment came this way. The previous owners used it for their in-laws, but they didn't need the furniture in their new place. Everything was nice and in good condition, so I agreed to buy it as part of the house purchase."

Chelsea listened as she explored the pretty apartment. A bouquet of fresh flowers sat on the dresser in the bedroom, and she thought it was awfully nice of Nicole to have done that. And there was a small balcony in the back, looking onto the neighbor's stand of evergreen trees.

"It's perfect," she declared, turning around. "Thank you so much. I'll take really good care of everything."

"I'm sure you will." Nicole handed a key to her. "Move in whenever you like. Right now, I need to get somewhere."

Chelsea's fingers closed around the key as if it was a lifeline. In a way it was—a lifeline that would help her stay away from the dark memories lurking around every corner in Los Angeles.

"Look around some more," Jordan said when they were alone. "I need to check on something."

He hurried out the door.

Curious, Chelsea went to a front window and saw him catch up with Nicole on the front walk. He seemed to be talking very fast and she bobbed her head before hurrying toward the house. A few minutes later a sleek silver-gray car appeared, practically below Chelsea's feet, backing down the driveway.

Jordan was still standing at the side of the drive and the vehicle stopped. He put a hand on the sedan's roof and spoke again. Even from her vantage point Chelsea thought he looked tense and she wondered if something was wrong.

Letting the curtain drop in place, she tried to stop trembling. How could she be twenty-seven and still feel like a scared child all the time? Over the past year Terri had been saying that Ron was gaslighting her, making her believe that everything was her fault. She'd finally realized her sister was right, but it wasn't easy to stop feeling as if she was the one who'd done something wrong.

"You okay?" Jordan asked when he returned.

"Fine." Chelsea loved her brother, but he'd always seemed so confident and bigger than life. He and Terri had reacted differently to the tension between their parents—they'd gotten angry and fought back. She was a mouse, which was something a lion like Jordan probably couldn't understand.

"What's that?" he asked, gesturing to the sheet of paper she was examining.

"The bus schedule. Nicole must have printed it out for me. She offered to give me rides when her schedule isn't too crazy, but I want to use mass transit until I get my car up here."

"*I'll* give you rides," Jordan said firmly, but Chelsea shook her head.

"Taking the bus will give me a better feel for the city."

"All right. This place seems move-in ready. Let's have dinner, then pick up whatever you need to get settled."

She followed, locking the door carefully behind them. Maybe she was just fooling herself, but moving to Seattle really did seem to be a good decision.

So far.

Tears threatened at that mental caveat. She desperately wanted to feel like a normal person again…someone who wasn't always expecting something horrible to happen.

NICOLE DROVE TO the agency where she and Adam were having a conference call with Rachel and Logan. She hadn't felt like dealing with Jordan's questions about Chelsea's employment beforehand, so she'd agreed to talk before her run the next morning. Right now he was meeting all her low expectations of reporters.

"Even bad press is still advertising," Logan quipped when she finished explaining the situation. He was in Venice for a wedding shoot. Weddings weren't his thing, but he'd known the groom forever and was doing it as a gift to the couple.

"Besides, we don't want to toady to reporters," Rachel added. "Kevin McClaskey never did." Rachel was at her home in Southern California.

"And his agency never grew," Nicole felt obliged to point out, troubled that her friends could be harmed by the way she dealt with Jordan. The only consolation was that *they* were the ones who'd urged her to do the interviews with *PostModern*. "I don't want to mess this up for you guys."

"You aren't going to mess anything up," Logan assured her. "Kevin wanted Moonlight Ventures to stay a mom-and-pop type of business. That's why it didn't grow. We can't worry about every biased reporter out there."

"We knew it was a risk to agree to the articles, no matter what they promised us," Adam said. "The editor wasn't playing straight to send someone who wasn't impartial, but it is what is. Besides, if we object, it'll just make us look defensive. We trust you, Nicole. Handle Masters the way your instincts say you should. Blow him off, argue, whatever feels right."

"I agree," Rachel added firmly. "Just be yourself."

"Except I've never been 'myself' with reporters," Nicole reminded them. "I've always put on a polite, distant act. That isn't going to be easy to do around Jordan." She didn't add that by the time she'd left modeling, she'd viewed reporters as conscienceless vampires who didn't care if they destroyed lives as long as they got their story. It wasn't fair, and she believed in a free press, but she just wished they'd stay away from her.

"Don't try to put on a polite show," Logan advised. "The magazine editor said Masters might want to talk with all of us. I think we should be upfront with him."

"There's also the issue of hiring his sister." Nicole pointed out. "Maybe I screwed up by letting Chelsea apply."

"I don't think so," Adam said. "I got great reports from her former employer and have a good feeling about her. Besides, it might be some form of discrimination if we hadn't given her a chance."

Nicole had wondered about that as well. It didn't seem likely, but there were a number of laws regarding employers and she was still learning.

"I don't think she'll operate like a spy," Adam continued, "though Masters may think *we* have ulterior motives for employing his sister."

Nicole made a face. "I already know he has questions about us giving her a job, but I doubt he trusts me regardless, so it probably doesn't make a difference."

"How about doing our own article?" Adam suggested.

She blinked. "Excuse me?"

"We're launching our *Beneath the Surface* blog before long. Why don't you write about Jordan and the process of being interviewed? You've always had good suggestions for fixing advertising material, so I'm sure you could do it."

Nicole frowned thoughtfully. Kevin McClaskey had published a quarterly trade newsletter and it had a respectable mailing list. They hoped to turn it into a magazine for the general public, but were still exploring the risks and possibilities. In the meantime, a blog seemed like a cost-effective way to gain an audience and it was something the others could work on, whether or not they were in Seattle.

It *would* be interesting to put the shoe on the other foot, so to speak, and turn the spotlight on a reporter. Jordan wouldn't have to be referenced by name, though it might be pointless not to do so. Once the *PostModern* articles began appearing, everyone would know he was the one who'd been interviewing her.

"I'll consider it," she said.

AT 6:30 A.M. the next day, Nicole started for the park and found Jordan at the head of the fitness trail where they'd agreed to meet. He wore running shorts and a T-shirt that showed off his physique. Plainly he'd done more than swing in a hammock and sip piña coladas while in Fiji.

"Good morning," she greeted him.

"Hi. As I said last night, I want to talk to you about Chelsea."

"Is there a problem?" She began a series of stretching exercises in an attempt to appear relaxed and casual.

"It seems unusual to offer a job to someone you know nothing about."

"Are you suggesting we'll regret hiring her?" Nicole looked up, keeping her expression innocent.

"Not in the least. Chelsea was excellent at her last job and only left because someone she, er, needed to avoid was employed there, too."

It fit what Nicole had suspected, that something particularly intense was going on in her new office manager's life. Jordan obviously didn't want to elaborate.

She nodded briskly. "Chelsea heard we needed someone and asked if she could apply. One of my partners is in town, so he interviewed her, then phoned for a reference and got a positive report. He was quite happy about hiring Chelsea, and we urgently need someone."

Nicole didn't think it was appropriate to offer more since Chelsea was now an employee of the agency. Adam's only concern had been that Chelsea was overqualified and might not stay long for that reason. On the positive side, she might advance into being an agent for Moonlight Ventures; with her experience in human resources, she likely had the necessary skills. Adam *had* wondered if she would be able to deal with pushy or manipulative clients, but had still felt she should be given a chance.

Jordan didn't answer immediately; he seemed to be formulating his answer. "This is an unusual situation. I'm doing a series of magazine articles about you and the agency. Those articles will give Moonlight Ventures a lot of publicity, and now my sister is working there."

"Are you worried about your objectivity, or whether I'm trying to influence what you write?"

"Maybe both."

"We already know you aren't objective, so that's *your* concern. And since I don't think you trust me in any case, anything I say or do won't make a difference."

Surprise flashed through his eyes. "You don't seem offended by that."

"Why should I be? It's far from the worst thing a reporter has suggested. Besides, as kids you always made it clear you disliked me, so you're probably starting the interviews with a bad opinion of me, regardless."

Now Jordan seemed completely nonplussed and she wondered if he was going to deny it. "You don't believe I could have decided I was wrong about you?" he asked instead.

Nicole made a noncommittal gesture. "I haven't seen any evidence to think so. You didn't really *know* me when we were kids, but still disliked me. And from what I've picked up from my folks, our mothers still don't get along. I never knew what happened that broke up their friendship, but it must have been bad. I doubt your mother has ever said anything positive about me or my family since then. Years ago she even conducted a brief, but vicious, social media campaign against us."

Jordan looked appalled. "Mom?"

"Oh, yes. Apparently a few of her comments were rather libelous. She deleted everything after my dad's lawyer mentioned a lawsuit might be in the offing."

"I'm sorry, I had no idea."

Nicole smiled wryly. "I was frantically busy with my college classes and work, so I mostly heard about it secondhand. It helped that social media was pretty new then. That aside, I don't expect everyone to think I'm perfect, especially since I'm not. Everyone has different tastes, and personalities sometimes clash. That's life. So, do you genuinely think I'm trying to manipulate you by giving Chelsea a job?"

"I'm still not clear about why you hired her."

"One of my colleagues made the hiring decision. All I did was give Chelsea the application and take her back to his office. What was I supposed to do, tell her she couldn't apply because she was your sister? That wouldn't be fair."

"Agreed, but you also offered the use of your guesthouse."

"True, and I'd let her stay for free, but she insists on paying rent. I did it because we knew each other as kids and…" Nicole stopped. Perhaps she shouldn't offer an opinion about Chelsea as an unhappy kid and the impression that she could use some support now.

"And?"

"It doesn't matter."

"Maybe it does."

"Let's just say it looks as if she's had a rough time lately and I wanted to help out. But remember that I'm not obligated to tell you everything I think, even during the interviews for *PostModern*."

"I don't expect you to. By the way, can we start them today, instead of waiting until Monday?"

Nicole's nerves instinctively tightened. Since the interviews hadn't "officially" begun, anything she'd said to date should be off the record. But that was a technicality. He might not respect boundaries, so she may as well agree. And the sooner the interviews were over, the better.

She really *would* have to think about writing something for the blog the agency was starting. Jordan probably wouldn't like it, but since he thought it was hypocritical for her to want privacy, she could argue the same about him. After all, he was a prominent newspaper columnist, making his living on being in the public eye.

Except...what she wrote shouldn't be about turning the tables on Jordan. She'd have to think it over.

"How about it?" he prompted.

"Okay, we can begin the process right away, but at the moment I'm going to start my run."

He fell in at her side as she set off down the trail. Though she would have preferred running alone, she didn't object. They ran for an hour and he insisted on running the half mile from the park to her house. She noted that his breathing was strong, not heavy, despite their swift pace.

"What are you doing today?" Jordan asked. "Chelsea told me she's starting at the agency this morning. Will you be showing her the ropes?"

"For a few hours, but I think it's best if you aren't there. It would be easier on her. This afternoon I'm attending a high school play and I'll go again tonight to see their performance for the general public."

"Why both?"

"To double-check my impressions." Nicole took off the sweatband she'd put around her fore-head. Taking a key from her pocket, she unlocked the door. "The audience also makes a difference, influencing the actors' energy. The earlier performance is for their peers."

"Then you're going to recruit clients."

"I want to be proactive. Stacks of inquiries come into the agency, but sometimes the most talented folks may not know it. Besides, most of the portfolios we've received are for models, and we're also looking for performers."

"Is it okay for me to attend with you?"

Nicole hesitated, then nodded. "I'll clear it with the school. Just don't tell anyone why I'm there. The principal knows, but I don't want the kids getting hyper because an agent is present, and I'd rather not give them false hope."

"That's reasonable. What time?"

"Meet me here at twelve thirty. Also, please don't mention the name of the school or any of the students in your article."

"I understand." He started walking toward the park.

As a kid Jordan had been athletic, and despite his military haircut and gangly physique, quite appealing to teenage girls. His features were still clean and defined, but no longer angular. And his body? She let out a breath, annoyed that she kept getting distracted by Jordan's physical attributes. After all, she'd worked with equally handsome guys since they'd moved her from a child category into shoots for teen products.

As Nicole went upstairs and showered, she mused that she'd basically worked her entire life, yet Jordan seemed to think she didn't have any right to a normal existence.

It was true that she'd entered adulthood with sizeable investments, which had only increased through the years. She was skilled at handling her funds, which meant she was quite comfortable. But money didn't solve all problems. Being in the public eye all the time was tougher than people thought.

Her so-called fame had been the problem when she and Vince had started dating. He'd been her first serious love and was the only guy she'd gone out with who hadn't expected her to be a polished supermodel all the time. But after a while he hadn't been able to take the notoriety and had broken off the relationship. Her heartbreak had become fodder for the media, including months of speculation that she was pregnant…even long after it would have been obvious that she was not.

Nicole stepped out of the shower and went into her bedroom. It was nicely furnished, her money allowing her to decorate exactly the way she wanted. Yet she had no one to share it with, something she seriously doubted would change anytime soon.

She stared at a painting on the wall and wondered how many people would trade her modeling success for love. Her stellar career was partly luck…luck to be born with what the world called beauty, and luck in having parents who'd known exactly how to market her appearance. She'd also had talent, worked hard and tried to act professionally, but she knew luck was always a factor. That was true of Moonlight Ventures as well, but it still needed her hard work and judgment.

Was that something she could explain to Jordan for the articles, or would he just see it as trite and clichéd?

What if it actually *was* trite and clichéd?

BY THE TIME Jordan got back to the park, where he'd left his car, he was still thinking about his sister working for Moonlight Ventures. His instincts told him Nicole wasn't out to hurt Chelsea, despite the past problems between their families, but he couldn't help being concerned.

It was impressive how rational Nicole seemed to be about criticism and the probability that some people disliked her.

He winced, recalling what she'd said about his mother's social media campaign against the Georges. How could Mom have behaved that way, when *she* was the one who'd thrown herself at Nicole's father? Wounded pride at being rejected? Or maybe it was just the insanity of spending so many years in a destructive marriage and resenting one that wasn't.

He'd been an unwilling, unknown witness to his mother's folly and had never told anyone what he'd seen. What he *hadn't* known was whether Nicole had learned about the incident from her parents.

Apparently not.

Jordan stuck his head under a spigot at the park picnic area and washed the sweat from his face. The water was cold and helped clear his mind.

After getting home the night before he'd called Terri and told her about the latest development. She'd decided to immediately leave for Seattle in Chelsea's car with a load of her things—they both wanted to ensure their sister's ties with Ron were well and truly cut. Terri might be tough and negative a lot of the time, but deep down she was fierce about the people she loved.

Back at his condo, he phoned Syd and explained the newest wrinkle in the situation. She felt it would give an added human interest twist, provided he was transparent about the circumstances.

"Our readers know life is messy. They'll be interested to see how you handle it," she told him.

"These articles aren't about me," he objected.

"Maybe they will be, partly at least. It's an intriguing angle."

Jordan hung up, ready to pound the wall. Was it possible that Syd was trying to maneuver him into writing a regular piece for her magazine? Before she'd become the editor, *PostModern* had asked him to do a monthly column, but he was happy with the way things were. While he might write a book someday, in the meantime he had the footloose and fancy-free life he'd always wanted.

AT TWELVE THIRTY SHARP, Jordan knocked on Nicole's door. "Shall we drive together?" he asked.

"Sure. That way we'll look like parents showing up to cheer on their kids. It should elevate the anonymity level."

"You don't want anyone recognizing you?"

"That's why I plan to slip in as the play starts. It cuts down on the potential. Plus, I have these."

She pulled out a pair of studious glasses and put them on. They changed the look of her face, especially since he'd never seen her wear anything other than sunglasses.

"Do you actually need your vision corrected?" he asked.

"No, but I've had these for years. They're good for misdirection."

Without makeup and in an oversized shirt, it was possible she wouldn't be recognized, though no one would mistake her for anything except an extremely beautiful woman.

"Will I pass?" she asked.

"I suppose. You really think we'll look like parents?"

"They can't see how we really feel about marriage and each other."

"I've been upfront about my disinterest in becoming a husband. So you feel the same way?"

She grinned. "I definitely don't want to become anyone's husband."

He groaned. "Come on. Do you always misdirect?"

"Is this for the article?"

"I don't know. Everything's a possibility. Plenty of speculation has gone on about your decision to leave modeling. A husband and kids were large question marks."

"Well, I'm not interested in getting married," she answered in what seemed to be a deliberately light tone. "The advantage of having a dog instead of a husband is that they don't think something is wrong if you aren't wearing makeup."

Jordan was sure there was something deeper being hinted at, but doubted she'd say more at the moment.

"Your editor mentioned wanting pictures for the articles," she continued. "But I hope it isn't necessary to include one of me dressed this way.

Going incognita is the best way to give these kids a fair shot."

"I understand."

Nicole walked to her car, parked in the driveway, and Jordan knew it made sense for her to drive since she'd probably visited the school already. They arrived a few minutes before 1:00 p.m. and she led the way to the auditorium, arriving as the curtain on the stage was going up.

Throughout the performance, she watched attentively, occasionally checking the program, though without making any notes. Presumably she wasn't seeing anyone she felt was promising. Jordan had to give her credit for appearing conscientious. His own attention kept wandering, unfortunately drawn by the scent Nicole wore, the line of her cheek, and the way her slight movements made him aware of the curves that had so often been displayed in a bikini or lingerie.

Perhaps that was the problem. Pictures were just pictures. But now she was here in the flesh and even though those curves were completely covered by a casual shirt, he'd seen enough photos of her in scanty clothes to know what lay beneath.

Shifting in his seat, he told himself the whole thing was basic human chemistry and could be overcome by rational thought.

Toward the end of the last scene, she stood and gestured for him to follow. They slipped out of the auditorium and walked briskly to the car. With the way they'd arrived and departed, he thought it was unlikely anyone would have noticed Nicole, even if she hadn't been in disguise.

"At least you don't have to attend tonight," he commented as she drove from the parking lot.

"Excuse me?" She cast a surprised glance in his direction.

"There wasn't much for a talent agent to explore."

"Did we see the same performance?" she asked incredulously.

"What are you talking about?"

"For one, the kid who sang a song in the third act. Her role was too small to see if she has any acting ability, but her singing was excellent."

Jordan frowned, remembering the short girl with stringy hair who had sung a few lines before getting interrupted by other onstage action.

"That kid isn't exactly a star in the making."

"Is that based on your prejudice against girls who aren't your idea of sex goddesses, or because you think the agency can't be interested in people who don't fit the world's limited concept of beauty?"

Whatever else Nicole might be, she was sharp enough to analyze his response and require him to define his intent.

He shifted in his seat. "If anything, I figured

Moonlight Ventures would only be interested in clients they can develop as supermodels or into major acting stars."

"Actors and models don't have to fit a particular idea of good looks and I'm not interested in stereotypes."

He shook his head, bemused by Nicole's relentless logic. "Okay," he said, deciding not to pursue the subject further, "the girl has a good voice. Is that all you got out of it?"

"The play itself was authored by one of the seniors."

"It was?" Jordan had thought the show was well-written, despite the often excruciating performances.

"Yes. According to the principal he's been a rebellious screw-up and had to write the play to get enough credit to graduate. I thought it was good and we may be interested in writers. Adam is exploring development of a literary division in the agency. I don't know if that will work, but other agencies have done it and he's been making editorial contacts. If anyone can pull it off, he can. At the very least we could refer the play's author to one of our connections."

"Isn't it unusual for a talent agency to divide its focus?"

Nicole waved her hand. "Right now, maybe, since I'm still the only one working full-time. But once all of us are on board, it might make sense to diversify. We have varied interests and know there's a wealth of talent in the Seattle area. Eventually we'll hire other agents as well. The kid who wrote that play may have the ability to go all the way. Talent often emerges young. Walter Farley wrote his first Black Stallion book in junior high school, and there are a number of other authors who also began early. Adam is bugged by the idea that there could be a great author out there who might never realize their own potential."

"Why is that Wilding's special area of interest?"

"His mother is a writer, though she's never tried to get published."

Jordan hadn't thought that much about Nicole's partners. The focus of the articles was supposed to be on her as a supermodel changing her life. If he could schedule conversations with Nicole's partners, it would mostly be for getting information that was related to her.

"So the agency might get a writing client for a potential literary division, and perhaps a singer. But do you need to go back again just to listen to amateurs reciting good lines?"

"I like to give them a second chance. It's hard to perform at your best in front of fellow students. But if it's too tedious for you, feel free not to attend this evening. After all, you've seen what I'm doing there and it isn't world-shattering."

"I'm going," Jordan asserted, stung by her "tedious" remark.

One thing was clear, the assignment was turning out to be very different from what he'd anticipated.

CHAPTER FOUR

NICOLE COULDN'T INTERPRET the expression on Jordan's face and decided not to try.

She pulled up in front of her house. It was after three thirty and she'd be heading back to the school in four hours. The schedule seemed rigorous for the kids, but the principal had explained the afternoon's performance was mostly intended as a dress rehearsal.

Considering how the agency had been inundated with people wanting to become clients, it might be silly to go out searching. But this was more dynamic—not to mention more fun—than sitting in her office looking at pictures or videos.

"What now?" Jordan asked.

"I'm going to sit on my new deck and breathe fresh air while I make notes about the performance."

"May I join you?"

"I suppose," Nicole said reluctantly.

It was ironic. If *PostModern* had sent a different reporter, she probably wouldn't be letting him or her into the house. So in a sense, being "herself" might actually be easier with Jordan. Well…easier on some levels, harder on others.

She went through the kitchen on the way out to the deck and took a bottle of mineral water from the beverage chiller.

"Help yourself," she offered. "Sorry, there isn't any beer."

He glanced into the compartment and selected ice tea. "I also see there's no wine. Worried about the calories?"

"I don't care that much for alcohol. The last time I had a drink was when we toasted the purchase of Moonlight Ventures."

Nicole spent a few minutes playing with Toby, tossing a toy while he fetched it and returned. The dog wriggled with pleasure each time she praised him. According to Toby's records, he'd been found as a hungry puppy near the Bainbridge Island ferry. It broke her heart to think of any animal being abandoned, but at least she could ensure this particular dog had a good life.

Finally he collapsed on the grass, panting and looking thoroughly pleased with himself. Some people thought cocker spaniels or corgis had the corner on adorability, but Nicole's money was on beagles. When he'd whimpered and looked at her from his kennel at the rescue center she'd practically melted. Until then she'd been considering a German Shepherd adolescent with enormous paws and a goofball personality.

She went back to her chair under the covered section of the deck and started making notes in her electronic notebook, periodically referring to the program from the play. The kids had seemed eager and sincere, though most of them weren't polished actors and actresses.

"I didn't know you liked dogs," Jordan said after a while.

Nicole reached down and patted Toby, who'd come over to sit next to her chair. "I couldn't get one before because of my travel schedule—it wouldn't have been right to kennel it constantly."

"That's why I've never adopted a pet or thought about family. I like being able to drop everything and head to another part of the world."

"Being free to travel is nice and I suppose a pet or a family would tie you down."

Though Nicole was glad she no longer had to be on the go constantly, she also missed it. But a business couldn't be run on an occasional basis.

Jordan's head cocked. "You have an odd expression."

"I was thinking about choices. This is probably the longest I've stayed in one place since I was a kid. It seems strange in a way."

His gaze sharpened. "Then that's one of the costs of your decision to change careers?"

Nicole didn't want to discuss what she thought or felt, but she had agreed to the interviews and intended to follow through.

"Yes," she said, "if you want to call it a cost. I'm responsible for taking care of the agency until there are more of us here to fulfill our commitments. Being more mobile the way I used to be might be nice, though I rarely had time to simply appreciate the locations where I worked. Still, I got to see a lot, even if it was on the fly."

Jordan had pulled out a notepad and written a bit before looking up once more. For a minute she was afraid he was going to imply again that she felt sorry for herself, which would tempt her to send his pad into the yard for Toby to use as a chew toy.

"Do you think you'll be able to resist the freedom of travel?" he asked instead.

"I don't intend to stay in Seattle three hundred and sixty-five days a year. Once the four of us are here, there will be some leeway. In the meantime, I made a choice about what I wanted to do with my life. It means I can't do some things, but can do others, such as have a dog."

Jordan looked at Toby. "He's a pretty nice choice."

"Yeah. Originally I wanted a large dog, but this guy charmed me into taking him instead. Maybe I'll get a cat to keep him company when I'm out."

"Two animals? I can imagine the look on Helen's face if she had to clean up after them."

"Helen?"

"She comes in once a week to clean my condo.

She jokes that I'm Felix Unger, the neat freak from *The Odd Couple*."

"But didn't Felix hope to get back together with his wife?"

"So I'm like him in some ways, not in others. Besides, I'm not exactly a neat freak, I just like to have everything in its place."

Jordan fell silent again and Nicole made a few more notes, trying to ignore his very male presence on her deck. It wasn't easy. Tension emanated from him, as if just sitting while she worked was taxing his patience beyond its limit. Though he'd claimed otherwise, she sometimes wondered if he'd already written the articles and if interviewing her was just a pretense.

Nicole mentally slapped herself. It was hypocritical to condemn the guy before giving him a chance to prove himself. If the *PostModern* articles turned out to be pure opinion, the same as his columns, *then* she'd know the truth.

She glanced at him from beneath her eye lashes. He was good-looking enough to be a model himself, though there was no telling how his looks would translate into photographs.

Saving her work after another half hour, Nicole looked at Jordan. "It's nice that you didn't just sit there watching me."

"No problem."

He exuded virile energy and she decided it was

best that he was a reporter. She had *never* dated one, considering it far too much of a risk.

She was always frustrated when lingering pangs of longing for love and happily-ever-after threatened her peace of mind. It wasn't that she wanted something like that with Jordan, but sitting on the deck with him was a reminder of the old dream.

Surely her disquiet was related to the radical changes she'd made in her life. She was no longer doing the work that she had enjoyed and her friends couldn't join her yet in the enterprise they'd planned together. Naturally she was unsettled.

"Something on your mind?" Jordan asked. "You have another odd expression."

"Nothing important."

"I'D LIKE TO SAY—even though we're understandably wary toward each other—" Jordan stopped and grinned at Nicole's wry glance. "I *am* worried about Chelsea. You're right that she's had a tough time and I appreciate your consideration toward her."

"I'm not being considerate, at least not in a sentimental way. One of our goals at Moonlight Ventures is to help people be at their best. The way I see things, that applies to our employees, too, not just our clients."

"So Moonlight Ventures is trying to develop talent, not just sell it?" he asked.

"Some people may need help to make their potential visible. Advertisers don't have time to look beneath the surface. They want someone who's already professional and able to project their best."

"Then basically being an agent is teaching salesmanship, like washing a car and doing a tune-up for a used car lot."

"That sounds cynical…which doesn't surprise me. What I've read of your columns suggests you have a jaded view of human nature."

His lips twisted. "The critics say I'm cynical, too, though I've noticed it hasn't hurt my readership."

"So you went from angry teenager to cynical columnist. Was it due to one grand event, or a process of continuing attrition?"

"A combination," he admitted, not wanting to discuss his parents and their inability to stay faithful to each other. But he also hadn't found life beyond his family's home to be much of a counterbalance to his attitudes.

All the same, he didn't think he was cynical—he was more of a skeptic, or perhaps a realist.

"In other words, you don't like talking about it," Nicole guessed. "That's understandable. Disillusionments are also about our vulnerabilities and most of us keep our most tender spots hidden."

"True. Do you plan on revealing any of your vulnerable spots?" he asked. He'd interviewed people who were experts at shifting the focus onto the interviewer and Nicole might be one of them.

She ran the tip of her tongue over her lip and he found himself wondering what it would be like to kiss her. Every move she made seemed to have a seductive edge to it, though he didn't believe she was doing it deliberately. Trying to bemuse or seduce a reporter didn't seem to be her style.

"No soft spots on display for a while," she said and he had to think a moment to recall the question he'd asked about revealing her vulnerabilities. "You have to really trust someone to uncover that part of yourself."

A flash of annoyance struck at the inference that she didn't trust him, but Jordan reined in his feelings. After all, she had no reason to find him trustworthy and he'd already revealed he had biases. A rational person *wouldn't* trust him.

"Is there anything I can do to gain your trust?" he asked.

Reaching her hands high in the air, she stretched and yawned. "Who knows?"

Jordan's muscles tensed. Her motions were alluring, but he still didn't think she was being consciously seductive.

One thing was for sure—Nicole hadn't dropped out of the fashion scene because her looks were fading, which was what a few disgruntled journalists had suggested when they couldn't get an interview. In fact, she looked better than ever, with naturally gold hair and the same vibrant blue eyes he remembered—no enhancement from colored contact lenses needed. She also exuded sexy vitality, so he didn't believe illness had led to her hiatus.

Another possibility was a personal issue, such as a love affair or a relationship that had gone bad. He'd tested those waters already and would return to it when the timing was right.

Settling against the high-backed chair, Nicole closed her eyes. "Don't you love a spring afternoon?" she asked. "It's still so fresh, the earth waking after winter. I didn't know it could be like that. Of course, everyone tells me this is a warm spring for Washington, so maybe it isn't typical, especially the hot spell that's been predicted."

"You act as if this is the first time you've ever seen springtime."

Her eyes opened. "It is in a way."

"Another thing you missed because of being an international model?"

"Stop barking up that tree," she said coolly. "This has nothing to do with me being a model. It's about having lived in Southern California my entire life. The weather down there is pleasant, as you know, but let's face it, the seasons aren't that definitive. They just sort of meander from one place to another. The seasons really make an impact up here. I'm loving the spring after winter."

Jordan nodded. He'd moved away from Los Angeles after college, wanting to leave the past behind and had lived in various places around the country. He liked the Northwest.

"Even in Seattle, seasonal changes aren't as definitive as they are back east," he said. "Spring also seems to come slower there."

"I suppose that's true. My friend Logan lived all over the world when he was a kid. He says it isn't until you've gone through a winter where trees and bushes mostly look dead, that you truly understand why poets rave about the coming of spring."

"Logan Kensington is the photographer in your partnership," Jordan commented, recalling the information he'd been given about Moonlight Ventures. "It's hard to believe he's giving up the artistry involved with photography to be an agent."

"It's nice to know you respect *photographers*."

He'd have to think about her inference that he didn't respect models.

"Are you and Logan involved?" he asked.

Nicole laughed and Jordan couldn't deny it was the kind of sound that could make a man lose his head, though he was determined not to be one of them.

"Logan and I are friends," she said. "We've

been friends for years and intend to stay friends for the rest of our lives. The same with Adam. Rachel isn't involved with them, either. It's amazing to me how many people struggle with the idea of men and women just liking each other without romance or sex being a part of it."

"Then there's no 'friends with benefits' going on?"

"Never." She let out a small laugh. "And I've been authorized to tell you that, despite your status as a journalist."

The humor made her face glow and Jordan had to remind himself that he was a journalist, not a randy teenager. The mystery was why he hadn't panted after Nicole all those years ago. Except maybe he had; now that he looked back, he had to admit it wasn't only irritation he'd experienced—beneath it had been a whole lot of old-fashioned lust.

The important thing to remember now was that he was capable of restraining himself.

"I'LL TAKE YOUR name and your son's portfolio, but I can't make an appointment," Chelsea told the determined woman in front of her. "If the agency is interested, someone will call."

Inside she was quaking, but was glad her voice sounded steady.

"I know they'll want to represent my son."

The woman grabbed the kid up hard next to

her and Chelsea saw how unhappy he looked. She winked at the boy, just slightly, and saw his shy smile.

"Thank you for bringing his photograph by for consideration," she said, deliberately putting the folder into a wire basket. "That's all I can do for you today."

"I... I'll find a way to report you to the owners for being obstructive."

Chelsea eyed the woman and realized she was one of the bullying stage mothers Nicole and Adam had warned her about. Well, she was tired of being pushed around.

"That's fine," she answered evenly. "Feel free to make any report you like. As I said, I'll pass the portfolio to one of the agents."

Snorting, the woman stomped out of the reception area with her child in tow. The boy turned his head and gave Chelsea a wave his mother couldn't see. Chelsea waved back; he was truly adorable. What a shame his mom was a nightmare.

As the front door shut behind her, Adam emerged from the back area. Chelsea couldn't stop the grab in her stomach, wondering if he was unhappy about the way she'd handled the situation.

"Good job," he told her instead. "Stage parents can be a royal pain. I've encountered them numerous times in my career and Nicole already has her own collection of horror stories to tell from here in Seattle."

"I guess I might have handled it better," Chelsea answered.

Adam looked reflective. "There's no way to know—each person is different. I only heard the last part as I came down the hall, but you did exactly what we told you to do. It's too bad you had to face a Gorgon on your first day."

"Uh, inside I'm just…melting gelatin salad right now."

"That's okay. A lot of us only pretend to be tough. But I like the image of melting gelatin salad."

Chelsea didn't know if he was just being nice because Nicole had known her before, but maybe it didn't matter. Nice was nice.

"It's past five, so let's lock the doors and go home," Adam was saying. "Can I give you a lift to Nicole's house?"

"That's awful considerate of you, but I want to practice with the buses. Luckily I'll have my car on Monday."

"Nothing like having your own transportation."

Later, as Chelsea approached the apartment stairs, an SUV pulled into the neighbor's driveway. A tall, studious-looking man got out and grinned at her. He had an armload of books and papers that started sliding, so she dashed to help catch everything.

"Thanks," he said. "I'm a teacher and my students wouldn't appreciate it if their work got lost or damaged."

"I imagine not. What grade?"

"Fifth. They still have a hint of innocence at that age. I get fewer wisecracks than when I taught older students."

"That sounds nice."

"It is. By the way, I'm Barton Smith."

"Chelsea Masters. I'm staying in Nicole's guesthouse for a while."

Barton was attractive, with broad shoulders, brown hair and blue eyes. He looked as if he was in his midthirties.

"Then we're neighbors. It's nice to meet you."

"Same here."

He started toward his house, before stopping and looking back at her. "Say, would you like to go out to dinner or a movie this weekend?"

"Sure. Oh, that is… I just got here and I don't know if my brother will want to do something. He lives here, too. I probably shouldn't make any plans. You know…while I'm getting settled. Some other time, maybe?"

She liked his smile and felt awful about her wishy-washy answer.

"Family first. I'll check back with you."

Barton went inside his house while Chelsea

scurried up the stairs to the front door of the guesthouse apartment. Perhaps she should have explained she'd just broken up with her boyfriend and didn't want to start dating right away. But would that imply that she thought he was especially interested in her? All he'd done was ask her on a casual outing.

Chelsea groaned and dropped onto the couch. Somehow she had to stop being such a limp noodle.

BARTON PUT HIS students' papers in his home office and went to the kitchen to make a sandwich. His new neighbor seemed nice, just like Nicole George. He'd hardly believed his eyes when he realized *she* was the one who'd bought the house next door. They'd talked several times and she was always friendly and normal, quite different from how he'd imagined a supermodel would act.

He hadn't considered asking her for a date though—it hadn't even occurred to him to think of her that way.

Since Ellyn had walked out on their marriage two years ago, he'd pretty much kept his head down and concentrated on getting through each day. But his brother, Peter, kept saying it was time to dive into the dating scene again. Barton hadn't been interested until seeing Chelsea Masters and the thoughtful way she'd helped save his students' tests and other papers.

Up close he'd seen bruises on her face, visible despite her makeup, and wondered if that *also* had something to do with her not wanting to go out for a while.

With a *mrrooow*, his cat, Spike, jumped onto the kitchen island. Spike had dry food in a bowl, but preferred human chow when he could get it.

"You aren't supposed to be there, pal," Barton scolded absentmindedly.

Spike purred. He'd lived a hard life before showing up at the school where Barton taught. There were several notches missing from his right ear, his tail was kinked in the middle, and a dip on one side of his jaw suggested it had been broken at some point. The students had named him Spike and fed him scraps, which had led to Barton taking the little con artist home, right before the Christmas break.

Grabbing Spike and his plate, Barton headed for the office, only to discover the cat had reached out a paw and filched a slice of roast beef from the sandwich.

"Fine."

Barton dumped the sandwich in the cat bowl and went to make another one. There was no point in getting annoyed with Spike—the cat had learned to survive any way he could. And at least he'd embraced a litter box and cushy indoor life with enthusiasm. His favorite spot to nap was a south-facing window where he could catch rays on sunny days and watch birds on the other side of the glass.

Adopting him had felt like closing the final chapter on Ellyn. She *never* would have tolerated an animal in the house, particularly a beat-up tomcat with the table manners of Attila the Hun.

For some reason Barton wondered how Chelsea Masters would react to Spike. She'd acted a little funny when he'd asked her out—was she trying to put him off with her excuse, or was he just being too sensitive? He didn't want to get seriously involved with anyone right away, but an occasional dinner or other outing would be nice—eating a meal with Spike just wasn't the same as eating with a human being.

He'd let his social ties slide after the divorce.

A couple of weeks ago, Barton had gone to dinner at another teacher's house where he'd met her husband and kids. While pleasant, it was awkward for a single man to spend time with a married couple. Still, it was a start. His brother was right. If he didn't start coming out of his post-divorce fog, he'd miss out on a lot.

CHAPTER FIVE

LATE IN THE afternoon Jordan stood and told Nicole he'd be back at seven thirty, ready for the second trip to the high school. Though he dreaded sitting through the same performance again, he respected her for wanting to give the kids a second look.

He went around to the entrance of the garage apartment and knocked. Chelsea was pale and shaky when she answered the door and he mentally castigated Moonlight Ventures for the hard day she must have had. He wasn't being reasonable and knew it, but she was his sister and he didn't want her upset.

"Ready for dinner?" he asked.

"Uh, sure."

"What kind of food appeals tonight?" he asked, as she locked the door and followed him downstairs.

"Whatever is good for you."

"Really, what would you like?" he persisted. When was Chelsea going to learn that she had a right to have what *she* wanted some of the time?

"Anything is fine."

He sighed. "How about Mexican? There's a place at the mall."

"I like Mexican."

Jordan knew she did, which was why he'd suggested it. Food choices weren't as important as not taking crap from a boyfriend, but it was a start. He wanted her to stick up for herself.

"How did your first day at the agency go?" he asked, trying to make it a casual query.

"Fine. Nicole is awfully nice and so is Adam. I wish he could stay, but he has a string of modeling jobs over the next several weeks."

Chelsea sounded sincere. After all, it wasn't necessarily the job that had gotten her upset. It might have been a phone call—no, scratch that. Terri had mentioned Chelsea's cell phone getting lost in the accident, unless she'd located it before leaving.

"Have you found your cell phone yet?" he asked.

"No."

"Might as well replace it. If we don't linger over dinner, there's a place near the restaurant where we can get one. I'd like to be able to reach you more easily."

"You don't need to take the time. I can manage."

Jordan shook his head. "Nonsense. I just have to be back here by seven thirty to shadow more of Nicole's work. She's attending a play to see if anyone involved with it has talent."

"Oh, right. She told me about that."

It was tempting to question Chelsea and see what she thought of the agency and the work they were doing. But it wouldn't be fair to his sister, or to Nicole.

At the restaurant, Chelsea seemed to relax. "Terri called. She's already on the road, bringing my car up here. I'll buy her a plane ticket to fly home."

"I talked to her, too. I've already bought her a ticket."

"Oh, I… I'm the one who should do it. She's coming as a favor to me. I'll pay you back."

"There's nothing to pay back. I've got more frequent flyer miles than I know what to do with."

Chelsea grew quiet again and Jordan wondered if she was brooding over her first day at the agency.

"So, do you think you'll like working at Moonlight Ventures?" he asked.

"Sure."

"What did you do today?"

"Just got used to everything."

"I see." Jordan felt as if he was slogging through an especially unproductive interview. "Did they tell you not to talk with me about the agency?"

Chelsea drew her head up, looking surprised.

"Not at all. It would hardly be necessary, anyway. I wouldn't tell anyone my employer's private information. That wouldn't be right."

"I'm not pumping you for information, just trying to find out how your day went."

"And I told you it was fine."

Jordan wasn't sure *what* was wrong, just that something seemed to be off. Later, when he tried to buy her a phone at the mall, Chelsea got upset and shoved her credit card at the saleswoman. Yet she seemed to get over it quickly; back at the guesthouse she waved and went up the stairs.

Nicole came outside a few minutes later. "You'll have to move your car so I can get out of the garage."

"I'll drive." He opened the door for her and she shrugged. Tonight she was wearing a black outfit that was dressier than her casual look earlier in the afternoon. But the stage prop glasses and slightly altered makeup was some misdirection.

He'd already programmed the school's address into his car's GPS, wanting to focus on discussion with Nicole rather than the twists and turns to their destination. But making conversation proved difficult; he kept worrying about his sister, wondering if he should have stayed with her instead of going with Nicole.

"Is something wrong?" Nicole asked.

"I was just thinking. Did you hear how things went with Chelsea today?"

"Are you checking up on her, or the agency?"

He tensed. "I'm concerned about my sister. We had dinner and she was even quieter than usual."

"Didn't you ask how things went?"

Jordan turned where the GPS said to turn. "Yes, she said everything was fine."

"Then why aren't you taking her at her word?"

"You don't know the circumstances. And I'm not going to tell you what they are," he added hastily.

Nicole made a disgusted sound. "Next time you might wait until I *ask* before rushing to say you aren't telling me something. It's Chelsea's information to share. She's an adult. If she wants to tell me, she will. I'm not going to treat her like a child who can't handle her life."

He felt a surprising impulse to explain how awkward the evening had been. Chelsea was such a sweet kid and he always seemed to be saying or doing the wrong thing with her. But why had she gotten so upset by a plane ticket and him trying to buy her a cell phone? He thought it was the kind of thing that big brothers were supposed to do.

As they arrived at the school, his nerves were tight and he thought longingly of the relaxing weeks he'd spent in Fiji. Right now, between worry for his sister, the *PostModern* article series, and the subtly provocative dress Nicole was wearing, he felt as if sandpaper was being rubbed up and down his spine.

This just wasn't going to be his month.

NICOLE TRIED TO ignore Jordan's mood and concentrate on the stage, confirming her impressions of the singer and the play's author. There was also a good comic moment that one of the freshmen pulled off. It hadn't worked in the afternoon's performance and was too short to know for certain, so she simply made a mental note of his name for future reference.

Yet the whole time she was aware of Jordan sitting next to her, and tried to visualize him as a huge, brooding question mark, rather than a man. She'd had little time for socializing lately, so surely it was natural for her to be more aware of him than normal.

During the final act, she stood quietly and they left the auditorium.

"Ms. George," a voice called as they walked through the entrance hall. She turned and saw the principal.

"Hello, Mr. Dougherty," she greeted.

"Good evening. Shall I keep you informed of future school events?"

"That would be helpful."

"I'm grateful for your interest in our kids." The principal glanced at Jordan. "Is this one of your fellow agents, or the friend you said would be attending earlier this afternoon?"

"He's, um, the childhood friend I told you about. He also wanted to see the public performance of the play. Good night."

"Oh, yes, the same to you."

Outside they got into the car and Jordan drove onto the street as a few other attendees were reaching the parking lot.

"Do you think Dougherty will *actually* keep it confidential when you're coming?" he asked. "Or that you were there today? I'm sure it would make him look good to parents and the school board if he told them you'd come to the performance."

Nicole rolled her eyes. Jordan was a true skeptic about human nature. "Obviously I can't guarantee it, but he's a concerned administrator who cares about his students. Regardless, if we contact any of the kids, they might tell their friends. That's probably a bigger risk than Mr. Dougherty spilling the beans."

They were nearing a small shopping area with a gourmet coffee shop and Jordan waved in that direction.

"I'd like a hot drink. How about you?"

"I suppose." She figured this was how it was going to work with him, lots of "casual" conversations, rather than formal interviews, which meant it would be awfully easy to let down her guard. Despite her partners' reassurances, she didn't want to relax too much with Jordan.

He pulled into the parking lot and stopped the car. They went inside and he ordered a tall black decaf, while she got peppermint tea.

Nicole noted how Jordan added a precise amount of sugar at the condiment bar and cleaned up after himself. Not unusual, but it went along with other things she'd observed. Jordan's car was spotless, inside and out. He made meticulous notes in his notebook, rather than hasty scribbles.

When he'd first appeared in his Harvard Guy getup, she wouldn't have expected it. But now, by his own admission, it was clear he liked everything to be under control. Yet he didn't seem neurotic, but appeared more like a man determined to have his life run the way he wanted. A wife, children, pets…they'd turn his orderly life into a circus.

"Are you planning to sign some of the kids from tonight?" he asked.

"I'll investigate the possibilities, but signing a client is also up to them. And for any kid under eighteen, their parents have to agree. Some might be opposed to the idea."

"That sure wasn't a problem with your mother and father," he said in a dry voice.

Nicole stiffened. She'd known Jordan a long time ago, but the kid—and later the teenager—she had sparred with wasn't the same person as the sometimes enigmatic man she was now encountering. And this was such an artificial situation with him interviewing her. Maybe it was inevitable that he'd bring up her parents since they'd had so much to do with her career, but she didn't find it easy to talk about them.

"They were astute about managing my career as a minor," she said. "It's interesting that you had such an odd tone when you mentioned them. Any particular reason?"

"Of course not." But Jordan had answered too quickly for her to believe his denial, and he may have recognized it because he sat back with a set jaw. "Okay," he continued, "it always seemed as if they were doing a rave review, as if they were saying 'Look how fabulous our daughter is doing, look how successful she is…isn't it a shame *your* kids aren't so pretty and in such demand?'"

"Unfortunately, you're probably right."

His eyebrows lifted in surprise. "I didn't think you'd agree."

Nicole drew a deep breath. "I'm going to level with you, but it isn't for publication. While my folks are good people, they *were* stage parents. I don't believe they ever tried to sabotage another child model's career, but they did everything possible to push mine."

"And you're okay with that?"

"I was a kid, Jordan, and to be honest I was a wimpy kid. I did what I was told because it was easier than facing the massive guilt trip about how I didn't understand how much they were doing for my future."

"You sound as if you resent them."

"I don't. Since they were high-end fashion buyers, they knew the movers and shakers in the fashion world, so when they saw opportunities, they pursued them for me. And like I said, you'd better not put anything about this in your articles. It's supposed to be about me changing careers as an adult, not my childhood."

"Granted, but I'm curious. You were such a little princess back then."

Nicole let out an exasperated breath. "Maybe, or maybe you just believed what everyone else said. I don't know how many times Terri's friends said I should try to get her a job as a model and that I didn't do it because I was a spoiled brat who didn't want the competition."

Jordan seemed to choke on a gulp of his coffee. "Terri? I can't picture her prancing down a runway."

"Your prejudices are showing. Prancing is a pejorative term."

"You don't have to use big words to prove you're intelligent."

She leaned forward. "I don't have to avoid them, either. Strobe lights, cameras and makeup don't progressively leach a model's brain into nonexistence. Or do you actually believe that people go into modeling because they lack the smarts or ability to do anything else?"

"Don't put words into my mouth," he protested. "Let's drop it and talk more about the poor kid with stage parents who pushed her into a career she didn't want, so when she grew up, she pushed back and left modeling behind forever."

Nicole tried to stay calm. "That's far too simplistic. Besides, I told you, I don't want anything about my parents in this article. They're decent people. Except for expenses associated with my modeling, they never touched a penny of the money I earned. It went into a trust fund."

"But didn't their pushing have something to do with your decision to change careers now?"

She stared out the window at the people coming and going from the nearby ice cream parlor and deli. Jordan might not be a full-time reporter any longer, but he still could ask questions that dug into a person's private thoughts and emotions.

"Well?" he prompted.

"Obviously I didn't choose my first career, it was chosen for me. That doesn't mean I hated it, and it doesn't mean I don't appreciate the advantages I have now because of it."

"You didn't give a real answer."

She sipped her tea. "It's the only one you're going to get at the moment."

"Then you're saying you might consider re-phrasing your answer in the future?"

"Possibly. No guarantees." Nicole set her cup aside. "Shall we go?"

"I'm ready if you are."

They got up and he held the door open for two customers coming into the café. One, a dark-haired woman about thirty, stopped midstep and smiled at Jordan with a flirtatious air.

Interesting. He was an attractive, unattached man and Nicole wondered if he would have tried to get the woman's phone number if he was alone. It must be putting a crimp in his social life to work on a Friday evening.

JORDAN STUDIED THE dark-haired woman, who smiled back at him with an inviting air. She glanced at his ring finger, then at Nicole, and back at him with another smile. Apparently his being accompanied by a gorgeous blonde didn't faze her.

"Shall we go, Nicole?" he prompted.

"Sure."

Outside she got into the car and fastened her seat belt. "It's too bad we didn't drive sepa-rately. You might have had company tonight if you hadn't needed to take me home. At least you could have gotten her number."

"I don't hook up *that* casually."

It was true. Even in Fiji, he'd taken the time to get to know his partner.

"If you say so."

"I *do* say so. I may not be interested in marriage or family, but I prefer knowing a woman at least a little while before sleeping with her."

"That one seemed both knowable and likable."

Jordan wasn't convinced about the likable part. "It's a moot point, regardless. Besides, wasn't she 'betraying the sisterhood' by coming on to me while you were standing there? We were obviously together."

"I suppose, but—oh, turn right," Nicole said urgently.

"What?"

"Do it."

He turned, drove straight a while, then made several more turns by her directions until they entered an open area and she told him to stop.

"Turn off the headlights and look," she breathed.

Lights were playing against the sky, as if invisible hoses were spraying liquid color far and wide. They got out and watched in silence, Nicole quietly drinking it in at his side. He looked at her. Even in the darkness he could see her rapt pleasure.

Finally, she sighed. "Have you ever seen the northern lights before?"

"Once, in Alaska. I'm more interested in visiting warm climates, than cold ones."

"When I learned they can sometimes be seen in the Seattle area, I figured out where this park was and I've been hoping. So I was awfully excited when I spotted them tonight. Thank you for sharing it with me."

Jordan sucked in a breath at her quick, impulsive hug. It might have been brief, but the softness of her curves felt imprinted on his body.

"It, uh, it's a remarkable sight," he said, annoyed that he was practically stuttering. Nicole wasn't the only beautiful woman he'd known, or the only one who'd hugged him.

"I've heard they can be even more intense during the winter. Isn't Seattle great?"

"You sound as if you've fallen in love with the area."

"I have," Nicole said simply. "It has a different kind of energy that's refreshing, though I don't have anything against Los Angeles. The LA area has all sorts of things that make it an exciting city—Disneyland, the Tar Pits, the Getty and the Coliseum, to name a few."

"Don't forget the Dodgers and Angels baseball teams."

"True, but up here I'm cheering for the Mariners. I've got a soft spot for people who've endured long losing streaks."

"Ah, so you like underdogs."

"Everyone roots for winners. Somebody needs to care about the losers."

"Is that one of the philosophies behind your agency?"

Her low, sultry laugh sent blood surging into his groin.

"Jordan, stop being an interviewer for five minutes and just watch the northern lights. This is a rare opportunity and you aren't taking advantage of it."

He made mental notes, trying not to think of Nicole standing there in the close, intimate darkness, or the heated imprint of her body against his. A cool breeze across the park did little to dispel it.

Focus, he ordered silently. For example, he should ask why she and her partners had chosen Seattle when there was such an active fashion industry in Southern California. Hollywood was there, too. Considering Moonlight Ventures was obviously interested in areas beyond modeling, they were a significant distance from some of the most lucrative markets to place their clients.

"You can't do it, can you?" Nicole asked. "I can practically feel the tension emanating from your body, as if the questions are charging through every cell and exuding from your fingertips."

Actually, it was hormones charging through his system. Focusing on journalistic questions was the only thing keeping him sane.

The devil with restraint. He tugged on Nicole's arm and pulled her close. Lord, her lips felt good and her soft, sweet scent filled his nostrils. Threading his fingers through her silky hair, he deepened the kiss. Her mouth opened and he could swear the lights in the sky had gone shooting through his veins.

Nicole gently pushed on his chest. He let go with a gasp, barely hanging onto his self-control.

"I'm afraid that was my fault," she said, her voice almost even. "I gave you the wrong idea when I hugged you."

"Oh, that's …don't worry about it."

"Maybe we should leave now."

"Sure." Jordan took deep breaths, willing his body to calm as they got back in the car. He started the engine and programmed the GPS for Nicole's address.

Back at the house she got out quickly. "Sorry for the misunderstanding."

Scrambling from the car himself, he hurried to the porch with her.

"You aren't invited in," she told him.

"I didn't think I was, but it's only right to walk you to your door."

"Such a gentleman."

Her faintly mocking retort was annoying. Besides, Jordan didn't *feel* like a gentleman. He felt like a caveman—or a skunk for letting Nicole defuse the situation with that excuse about a hug.

Perhaps the kiss *had* been partly prompted by her spontaneous act, but he wasn't innocent in the situation.

Nicole opened the door and he heard the beeping of a security system. The latch clicked behind her and he strode back to his car. No point in bemoaning his lack of restraint. The kiss had happened and he couldn't pretend it hadn't. But it didn't have to happen again.

He grinned at himself and thought of how Syd would chide him if she knew. He'd love to back out of doing the article, but he couldn't. The two of them had been through hell together more than once in his early days as a reporter. She'd been the veteran and taught him a lot. Once, when they'd been faced with a drug dealer, she had talked them out of a dangerous standoff, possibly saving his life. The least he could do was hit the off switch on his hormones and write the articles she needed for *PostModern*.

NICOLE TURNED OFF the security system and reset it. The first thing she'd done after escrow closed was hire a company to wire the doors and windows. While she didn't want to be paranoid, she'd had a security system ever since dealing with an obsessed fan years earlier.

With a yelp, Toby sped through the house and she leaned over to receive his frantic welcome.

It helped her resist the urge to peek through the curtains and watch Jordan drive away.

"Hey, it's all right," she soothed the dog.

This was the first time she'd been out so late since adopting the little guy. No wonder he was relieved to know he hadn't been abandoned again.

"Maybe I *should* get you a friend," she said. She'd heard of taking a dog to the shelter and letting it pick out a feline companion. At the very least, it would tell her whether Toby was okay with cats. On the other hand, adopting another animal might be too much to handle at the moment.

Toby stuck with her as she got her computer out to check emails. She'd kept her phone turned off; it felt rude to constantly check an electronic gadget while viewing a performance or spending time with someone.

There was a message from Rachel, inviting her to call and talk if she needed to vent about Jordan. Nicole might have phoned...if it hadn't been for the kiss. She needed time to deal with her thoughts.

It was partly her fault. She should have simply ignored the signs of the northern lights. Going to a quiet park had prompted an intimacy that wasn't real, even if it had been charged with sexual tension. As a reporter doing a story on her, Jordan shouldn't have succumbed, but Nicole knew she should have been smarter as well.

Upstairs she ran a bath in the jetted tub, undressed and sank into the deep warm water.

Since it was big enough for two people, the tub was another reminder that she was alone. The Realtor had almost cooled the deal when she'd raved about the amorous possibilities. Nicole had brushed it off, joking that she preferred thinking of the bathroom as a fortress of solitude.

Turning on the jets, she tried to lose herself in the sound of the water and the warmth of its swirling currents.

Jordan had definitely improved in the kissing department. But while she'd been tempted to let it go further, she had pulled herself under fierce control. He might question her motives for helping Chelsea, but *she* questioned why he'd kissed her. There didn't have to be anything ulterior in it, but she couldn't take a chance. For the sake of her friends as well as herself, she had to keep her head.

The truth was, she had a naturally romantic nature…which put her at a disadvantage. As a model, her image had often been used to promote the romantic possibilities of certain products. But roses and candlelight, kisses in the rain, sexy lingerie…nobody lived that way twenty-four hours a day. To keep from getting sucked into what other people seemed to expect, she had been forced to keep her romanticism in check.

A cold nose nudged her elbow. Toby was on his hind legs, looking into the tub. She fondled his ears and he didn't seem to mind her damp fingers. What a sweetheart.

Being alone and heartache-free, having fun with her dog and her friends…that was the right choice for her. Discovering that physical needs weren't easily ignored didn't change her mind on the issue. Maybe someday she'd consider other possibilities if she was sure the guy in question was grounded in reality and could see past her bustline and polished photographs. She needed a man who could deal with life being messy and sometimes out of control.

That hypothetical man definitely wasn't Jordan, no matter how good his lips had felt against hers.

As she pulled up old memories, Nicole recalled how defiantly he'd pretended his family was happy and normal as a kid. Since their parents had been friends in the early years, she'd picked up on some of the pain and ugliness. She had known he was putting on a show. Old habits died hard, and even from the little she had seen, it looked as if he enjoyed being a bachelor, with everything in his life organized and controlled. Definitely not the guy for her.

So the thing to do was treat the kiss as an aberration. He surely recognized it as such, and there was no need to discuss the matter; it had nothing to do with the magazine articles.

She relaxed into the swirling bath water and told herself once again that she was better off single.

CHAPTER SIX

LATE SATURDAY AFTERNOON Barton came home from a day of hiking with his brother, who'd once again harangued him about getting back in the dating game. Peter was a fiend on the subject and had been for nearly a year.

"So things went bad with Ellyn," Pete kept saying. "It happens. There are plenty of other women out there."

Barton hadn't told him that he'd tried asking his neighbor out for a date, though maybe he should—at least it might shut Peter up.

The doorbell rang a few minutes after he returned. It was Nicole George.

"Hi. Is everything okay at your place?" He'd told her to feel free to ask for his help at any time. Being a good neighbor was important to him and he'd learned a great deal about repairs after fixing up his property.

"It's fine. I came by earlier, but you weren't home. I'm having a few folks over for dinner tonight and hope you'll come also."

"I don't like horning in on a group of friends."

"Don't worry, they're more acquaintances than

friends. One is Chelsea Masters, the woman staying in my guest house."

A surge of anticipation went through him. "I
met Chelsea the other day."

"Good. Another guest will be her sister, Terri,
who just arrived after driving Chelsea's car up
from Los Angeles. Their brother is also coming.
I knew the Masters family when I was a kid, but
hadn't seen them until recently when Jordan was
assigned to do some articles on the agency. You'd
actually be doing me a favor to come over and
add to the mix."

Barton didn't know if Nicole was simply being
gracious, but could see how the gathering might
be an awkward combination. Besides, the best
thing he had to eat in the house was four-day-old
pizza in the fridge. Even Spike turned his nose
up at four-day-old pizza.

"That would be nice," Barton said. "Can I get
something at the store to contribute?"

"Nope, just bring yourself. Say in an hour?"

Once she was gone, he ran upstairs to shower.
This would be an opportunity to learn more about
Chelsea without making it a big deal. Peter was
right that he needed to come out of his shell and
get back to normal; he just hadn't felt like it until
meeting her.

Spike sat on the bed as he dressed, seeming
grumpy at the sign his human companion was
getting ready to go out again.

"Bad luck, pal," Barton told him when the cat glared. "I got a better offer for the evening."

At six he rang his neighbor's doorbell and Chelsea answered. The bruises on her face were still visible beneath her makeup, but he could tell they were starting to heal.

"Hi," she greeted him. "Nicole is in the kitchen. Come out to the deck."

"I understand your sister drove your car to Seattle."

"Yes. I flew north to visit my brother and ended up getting a job my first day. Terri offered to bring my car and some of my stuff."

"You must be the impulsive type."

She looked charmingly pretty with her dark hair pulled back in a ponytail and wearing a pair of trim black shorts and a blue T-shirt. Her figure was appealing, but he especially liked her deep brown eyes. They were soft and warm and vulnerable.

Chelsea shook her head. "As a rule I'm not the least bit impulsive. But… I don't know what happened. It seemed like a good idea and I think it's going to work out well."

"There's an exception to every rule, right?"

"Yes." She brightened. "That's probably it."

Barton had been cured of his own impulsiveness. He and his wife had married after a short courtship. They should have made sure they were committed to each other through thick and thin, and most of all, that they shared the same values and vision for the future. It was a mistake that had cost him dearly.

Now he believed in slow and deliberate decision-making.

Another brunette was sitting on the deck. Although she was attractive and shared a resemblance to Chelsea, she had an almost mocking hardness in her features. Chelsea's face was much gentler.

"This is Barton Smith," Chelsea introduced him. "Barton, my sister, Terri Masters."

"It's a pleasure, Terri."

Nicole's beagle dashed up the steps from the yard and Barton bent to pet the eager little animal.

"He seems to like you," Chelsea said.

"We've met before and he probably smells my cat, Spike."

"You're a cat person?"

"Spike decided I was going to be," he replied, "whether I wanted to be or not."

She laughed.

The large deck was a pleasant spot for a gathering. There was even a well-equipped cooking area at one end, with a chimney to vent the smoke from the built-in barbecue.

Nicole hurried out and started the flame on the gas grill, then came over and greeted him.

"I'll be back and forth for a while. Help yourself to something to drink," she invited, gesturing to the refrigerator in the outdoor kitchen.

She disappeared inside again while he collected a bottle of sparkling cider and sat next to Chelsea.

"How did grading the tests and papers go?" Chelsea asked.

"Terrific. I'm pleased with how far my students have progressed this year."

"Nice to know you didn't waste all that time on the little beasts, right?" Terri interjected with a sardonic note.

Chelsea cast an uncertain glance at her sister before turning back to him. "I think teaching must be a satisfying job."

"It is for me."

The doorbell rang again in the house and Chelsea ran to answer it. A minute later she returned with a tall, imposing man who had the same watchful hardness in his face as Terri. It had to be the brother that Nicole had mentioned.

"This is my neighbor, Barton Smith," Nicole said, coming out of the kitchen door again. "Barton, this is Jordan Masters. And I'm sure Chelsea has introduced her sister. As you can see, you're here to help provide balance against the Masters of the Universe."

Barton grinned at the superhero reference along with Chelsea, though Jordan and Terri barely cracked a smile.

"Don't mind them, Barton," Nicole told him, "these two can be too serious for their own good."

"Are you implying that I don't have a sense of humor?" Terri demanded.

"Not at all," Nicole answered. "I just think it struggles to escape at times—at least it did when we were kids."

Both Terri and Jordan appeared surprised by Nicole's comment, but she'd said they hadn't seen each other since childhood and Barton suspected it hadn't always been a comfortable relationship.

Chelsea sat down once more and Barton thought again about how nice she seemed. Nicole had said he was doing her a favor by coming to dinner, but he was the one who felt as if he'd been given something.

AN HOUR LATER, Jordan looked at the gathering around the patio table and felt a headache developing, even though the conversation had remained relaxed. Nicole seemed to have things well organized as she set out bowls of food and a platter of shish kebabs fresh off the grill.

He *did* wonder if she had invited her neighbor with matchmaking in mind, but his sister was unlikely to jump into another romantic entanglement right away. Besides, Nicole might be interested in Barton herself. An unpleasant sensation surged through him at the idea and he was stunned by the desire to tell her neighbor to back off.

Jordan swallowed the feeling even as he stifled a yawn. His eyes were gritty from lack of sleep—cold showers could do that to a guy. Then that morning he'd gotten a text from Chelsea saying that Nicole had invited them all to dinner and she'd see him then. It was the last thing he'd needed.

After reliving the previous evening's kiss, he wasn't sure what to think. Nicole had responded—not enthusiastically, but she'd definitely returned the kiss. And she'd kept her cool better than he had, cutting it short and not overreacting.

He ought to be grateful.

Barton Smith leaned toward him. "Nicole says you're doing a series of magazine articles about the talent agency. I've always heard about the importance of being objective in journalism. So what do you do when you're assigned to cover someone you knew as a kid and you can't be totally objective?"

With a wickedly amused expression, Nicole turned to him. "Yes, Jordan, tell us how that works."

Hmmm. She was enjoying his discomfort far too much.

"I'll be up-front about us knowing each other," he explained. "*PostModern* isn't a typical publication, and they're always looking for new approaches to a story."

"Maybe the editor wants you to explore a new style," Nicole suggested.

"It's possible," he admitted.

Actually, it was not only possible, but likely. Nicole's remark had reminded him of Syd's prodding over the past few years, saying she wanted him to stretch more often beyond the short, pithy commentary he did for his columns. She liked his longer work and believed he should do more of it, lest he grow hidebound in one style. Now that he thought of the trial paragraphs he'd written so far on the article, he knew they weren't what Syd wanted.

He straightened, a sense of determination filling him. He could do this.

Nicole served salad onto her plate. "I suppose it's impossible to ever be completely objective. We look at life through the lens of our culture and our experiences."

"That's what I want my students to understand," Barton said. "Some of them originally came from other parts of the world, and I think it's wise for everyone to find out that there isn't just one way of doing things or of thinking about them."

"You want to teach them tolerance," Terri remarked.

"Maybe more than that," Chelsea suggested.

"Definitely more," Barton agreed. "I don't think tolerance is a high enough standard."

"Me, either," Nicole said. "It's better than nothing, but surely we're ready to go beyond it."

"Like respect and appreciation," Chelsea added.

It wasn't the discussion Jordan had expected over dinner on Nicole's deck. So...what *had* he anticipated? Something light and fluffy? A review of fashion or the latest blockbuster film? Or maybe Nicole was just trying to prove she could be a serious thinker.

His head began pounding in earnest as he forked up a chunk of beef from his shish kebab. It was delicious, he thought absently, marinated just right and grilled to perfection. Nicole might not have had much time to cook over the years, but it appeared she knew what she was doing.

"Did you?" Terri asked, poking his shoulder, and Jordan realized that he'd lost track of the conversation.

"Sorry, I was miles away. Did I what?"

"See the latest *Star Wars* film. Nicole says it was good."

Irony struck him at the much more casual subject. How had they gone from a discussion of social and educational policies to movies?

"No, I missed seeing it." He listened more carefully as the conversation shifted to baseball.

Barton was proving to be a good addition to the dinner party, helping make the evening more comfortable, or perhaps more casual. There was too much history between the Masterses and the Georges, not that anyone except him knew the full story. But even without that, Terri could make things awkward and all the events of the past week added to the potential for tension.

Jordan glanced at Barton, still wondering if Nicole was hoping to fix him up with Chelsea or had a personal interest in the guy. Or was Nicole's joke about having an ally against the "Masters of the Universe" the real explanation?

Funny. No one had used that line on him before, though Jordan had heard other jokes about his supposed arrogance. But then, he wasn't entirely sure whether the Masters of the Universe were the good guys or the villains.

Nicole was sharp and he was confronting her intelligence in a way he never had in the past. It wasn't that he'd believed she was dumb, it was more that deep down he'd assumed she hadn't *needed* her brains.

Resignation went through Jordan. He'd said some stupid things about Nicole when they were kids…things that would have gotten back to her. She was probably going to spend their time together trying to expose his biases.

Her fingers brushed his as she handed him a basket of garlic bread, and he ignored the warm flush up his arm…that is, he almost succeeded in ignoring it.

NICOLE WONDERED WHERE Jordan's mind kept wandering to; he didn't seem to be paying much attention to the discussion.

Something touched her foot and she saw it was Toby. He stared up at her with wide, pleading eyes.

"I wish I could, baby," she told him, "but the rescue center told me it's best if you don't get table scraps."

"He does a great job of acting like an orphan without means of support," Jordan observed, seeming to come out of his reverie.

"I know. I fed him twenty minutes ago and still feel guilty." She leaned down, grabbed one of Toby's toys and tossed it into the yard. Delighted, he went tearing after it, only to be distracted by a butterfly.

Everyone had finished eating, so Nicole headed into the kitchen to fetch dessert. Jordan followed her.

"Can I get something for you?" she asked brightly.

"No, but I've been wondering why you invited your neighbor. He seems nice and the conversation has gone smoothly, partly because of him, I suppose, but I still can't help wondering."

"Wow, the conversation has gone more smoothly because of Barton," she said in a dry tone. "Isn't that enough reason to issue an invitation?"

"You must know him fairly well to realize he'd be helpful."

She raised an eyebrow. "I only moved into the house a short time ago. But I made a good guess, with no ulterior motives involved. I asked a couple of other neighbors as well, but they had plans. What's so important about who was invited to dinner?"

Jordan looked conflicted, his brow creased. "It doesn't matter. I'm a reporter, I like to know things."

Her smile flashed unexpectedly. "Oh, you're a reporter now? You didn't appreciate being called that the other day."

He sighed. "I've been thinking about what you said, that Syd wants me to stretch as a writer. She's always kept an eye on my career. We went through some tough times together when we were both reporters, including two days as hostages when we were covering events in the Middle East."

"Good heavens." Nicole felt an odd flutter inside as she considered the possibility that Jordan could have been murdered and they would have never met again. "That must have been an awful experience."

"I wouldn't recommend it to anyone, but going through it together forged a bond we'll never lose. Syd kept her head, probably a lot better than I did."

Nicole pursed her lips. "It seems out of character for you to reveal information to me. Perhaps you're the one with an ulterior motive. Are you hoping to win sympathy and get me to drop my guard?"

"In case I haven't made it clear enough yet, this isn't an exposé."

"You'd just ignore a juicy tidbit that might boost *PostModern*'s circulation?"

"There's a difference between looking for a scandal and reporting something you happen to learn."

He ran his fingers through his dark hair and Nicole wondered if his lovers did the same thing. The time they'd kissed in high school, his hair had been short and prickly against her palm. She'd figured he was going for a tough square-jawed I-can-take-anything persona.

Shaking her head to clear irrelevant memories, she filled her whipped cream canister.

"Do you see the difference?" Jordan prompted.

"Not if the information you 'learn' isn't relevant or necessary to reveal. And especially if it isn't even reported correctly."

"The subject of an article isn't always the best judge of what needs to be reported, or what the readers like to know. Don't you believe in freedom of the press and free speech?"

"Definitely. In fact, we're starting a blog for the agency. My partners suggested I write about what it's like to be interviewed by you for these magazine articles."

His gaze sharpened. "Are you comparing a blog to freedom of the press?"

"Who's to say what a blog is? They're still figuring out what things on the internet represent and even after they do, I bet they keep redefining it. Besides, no matter what, it's about freedom of speech."

He was massaging the back of his head and neck, a drawn expression on his face. "Okay," he agreed finally, "you have a point. But why do you need to write about me?"

"Maybe you aren't the best person to decide what our readers may find interesting."

"Don't use my arguments against me." His voice sounded rueful. "That isn't a fair tactic against a guy with a headache."

"Never let it be said that I didn't give aid to someone in pain." Opening a cupboard, she grabbed a bottle of aspirin and handed it to him with a glass with water. "Help yourself."

Jordan swallowed two aspirin tablets. "Thanks."

"You're welcome." Picking up a tray with shortbread, a bowl of sliced strawberries and the whipped cream, she nodded at another tray with bowls on it. "Can you bring that one for me?"

"Sure."

"That looks fabulous," Chelsea said as they approached.

"I'm addicted to anything strawberry, especially in spring when the berries are at their best," Nicole answered.

"I agree." Barton picked up the canister she'd filled with cream. "What's this?"

"A gadget that makes whipped cream. You just pour in the cream and use a gas canister. Ain't modern technology wonderful?" She gave Jordan an innocent look. "Is whipped cream a frothy enough topic for a model?"

"Very amusing."

"I do my best."

It probably wasn't very nice to keep yanking his chain; the guy *did* have a headache. She'd have a headache, too, a permanent one, if she lived in the tiny condo that Chelsea had described. It obviously suited him. Jordan wanted a carefree bachelor life—the apartment-style condo would have told her that without the little she'd picked up from his column and his remarks the previous evening.

Nicole sighed. Jordan had created a life that worked for him and she felt a hint of envy to realize he had everything together, a little too much perhaps for her taste, but he did seem to have things under control. By contrast it seemed as if she was racing to catch up with herself.

Then good sense kicked in.

For years she'd fashioned her own life to suit her, as much so as Jordan was doing. The only reason things were more chaotic now was because she had made a decision to *change* her life and it took time to settle into a new home, a new city and a new career…not to mention having to deal with a reporter while she was doing it.

And the reporter was Jordan Masters, who'd turned into a sexy and dynamic man who was disrupting her satisfaction with her platonic lifestyle. That just added insult to injury.

CHELSEA FOCUSED ON her bowl as she carefully arranged a layer of strawberries over a slice of shortcake. The dinner conversation had been awfully pleasant and Barton seemed as nice as she'd first believed him to be.

But she couldn't forget that she'd also thought Ron was nice in the beginning, so she needed to be careful the next time she got involved with a guy. Not that it was an issue with Barton; it was far too soon to think about romance, even if he was interested, which he probably wasn't. Well, he *had* asked her out, but she'd also gotten the impression that he'd been hurt in some way. So inviting her to dinner or a movie could have just been him being neighborly.

Annoyed with the way her brain kept churning, Chelsea accepted the whipped cream gadget from Terri and squirted out a generous amount.

"How can you do that?" Terri said, peering at the tiny dollop in her bowl. "It's like having a little strawberry with your whipped cream."

"I disagree," Barton returned firmly, "your sister is a woman who knows how to eat strawberry shortcake." He put an equal amount on his own dessert.

Chelsea didn't know if he was just being nice, but she appreciated his support. While she loved her sister, Terri was tough and had edges...the same as Jordan. They were both strong and never seemed to be afraid, the total opposite of her.

"Where are you from originally?" Terri asked Barton.

"Seattle, born and bred," he told her.

"That makes you the only Northwest native here," Chelsea said. "What's the best part of living in Washington?"

"I hesitate to say. I'd hate getting into an argument."

"Why would we argue?"

Nicole pointed to the ribbon around her neck. "He may be referring to baseball, Chelsea. Your keys are on a lanyard with the Angels' logo."

"Oh."

"There's nothing like watching a baseball game at Safeco Field," Barton said. "But I suppose you feel the same about the Angels' stadium in Anaheim."

"They're the Los Angeles Angels now," Terri objected.

"Except they didn't actually move out of Anaheim."

Chelsea was glad that Barton didn't seem put

off by Terri's attitude. She wondered why her sister was always so thorny. Maybe Terri did it to keep people at a distance.

Terri looked ready to continue the debate and Chelsea felt a familiar clench in her stomach.

Nicole waved a spoon mounded with whipped cream in the air. "While I'll never abandon my first love altogether—and I'm talking about the Dodgers here—there's room in my life for a new friend. Safeco Field is a great place to bond."

"That's right," Barton said approvingly. "The next thing you know, it'll be season tickets and a Mariners flag on your garage. I understand the team has one of the biggest female fan bases in major league baseball."

"I've heard that, too, and I'm ready to fall in love again."

Sinking back in her chair, Chelsea ate a bite of strawberry. She was grateful for the way Nicole had defused the tense moment. If only *she* were so adroit.

If she had the nerve, she'd ask Barton if he had a season ticket to Safeco Field and how often he went to home games, but it might have looked as if she was hinting for a date. She wouldn't have been, though having him as a friend would be nice.

JORDAN'S HEADACHE STARTED easing off as the evening wore on. He should have taken something when it first started instead of playing iron man. Of course, he was still uncomfortable in other ways.

Some of it stemmed from his attraction to Nicole, which he couldn't completely ignore. It wasn't that there was something terribly wrong with her. In fact, she was proving to have an interesting personality, though it was inconceivable to consider them getting together. But he would feel that way about any woman. He didn't want ties. He wanted to be free to live life on his terms, and generally spent time with women who wanted the same.

The other part of his discomfort was professional. Nicole's light comment about being ready to fall in love again had been offered playfully to ease the social awkwardness that Terri sometimes created. But a moment after the words had left Nicole's lips she'd sent him a cool, challenging stare. It was as if she was daring him to take the words out of context and tell the magazine-reading public that Nicole George was anxious to find love. That kind of thing probably *had* happened and was a reminder of the gray areas involved with his work.

"Mount Rainier is incredibly beautiful," Nicole said and he realized the conversation had shifted once more. "My friend Logan does photography up there whenever he has time."

"My folks used to take us to Rainier to pick

huckleberries," Barton said. "We'd bring a picnic and spend the day picking."

"I've heard of huckleberries, but what are they like?" Chelsea asked.

"Mostly they look like miniature blueberries. They taste great, but loganberries are my favorite."

"Where do you pick those?"

"I don't think they grow wild. Mom buys flats from a grower to make jam, and to freeze for pies and cobblers."

"It…it sounds as if you have one of those old-fashioned mothers who cooks and bakes."

His sister's face was wistful and Jordan remembered how she used to play house when she was little, concentrating on it as if she could create a different kind of life for herself. It hadn't worked. Nor had his attempt to escape reality as a teen through sports and girls. Only time and maturity had moved him to a better place.

"My mother is both modern and traditional," Barton told Chelsea. "She's an engineer in the aircraft industry and also loves the home arts. She cans, freezes and dehydrates fruits and veggies in the summer and fall. She also sews and enters stuff in the Puyallup Fair."

"She sounds busy," Nicole commented.

"A regular Suzy Homemaker." Terri's voice was dry.

"Right," Nicole agreed. "She's deciding what a homemaker is on her own terms. I admire that."

Jordan wanted to admire how she handled the awkward moments in the conversation, so why did he hesitate to acknowledge graciousness when it was wrapped up in a sexy golden-haired former model?

He smiled, though his facial muscles were tight. "Nicely said."

"Which one of us?" Terri challenged.

He shrugged. When Terri was in one of her moods, it was best to let it go. And he suddenly wondered what had gotten her going. Was she upset about Chelsea moving out of the Los Angeles area? She wanted the best for their sister, but maybe she was suddenly feeling alone. Or it could be something else. He had to admit to sometimes being clueless when it came to his sisters. What he did know for certain was that when Terri was unhappy or scared about something, she usually turned to argument or anger to deal with it.

"Would anybody like coffee?" Nicole asked. "I can make a pot of decaf."

There were nods all around and she stood.

Terri got to her feet as well, a strained expression on her face. "Let me help."

Nicole smiled. "How nice."

Jordan stood to join them, only to see a warning glance from her. Or at least he thought she was warning him. A sophisticated supermodel didn't need protection from his sharp-tongued sister. As for Terri, she was able to hold her own and wouldn't accept big-brother protection, regardless.

He dropped back into his chair.

"Barton, I apologize if Terri is…" Chelsea's voice trailed before she took a deep breath to continue. "My sister doesn't mean things the way they sound."

"Don't worry about it," Barton answered. "You should meet my cousin. When Greg found out Nicole George was my next-door neighbor he speculated whether she did topless sunbathing in her backyard. He actually said that to her face. I could have slugged him, but she was classy about it."

"She would be."

Jordan seriously doubted that Nicole would do nude sunbathing where anyone might see her, though the image that popped into his head put him in acute pain.

Surreal. That was the only word to describe the evening. It wasn't often that the past and present collided this way.

He again wondered if his attraction to Nicole was something he should mention to Syd, only to promptly decide the answer was no. She'd just be surprised to hear him say he hadn't felt that way before and likely claim he'd just been fooling himself until now.

Pushing to his feet, he started gathering plates

and utensils, anything to keep from thinking. At least he wouldn't be rushing into the house immediately; a decent interval would have passed.

AFTER NICOLE TURNED on the coffeemaker she looked at Terri, who was taking cups down from the cupboard and putting them on a tray. Along with the rest of the Masters family, she'd played a part in Nicole's childhood, though Nicole had spent as little time around her as possible. Chelsea had inspired sympathy, but Terri had usually been a pain with her angry defiance about everything. Jordan could be the same way.

"I know, I know," Terri said with a twist of her lips, "I'm a witch, spelled with a 'b.'"

"You were always forthright."

"What you're saying is that I never grew up. You could be right—maybe I'm still fighting trolls and demons."

Nicole poured cream into a small pitcher, glad she'd taken time that morning to unpack the rest of her kitchen supplies. "Most of us have a few."

"I suppose, and they dog our footsteps at every turn."

"But we don't have to offer them permanent residence in the guest bedroom."

A burst of laughter came from the other woman. "Lord, Nicole, you're quick. How did I miss that all those years ago?"

"We didn't know each other very well. You and Jordan were friends with my sister, not me."

"Yeah. I never understood why Emily put up with my crap."

"Em has a genius for friendship."

"She certainly does," Jordan said, startling them both. He stood at the kitchen door, holding a stack of plates and silverware. "I'll put these in the dishwasher."

He seemed full of suppressed energy and Nicole decided it was just as well to let him have something to do.

As part of her own research she'd gone online to read the last two months of Jordan's columns, available on a number of major newspaper websites. In them, he'd lauded the pleasures of the tropics, with mentions of Hawaii where he had a vacation place. They gave the impression he was a laid-back guy with a sardonic wit, but there was nothing laid-back about Jordan. Even now, putting the dishes into the washer, he was as precise as if he'd written a manual on the subject. Jeez, he even rinsed the plates and silver, while she just tried to put things in so they didn't hit and break.

On the surface, inviting the Masters family to dinner *hadn't* been logical. They were barely acquaintances any longer, and had never been friends. Now she mostly felt bad for Chelsea, who plainly struggled with self-confidence.

Suspecting Chelsea wasn't eager to have too

much "alone time" with her brother and sister, Nicole had invited everyone to dinner to "inaugurate" her new barbecue. But her motives weren't entirely altruistic…she'd mostly done it to ensure she and Jordan had other people around the next time they saw each other. This way they could slide over the awkwardness of a kiss that shouldn't have happened.

He finished loading the dishwasher while she put spoons and napkins on the tray with everything else. Without a word, Terri picked it up and carried it outside.

Jordan's forehead was crinkled with tension, his jaw tight.

"Something wrong?" she asked lightly, hoping he had enough sense to avoid mentioning the previous evening.

"No, it just seems strange for us to be here, so far from Los Angeles and so many years since we were kids."

"Odd things are often the rule, rather than the exception. Once I ran into one of my college professors in London. I had no idea she'd be there, but she had flown in for a conference on international corporate relationships and was sightseeing."

"That fits. The biographical material said you'd earned your degree in business administration—if they got it right."

Apparently he remembered what she'd said about inaccurate research.

"That's right," she confirmed, "with a minor in finance."

"Then running a business was always your plan?"

The coffeemaker had finished, so Nicole poured the coffee into an insulated carafe. "No, but I had to choose something to study. Business and finance interested me. Does that seem equally strange to you?"

"I might have expected you to choose the arts or develop a perfume or makeup line. Or perhaps clothing design."

"Dressed by George, you mean?" she asked lightly.

He grinned. "That would be a catchy label—even better if you were British."

"My parents came up with it. They suggested I try design as an alternative to a talent agency." She frowned.

"Something wrong?"

"I still don't want my mom and dad to be part of the articles. I know I'm the one who mentioned them, but I didn't invite you to dinner as the reporter writing a story on me. You're here as Chelsea's brother."

Jordan crossed his arms over his chest. "Yet our families form part of who we are and the choices we make."

"Maybe, but how would you like the spotlight

turned on you and how *your* family has affected your life choices?"

A tight expression crossed his face. "I wouldn't."

"And in the average article on a successful business*man*, his parents' influence probably would not be brought up in an interview."

"You think women are treated differently?"

Nicole rolled her eyes. "You know they are."

"I'm not claiming that's how it should be."

"Then don't drag things into this that you wouldn't if I was a man."

Though the conversation shouldn't have been provocative, it was becoming that way. The importance of women's rights and equality didn't change the reality that they'd kissed the previous night…or that a part of her wanted to repeat the experience.

Jordan followed her onto the deck and Nicole forced herself to breathe normally. Once the *Post-Modern* articles were finished, her contact with him would be limited. She doubted he'd come to the agency very often, even with his sister working there. They might cross paths while running, but not much more.

If she had to, she'd put a reminder on the bathroom mirror that Jordan was merely a temporary part of her life.

JORDAN FELT AS if the evening would never end, even though Terri had relaxed and was joining more normally in the conversation, which had shifted to organic food. It wasn't a debate since everyone seemed to agree that it might be a good idea.

Nicole leaned back in her chair while she drank from her glass of soda water. She wore a black T-shirt with close-fitting black jeans. Her famous "spun-gold" hair was fastened into a ponytail. There was nothing supermodel-ish about her, although even such casual clothing was clearly from the high end of the fashion world. Or was it the way she wore the clothes that made them seem that way?

The late Northwest evening stretched daylight past eight before it began fading.

Barton glanced at his watch. "Guess I'd better get going. Nicole, thank you for a great evening."

"My pleasure. I'm glad you could come."

Chelsea stood also. "It's been terrific. Can I help clean up?"

"Nope, everything is in good shape. Besides, doesn't Terri's plane leave early tomorrow?"

That gave Jordan the excuse he needed to get out of there. "Yes," he agreed, "I need to have her to the airport by seven."

"I'm taking her," Chelsea said.

"I…" He paused, suddenly remembering Nicole's assertion about not treating Chelsea as a child who couldn't handle her own life. His sister had made a huge independent step, and he probably *wasn't* helping by rushing in to take care of things. "That's great, but I'd like to see her off, too. May I tag along, and then we could all get breakfast at the airport?"

"That sounds nice."

"Sure," Terri said. She was staying with Chelsea for the night and suggested they pick him up in the morning.

A few minutes later he was in his car and Nicole was waving a courteous farewell to all her guests before disappearing inside. He wondered if she was breathing the same sigh of relief as he was.

CHAPTER SEVEN

NICOLE ARRIVED AT the agency by 6:00 a.m. on Monday. With the time required to work with Jordan for the *PostModern* article, she needed extra hours in the office. There wouldn't be any backup this week, though Rachel was flying in the next weekend for a five-day stint. Having her partners there a portion of the time helped her while giving them more of a feel for the way things were developing.

Fierce concentration should get her through a respectable section of the paperwork that always waited for her. Fortunately, the financial side of the business was in the hands of an expert accounting firm that Kevin McClaskey had used for years. They handled income and payments so all she had to do was review it.

By ten thirty Nicole had finished the previous week's financial review, set up several photo shoots and go-sees, earmarked three files for interviews as prospective clients, and even scribbled a few thoughts for the blog article Adam had asked her to consider.

Jordan was coming in at eleven and she decided to take a break and run next door for coffee, stopping on the way to see if Chelsea wanted some, too.

"That's nice, but they filled a thermos for me this morning," Chelsea told her.

Nicole laughed. "The original plan was to have a pot always going in the lounge area in the back, but the coffee at the Crystal Connection is so good, I usually don't bother."

"I could make coffee if you want me to."

Chelsea's eagerness to help was sweet, but Nicole didn't want to take advantage. At any rate, the office manager job was already loaded with gofer duties. "Not right now, but I might take you up on that offer when there's a lot of activity and we don't have time to go out for it."

"Whenever you want."

The property that Nicole and her partners had bought from Kevin McClaskey was a large converted industrial building. Some of the shop spaces rented out to other businesses were accessed through an attractive atrium, although the Crystal Connection and Moonlight Ventures fronted on the parking lot.

"Hello," Penny Parrish greeted Nicole as she walked into the shop. Penny and her husband sold beautiful crystals and polished rocks, but had added a coffee bar to bolster their profit margin.

"Hi," Nicole replied. "I desperately need caffeine."

Eric Parrish was already in the coffee bar. "Your usual?"

"Yes." She handed him the insulated mug she'd brought.

It was amazing how well the Parrishes remembered their regulars' preferences. Eric was the elder of the couple by sixteen years. Though now eighty, he showed no sign of wanting to retire. While Nicole admired his persistence and hoped to be equally as sharp mentally and physically at his age, it posed a potential issue for the agency. The Parrishes had a long-term lease in the location where she and her partners wanted to expand the agency, but that was something to worry about in the future.

The bell over the door tinkled and Jordan's voice startled her. "Hey, Nicole."

She swung around to face him. "Hi."

"Chelsea told me you'd gone for coffee. I thought I'd pick some up, too."

"The Crystal Connection has the best around."

"Thanks for the vote of confidence," Penny said.

Eric handed Nicole the cup filled with her favorite medium roast and she added a small amount of sugar with a larger share of cream. After learning how she liked it, they always left room for her preferences.

"How are things going at the agency?" Penny asked while entering the purchase into the computer register. For regulars, there was a running tab that got paid once a month.

"Great."

"I met your new office manager. She seems nice."

"She is."

Nicole didn't mention that Jordan was Chelsea's brother. She waited while he paid for his order and they walked back together.

Chelsea looked up as they came through the door. "The general phone line has done nothing but ring since you left," she said. "Some of the callers asked for you, but I took messages instead of sending them through to voice mail. Is that okay?"

"Definitely. Callers should be screened for the ones who have a relationship with the agency and for anything you can handle yourself. Besides, it's faster for me to check written messages. Some of our clients can spend several minutes on voice mail trying to explain what they want without ever getting to the point."

"The message slips are on your desk. None of them seem urgent, but you'll want to check in case there's something I missed."

"Thanks."

Leading the way back to her office, Nicole waved Jordan inside. He glanced around the room she'd designed for quiet elegance and functionality.

"Very polished," he said. "The agency must be doing well."

"Moonlight Ventures has always been a solid concern, and as I mentioned last week, we are working on expanding the business. Until my partners get here, that part is slow, but it's part of our plan."

She saw no reason to discuss the growing profits at the agency.

He sat in one of the comfortable chairs at the end of the office, away from her desk. Nicole recalled a seminar she'd once attended; the leader had talked about taking control of a situation by choosing where to sit in the room. But to protest Jordan's choice of seat might seem petty, or make it appear she was on the defensive. So she just went to her desk and picked up the messages Chelsea had mentioned. Three were from people pushing to become clients of the agency. Chelsea was correct that nothing was urgent. That was a good sign. Some people thought everything was a crisis and it would be a godsend if Chelsea had enough judgment to tell the difference.

Seating herself on the opposite side of the small circle of chairs, Nicole smiled evenly at Jordan. Luckily she had oodles of practice looking comfortable in the most uncomfortable of circumstances. "Is this our first formal interview?"

"Yes, though I'd also like to see more of what you do in action."

She'd anticipated that and had a few ideas that might bump him further out of his preconceptions. "That's fine," she agreed, "provided it doesn't violate anyone's privacy."

"That's a given. I realize you've only been an agent for five or six months, but what part of the work do you enjoy the least?"

"Having to tell someone the agency isn't interested in representing them," Nicole said promptly.

"I wouldn't like that, either."

"Some are rather arrogant or wildly ambitious for themselves or their children, and saying 'no' can spark an argument from them, so that isn't pleasant. But the ones I hate turning down the most are the shy hopefuls, the people who long to be recognized as pretty or handsome or talented."

Jordan's face seemed carefully devoid of expression and she didn't know if it was because he was trying to be aloof, or if he'd taken exception to something she'd said.

"It must be hard knowing how to say no tactfully since you've never been on the receiving end of that sort of message."

She chuckled. "Is that what you think? I've been turned down my share of times. I even showed up once for a commercial and the director told me flat out that even though the advertiser had requested me, I was completely wrong and could just go home."

"I can't imagine why he felt that way."

"That sounds suspiciously close to a compliment."

"I'm simply aware that your type seems universally popular."

"My type?"

"Golden-haired, sexy and classically beautiful. I'm not saying that to be flattering. You know what you look like."

Nicole sat back in her chair. She wasn't flattered. Jordan was right about how she'd been marketed and it would be hypocritical to pretend otherwise.

"So what does that have to do with this interview?" she asked.

"I wonder what it's like to shift out of a career where you were in demand for your beauty. You're behind the camera now, in a sense. That's a wholly different dynamic."

He'd led up to *that* question quite neatly.

JORDAN WATCHED VARIOUS expressions flitting across Nicole's face. Assumptions were tricky. Until a week ago, he might have assumed she was having trouble being out of the limelight. But that wouldn't make sense. She wasn't a fading beauty, desperately longing to stay the center of attention. She'd left the field while she was still stunning and demand for her image was high; leaving had been her choice.

After a few moments her head tilted to an angle he'd seen in a dozen advertisements. "In a way, it's a relief. There *is* a sense of loss, though I think that's natural when someone is adjusting to change. I'm still sorting it out."

The answer seemed straightforward, if not overly informative.

"Can you tell me what led you to make such a big change?"

"I couldn't be a model forever, could I?"

"Some have done it much longer. Look at Christie Brinkley and Cheryl Tiegs. They've redefined how the world looks at women past a certain age, along with actresses such as Meryl Streep and Helen Mirren."

"I know, but doing it now means I have more time to explore new possibilities. Helping other people succeed appeals to me. I've been lucky to have people help me and hope to do the same for others. Seems like a great way to make a living."

"So you want to do something noble?" he asked. He was trying to restrain his skepticism, not wanting to be influenced by years of sour comments from his mother.

The memory of his discussion with Nicole on Saturday returned with ironic force. She'd wanted to know whether he'd like revealing how his family experiences had affected him. He definitely wouldn't. On the other hand, *everyone* was affected by their past. Surely it was a legitimate line of questioning. Or was it? She could be right claiming a man in her position wouldn't be asked about parental influence.

"Becoming an agent isn't about being noble," Nicole said firmly. "I liked modeling and wanted a second career that would be equally interesting and mean something. This is what I chose."

Jordan thought there was more she wasn't saying, but he had plenty of time to get at the truth. If necessary, he'd just keep asking the same questions in different ways until he got the information.

"Planning a second career is common these days," he said. "But usually not by someone who's only thirty. That's pretty young, especially if you still enjoyed modeling. Other models in your shoes have started businesses and run them at the same time they've remained in front of the camera."

"Don't forget that I'd been modeling since I was a baby," she reminded him. "Three decades is a long career."

"It was also a line of work you didn't choose," he said, avoiding pointing out that her *parents* were the ones who'd put her in front of the camera. "Did having a personal choice about running an agency influence your decision-making process? You said yourself that you modeled from infancy. It isn't as if a baby says, 'Yeah, sign me up.'"

Instead of immediately replying, Nicole took several sips of coffee. Unsure if she was road-blocking him or simply thinking, he drank from his own cup. Chelsea had been right, the Crystal Connection's product was excellent. He hadn't expected much from a coffee bar run out of a new age shop selling rocks and crystals.

Nicole had made it clear that she wanted her parents left out of the article. But his question *was* pertinent. He also didn't think she'd mind as much if someone else was asking it.

Finally Nicole put down her cup. "Sorting out the motives for any decision can be complicated...and don't think I didn't notice that this is about my parents again and you've already asked about that. Although I had an agent, my folks made the final decisions for a long time. When I turned nineteen I took control of my career, which was a difficult adjustment for them. If I'd simply wanted to feel empowered, that would have been more than enough."

"I wasn't suggesting it was the only reason. *PostModern* wants a real examination of the complexities that lead someone such as you, who seemed to be living the dream, to make a change in her life. So I'm not looking for one-two-three explanations, because when it comes to the human psyche, there's no such thing as simple."

"I'll think about it and we can discuss it an-other time."

Jordan sighed. It had been ages since he had worked as a reporter. Even then it had been mostly about asking a few brisk questions and writing down equally fast answers. But Syd would never be satisfied with a standard story. This needed to be far more intimate and asking him to do it was just...

He scowled.

Okay, maybe he *hadn't* been the kind of re-porter who'd dug deeper. His professional goal had always been to write an op-ed column and everything else had become a stepping stone to his ambition. Syd hadn't approved, claiming he needed experience to have something worth say-ing, not just a clever way of saying it.

Nicole cocked her head. "What are you think-ing about? You've got a rather intense expression."

"That I'd like to send my editor to Antarctica."

"Should I be offended?"

"No. What it means is that I'm a completely normal person who, as it turns out, isn't crazy about being pushed out of his comfort zone."

"Few people are. Change can also be about growth, whether you like it or not. Maybe these articles are the fertilizer she's spreading to stimu-late your growth spurt. Or in your case, advance-ment on the evolutionary scale."

Jordan laughed reluctantly. "Hey, I'm not the focus of this interview."

"You are, in a way," she said before adding, "for the blog."

He might as well be honest with himself—at the moment he'd give a lot to have Nicole focused on him, with the rest of world locked out. She might be dressed in casual business garb, and didn't appear to be trying to attract his sexual interest, but she wasn't downplaying her looks. Her slim skirt and blouse showed her figure to perfection. It was a warm day and she wasn't wearing stockings, but her feet were shod in elegant sandals. Her hair fell in golden waves over her shoulders, one lock curling around her left breast...

He definitely had to stop noticing details like that.

It still didn't make sense to him. He'd seen Nicole pictured in dozens of ads that were far more provocative, with seductive poses, sultry angles, and simmering glances. Sometimes she'd been barely clothed, wearing scant bikinis or silk lingerie. If he was going to feel a personal attraction, wouldn't he have gotten at least a hint of it when looking at those shots?

Syd had kidded him about the possibility of hormonal interference and he'd assured her that it wouldn't be a problem. Now he had a feeling that the universe was laughing at him.

IN BETWEEN PHONE calls and filing, Chelsea spent the morning exploring drawers, cabinets and the computer. Nicole had apologized for not being able to provide more orientation and had promised they would be patient as she learned how the agency operated and what needed to be done.

Admittedly, the thought of meeting the rest of the agency's partners made Chelsea nervous. Nicole had been terrific and Adam Wilding seemed nice. But Rachel Clarion and Logan Kensington were unknown quantities. Still, it seemed unlikely that Nicole would be friends and partners with people who were jerks. Besides, there would be even more unknowns at a different company.

Chelsea pulled out a stack of papers that had been shoved behind supplies on a bottom shelf, a miscellaneous collection of paid invoices, bills of lading and other documents. Before Adam had left, he'd mentioned paperwork was missing; perhaps the temporary office help had never filed it in the first place.

From what she could tell, the original filing system had been excellent, it was the haphazard way it had been kept recently that was the problem. Chelsea sorted the unfiled paperwork and decided to start going through the physical files, A to Z. Getting everything into its right place would help her learn more about agency operations.

Her spirits rose as she worked.

She was starting to think she could be really good for the agency. It had been a long time since she'd felt that way, partly because of Ron's constant, insidious little comments. They'd chipped away at her confidence, bit by bit, until nothing had been left. Now, so far away from him, she couldn't believe she'd put up with it for so long. What was *wrong* with her? She sighed. Maybe nothing. Perhaps Ron hadn't realized what he was doing and they'd simply been a really bad match.

The phone rang. She was in the file and copier room behind the reception desk. Dashing out, Chelsea grabbed the receiver.

"Moonlight Ventures Agency."

"Chelsea? That's gotta be you."

It was Ron and she felt an instinctive surge of panic. Here she just been thinking about what he'd said and done and the next thing she knew, his voice was sounding in her ears. Forcing herself to calm down, she reflected that there was nothing weird about it. She'd thought often about him in the few days since they had broken up, so if he called, it was practically a guarantee that he'd hit a moment when she was remembering something about their time together.

"How did you know I was here?" she asked, keeping her voice even.

"One of your neighbors said where you were working."

Chelsea blinked, recalling that she'd phoned

a neighbor in Los Angeles to explain the situation and that she was moving to Seattle for her new job. She should have asked Marta not to tell Ron anything if he came around; she just hadn't thought he'd bother.

"I had to call—I couldn't believe you'd get a job so far away from me," Ron added.

She drew a deep breath. "What I do isn't your business any longer. I told you we're through."

"But you didn't mean it. You're always saying things you don't mean."

"I meant it. We're finished."

"After three years together? I put a lot of time and energy into our relationship. We love each other and—"

"And nothing," she said as firmly as she could manage. "Find someone else."

"But—"

Chelsea hit the off button on the phone, partly out of panic. But it also might be the only way to handle Ron—he always had an argument to make, could cajole and wheedle and send her on guilt trips and uncertainty searches. From now on when she answered, she'd check the caller ID to see if it was him.

Dragging in deep, calming breaths, she went back to work and forced herself to open and sort the next file. It helped that she was so far away. Ron might call long distance, but he probably wouldn't come north to see her in person.

Using logic to deal with her thoughts helped quiet her nerves, but she still couldn't ignore the stabs of guilt over what had happened...and a little anger as well.

Why couldn't she have met a nicer guy three years ago, instead of Ron? If it had been someone like Barton Smith, her life might be entirely different today. Then she reminded herself that she didn't actually know Barton was nicer and that in the beginning, she'd thought Ron was great, too.

AFTER AN HOUR of cautious discussion with Nicole, Jordan knew he wasn't close to getting the kind of insights needed for the *PostModern* articles. His frustration was pointless and unrealistic. It took patience to get through to some people. Syd must have expected this to be a challenge. She always said complex people were the ones their readers wanted to hear about; otherwise, they could get three paragraphs to skim on the internet.

He was the one who'd assumed Nicole wasn't multidimensional...a stupid notion based on his old ideas about her. It was becoming uncomfortably obvious that he wasn't putting aside his biases nearly as well as he wanted.

Nicole glanced at the clock on the wall. "It's almost noon and I need to check in at a photo shoot that starts at one thirty. So we'd better finish for now. Do you want to go with me this afternoon?"

Jordan couldn't imagine anything duller, but Nicole's blue eyes held a distinct challenge.

"Sure," he agreed. "Can I take you to lunch first?"

"I've got a call to make, so I'm going to eat something at my desk. We'll have time to get to the shoot if you're back by one."

He excused himself and went to the reception area where his sister was studying something in a file.

"Hey, how about taking pity on your brother and going out to lunch with me?"

"Uh, I'd love to. Just a minute." She put the file in a drawer, jumped up and collected her purse. She carefully locked the front door and followed him to his car.

"I need to be back in an hour," she said.

"No problem, so do I. There's a deli nearby that makes great sandwiches. We can eat them down by the lake. It's a warm day for late April, so sitting outside will be perfect."

"That's nice." Chelsea smiled, but still seemed pale and tense.

"Something wrong?"

"No, I mean, well… Ron called the agency looking for me. I didn't look at the caller ID, and…he recognized my voice right away."

"What the dev—" Jordan cut his exclamation short. "How did he know where you were?"

"Probably from my neighbor in Los Angeles.

I talked to her a few days ago and I must have… um…forgotten to say everything was confidential."

"What did he want?"

Chelsea sighed. "The usual. I told him to leave me alone."

"I'll call and reinforce the message."

"No," she said sharply. "I took care of it. Ron is my mistake. No one else should have to deal with him."

"I'm your brother. I know we haven't had much chance to know each other as adults, but I want to help."

She was silent a long moment. "Then let's *be* adults. Let me take care of this and if I need help, I'll ask."

"Okay."

Too late he recalled his resolution of the past weekend, that rushing to help her without permission wasn't a good idea. He wanted to respect Chelsea as an adult. But he wasn't sure what his role should be. He'd never been the protective big brother of novels and family TV programs and the Masters clan had never fit an idealized image. He'd gotten closer to Terri the past couple of years, partly because Terri had called often to discuss what was going on with Chelsea. She'd been really worried about their baby sister. It had brought into focus that while Terri had sharp edges and a tough exterior, underneath she truly cared.

"I think I'm going to like my new job," Chelsea said, breaking into his thoughts.

"That's terrific." He answered, remembering she'd already emphasized that she wouldn't say anything about the agency or Nicole. "I'd love to hear about it, but while I'm doing the articles, perhaps it would be easiest if we avoid talking about Moonlight Ventures."

"Yeah." Chelsea settled back into a more relaxed position. "You know, I'd like to get a cat after I find a permanent apartment."

"A cat?"

"Yes. I've always loved them and wanted to adopt a kitten two years ago, but I... I just didn't."

Right, Jordan thought, *Ron had probably objected.*

"Do you want company while you go looking for one?" he asked.

"Maybe. Nicole says there were a lot of kittens and cats at the rescue shelter where she got Toby, so I'll start there. Maybe you should adopt one, too."

"Not a good idea. I'd feel like scum having to kennel it whenever I go out of town. You know how much I travel."

"Except now you have a sister living nearby. I could take care of an animal for you."

"I'll think about it," he answered, mostly to get her off the subject. He didn't want to adopt a dog or cat any more than he wanted any other permanent involvements.

His life worked fine the way it was.

CHAPTER EIGHT

AFTER A CALL with Rachel to discuss agency business, Nicole took the salad she'd brought for lunch out of the refrigerator and did paperwork as she ate. Some of it was stuff Chelsea would eventually learn to do, and Nicole could hardly wait to surrender it to her.

"Isn't it important to relax over lunch?" Jordan's voice interrupted her concentration.

She glanced up to see him in the doorway of her office. "Right now I need to use every minute I can." She refrained from mentioning that the interviews were one of the reasons her schedule was so full. The timer chimed on her desk, reminding her of the next task.

"An alarm?" Jordan asked.

"Sure. I get absorbed in what I'm doing and set an alarm so I don't have to break my concentration to keep checking the clock."

Nicole stood and stretched and saw heat flare in his eyes. She swallowed; it was best to ignore any hint that he might think she was attractive. The relationship with Jordan was strictly business, and temporary at best. Nor was there anything unusual in a man finding her desirable. She'd been fortunate to be born with good looks and it wasn't anything to be smug about. After all, her appearance wasn't an achievement. While she'd learned how to present herself, it wasn't the same as her business degree, which had required hard work. Well, she had to exercise and be careful about eating, but that wasn't quite the same.

"Ready to go?" Jordan asked. The husky note in his voice sent tingles up her spine. Obviously her body wasn't cooperating with her wish to stay free of entanglements.

"Just about," she answered as casually as possible. "I need to check with Chelsea before leaving."

He followed as she went out to the reception area.

"Chelsea, I'm going to that photo shoot now. Do you have any questions about what you've looked at so far?"

"No. But I'm working on a new way of recording the hours our clients are on assignment, rates and such. I found the note from the accounting firm saying they'd like a new format."

Nicole frowned. "That never got to me. Could you let them know we've had staff changes and that you'll work with them on a process that meets both our needs?"

"I hope it's all right, but I already emailed and told them that I didn't think you'd seen the request and I would bring it to your attention once you were free."

"That's terrific. Things are already going smoother with you here."

Chelsea's face glowed pink with the compliment. "If anybody calls or stops in to see you, what shall I tell them?"

"Just that I'm out on business and you'll give me the message. Call or text with anything truly urgent."

Nicole was acutely aware of Jordan's presence as they walked outside to her car.

Renewed tension crawled through her. Perhaps she'd feel the same with any other reporter, but it was more intense because it was Jordan and the new office manager was his sister. All the same, she didn't believe she would have interacted with Chelsea in any other way. A word of approval had seemed appropriate, though she hadn't been able to keep from wondering whether Jordan would think she was trying to get on his good side.

Yet it was also unfair to withhold a compliment to an employee just because she didn't want to be perceived as trying to butter someone up.

She breathed deeply to relax, wishing her brain didn't run in circles around itself. Unfortunately, the chase would probably continue at a fast pace until the interviews for the magazine article were completed.

BARTON PARKED NEAR the Moonlight Ventures Agency...out of easy view from the windows and double doors. The glass was tinted and had a reflective quality, so while he couldn't see inside, Chelsea could probably observe everything going on *outside*.

He wanted time to think his plan through again. In his pocket were two tickets to the Mariners game that night. Considering the discussion about the Mariners at Saturday's dinner, it seemed okay to ask Chelsea to go with him.

Heck, there was no point in overthinking everything.

Getting out of his car, Barton strode toward the door and opened it, hearing a soft chime as he entered.

Chelsea turned from the computer at the right side of the wide, curving reception desk.

"Barton. Hi." Her face was pink, perhaps from surprise. "Why aren't you teaching your class?"

"A truck hit a transformer near the school and knocked out the power, so we closed early. I hope it was okay to drop by to see you."

"It shouldn't be a problem. What's up?"

"A parent gave me tickets for the ballgame when he came to pick up his son—they aren't able to go themselves—so I was wondering if you'd like to see Safeco Field tonight."

"Oh." She bit her lip. "Doesn't someone in your family want to go with you?"

"Naw, my brother has season tickets and my folks aren't into baseball. Please come. It's more fun watching a game with a friend."

"Oh. That's awful nice of you. I'd love to."

He grinned. "Great. This is my chance to win over another fan for the home team."

She laughed. "Subversive tactics?"

"At least I'm being up-front about my motives." Yet he knew he wasn't being *completely* up-front. After a long period of keeping his head down and ignoring the possibility of making new friends, he wanted to get back to his old self. Maybe not jump into romance, but friendship seemed good. Easier said than done, though.

"What time?" Chelsea asked. "I don't get off until five and it takes fifteen minutes to drive home. Longer if I hit traffic."

"We'll leave as soon as you get there. The game starts after seven, but earlier is better for parking."

"I wouldn't want to hold you up or anything, so go without me if that's best."

"We'll make it work. Don't eat anything. Safeco has great food for dinner."

"I've heard about the garlic fries."

"They're terrific." Barton began relaxing. Chelsea was treating this like two friends going to a game. He'd once taken a woman on a first date to Safeco and she'd acted as if even suggesting garlic fries was death to romance. At least he'd found out right away that they weren't compatible. As for Chelsea's views? There was no way of knowing, but he was ready to let a friendship develop without pushing another agenda.

"I'll get out of here so I don't interfere with your work," he said. "I come this way from the school, so I took a chance on dropping by instead of waiting to call once I got home."

"I'm glad you did."

He left with a wave and drove to his house whistling. This was definitely better than the funk he'd been living in for so long.

Leaving the car in the driveway for a quick departure later, he went through the front door to find Spike careening through the house with a yowl.

"Hey, buddy."

Spike turned his big striped head to one side, then suddenly leaped into the air. Barton barely managed to catch him. The cat had never done it before, but now he looked self-satisfied and purred his loud motorboat rumble.

It might be a coincidence, but maybe Spike also recognized his human was feeling differently. For a while after Barton's marriage splintered, it had seemed as if nothing would be normal or good again.

It was nice to know he'd been wrong.

JORDAN WIPED PERSPIRATION from his forehead.
The unseasonably warm weather shouldn't be a
problem; after all, he'd just gotten back from Fiji
where he'd never dressed in more than shorts and
a T-shirt. Maybe his discomfort was from com-
miseration with the models, who were wearing
heavy winter jackets under hot lights.

Nicole was consulting with her clients, giving them last-minute pointers. With her experience in the field, she seemed to be interpreting
her role as an agent *and* coach. It reminded him
that she'd claimed one of her interests was helping people be at their best.

"Remember," Nicole finished, "though the
final decision belongs to someone else, you can
make diplomatic suggestions. Don't be a com-
plainer about things that don't make a difference,
but it's all right to say if something makes you
uneasy. The most important thing is listening to
the people around you."

The photographer approached and she stepped
away from the set that held fake snow and a winter backdrop.

"Some of what you told them didn't mean
much to me, but the last part sounded like sensible advice," Jordan said. "Do models turn into
prima donnas very often?"

"It's an occupational hazard. After all, it seems
as if you're the center of attention, the focus of
the world, when it's actually the image or prod-

uct that they want to sell. Nothing damages a career faster than to turn into someone nobody wants to work with. At the same time, I want to protect my clients from feeling as if they have to put up with any treatment to get ahead. It's a delicate balance."

The next hour passed slowly as the models posed, took one coat off in obvious relief, only to sigh as they put on another one. The photographer tried using a fan to make it cooler for them, but it blew the fake snow around too much.

Nicole helped a few times, unobtrusively, but other than that, she watched carefully and made notes. After an hour and a half, she waved goodbye to the photographer and models.

"We can leave now if you like," she told Jordan.

"Do agents usually spend a lot of time on the set with their clients?" he asked as they drove back to the agency.

She hesitated, though he wasn't sure if it was the traffic making her pause, or if she was formulating her answer.

"Not usually," she said at length. "When you have a large number of clients, it isn't even possible, though the previous owner of Moonlight Ventures made a valiant effort. But these were all first-timers and the photographer was also new to me. I like to have some confidence that the situation is okay for our clients."

"None of them seemed the type who'd do anything inappropriate."

"You can't tell just by looking." An expression of distaste twisted her soft lips before her face smoothed out again. "Besides, that isn't the only hazard to a model. Improperly managed equipment, for example, can be dangerous."

"I'm sure your clients are grateful that you watch out for their welfare," Jordan said, making a mental note to ask more about how her experiences as a model were influencing her actions as an agent. He had a feeling there was a history. And now that he thought about it, he remembered one of her partners at the agency had been badly injured on a set.

"It's my job to do as much as I can."

"Did your agent do the same?" he asked, deciding to probe while the subject was open.

Another pause as she navigated a left turn at a busy intersection.

"They didn't spend much time on location, but I had good agents. The one I had the longest retired three years before I did. While the woman who took over was competent, it made me think about what I appreciated most in an agent."

"So that helped fuel your choice of a second career?"

"I hadn't thought of it before, but I'm sure the contrasting styles were a factor."

Jordan began envisioning the sort of situation where a young woman might be vulnerable. Scantily clad girls with men having power over their career? The potential for problems was distasteful, and he was too realistic to believe they never happened. The question of whether it had ever happened to Nicole disturbed him as well. It was probably because he knew her; for anyone else it was theoretical.

"You've been in a dark reverie," Nicole commented as she parked in front of the agency several minutes later.

"I've been thinking about the potential risks to people in your former line of work, especially when men have power over a woman's career. Did you experience any sexual harassment?"

"Not often. I did have a close call with a photographer who thought sex with models was part of his compensation." Her face was grim. "I got him fired from that particular job and later someone else went further. I understand he's in jail now."

"Good."

"You said that passionately."

"I don't like victimizers. Taking advantage of someone with less power is contemptible."

A smile turned up the left corner of her mouth. "That's an excellent ethical standard."

"Does it surprise you that I have ethical standards?"

"Not so much now, but it might have when we were kids."

It had never occurred to Jordan to wonder what Nicole had thought of him when they were growing up. He'd called Nicole "the little princess" and hadn't meant it in a complimentary way. To his friends he'd groused about his mother's awe when it came to the girl who was pictured everywhere, though he'd never mentioned the spite his mom had later developed. But he had never thought about whether Nicole's attitude toward him was positive or negative.

"So, what *did* you think of me back then?" he asked.

"When we were kids, you came off as a brat who didn't care who he ran over or whether he hurt anyone. Literally, like the time you mowed me down when I was trying to learn how to skate. When we were older, it still seemed as if you didn't care very much if what you said or did injured me or other people. You were also full of yourself, anxious to have sex with girls. Now I think you were trying to run so fast your feelings couldn't catch up with you."

As Jordan stared through the windshield, he wondered if Nicole had hit the mark.

"Really," he said noncommittally.

Her head cocked. "It's possible. Anyway, teenage boys tend to be driven by their hormones, which explains some of it."

Curiously, Nicole wasn't showing rancor over

his past behavior. The quirk in her lips indicated humor instead.

"When did you stop holding my youthful transgressions against me?"

"Who said I have?"

"It's obvious, or at least it seems that way."

She unfastened her seat belt. "Everyone has to choose what portions of the past are going to matter. It's part of growing up."

"And I wasn't significant enough to matter?"

"Heck, I never expected to see Jordan Masters again, so my memories of you got mostly sanitized. You know, bleached bones of history or something like that…something poetic." There was a glint of amusement in her voice and eyes.

There was no denying that Nicole was entirely different than he had expected, and he shouldn't have had expectations about her in the first place. Maybe he'd fallen into the trap of viewing her as two-dimensionally as a magazine layout. For one thing, he'd never imagined she had a sense of humor, or that she was rational and mature enough to shrug off old injuries.

Stupid of him.

He sighed. Maybe lingering guilt was responsible. After all, outside of the parties involved, he appeared to be the only one who knew what had really happened between their parents. Not that it mattered anymore. Nicole might not even care that his mother had tried to seduce her father.

But he wasn't sure. It was something he'd kept to himself for a long time, something that didn't seem right to share. Now he wondered, particularly since learning his mother had taken the feud to social media, however briefly.

"Sorry, I have to cut this short," Nicole said. "I need to get inside and finish up some work."

"Of course."

He climbed from the car, aware of her graceful movements as she did the same.

"There's something else," Nicole said after locking the vehicle. "I'd like to suggest that if we go somewhere together in the car, we don't do interview questions while driving."

"Why not? Multitasking gets more done."

She shook her head. "Not everyone agrees that it's productive. I've always had a preference for concentrating on one task at a time, and some recent studies indicate that it's healthier."

"Okay, we'll play by your rules."

"Not rules, just a mutual agreement. Okay?"

"Sure," he said, knowing it would be useless for him, at least. They might agree to focus on a single task or subject at a time, but he had a feeling one track of his brain would be required to continue dealing with his libido—some things were inevitable.

"Great. When should we get together again?"

"How about tomorrow morning or afternoon?"

"Let me check my schedule." She pulled out

her phone and looked at it. "Tomorrow isn't good and Wednesday afternoon I have another photo shoot. Also, at 11:00 a.m. Thursday I meet with a potential new client."

"Could I sit in on both?" he asked, wondering if he was a masochist.

"I'll check to see if it's okay. The photo shoot isn't a problem. It's at a gym, so it's a public location. Hopefully it will be cooler than today."

"Uh, that sounds good." He was disappointed that it wasn't outdoors, but it would still be a more relaxed setting than a photographer's studio. "What time?"

"I need to leave just before 1:00 p.m. to allow for traffic. The shoot starts at 2:00."

"Sounds good. See you then."

He indulged himself by watching her walk toward the front door of the agency. The hardest part was where to let his gaze linger. Nicole had plenty of attractive curves and a single-minded focus on them would provide a man with a huge amount of fuel for his imagination.

NICOLE SAW JORDAN'S reflection on the window as she walked across the small parking lot. She wondered if he realized she could see him in the reflective coating on the glass almost as well as he could see her.

It was tempting to turn around and do something outrageous, but she couldn't think of the right gesture. Besides, it would be childish.

Yet for some reason she thought about something she'd seen at Emily's wedding. The groom's brothers had painted "Thnx" on the sole of one shoe, and "Em" on the other, so when the pastor asked them to kneel at the altar, the words were visible to the guests. It had appealed to the sentimentality Nicole tried to keep hidden. Her parents must have guessed part of what she'd felt—which might be one of the reasons they'd believed the wedding had influenced her to change her life.

As she went through the door, Nicole reminded herself that she didn't need romance. Still, she flicked a glance backward and saw that Jordan was now headed for his vehicle. His standing there, seeming to watch her walk away, probably hadn't meant anything; most likely he'd been contemplating whether he wanted to go in and say hello to his sister.

"Hi, Chelsea," she said, stepping into the cool reception area, heartily glad she'd insisted they have air-conditioning installed. In Seattle it might not be needed on a regular basis, but when it was needed, it was *really* needed.

The new office manager's face was pink and excited.

"Something happen?" Nicole asked.

"Oh, nothing. For the agency, that is. Um, Barton Smith dropped by this afternoon to see me. I hope it's all right."

"It's fine," Nicole assured her. "What did he want?"

"He had extra tickets to the Mariners game tonight and asked if I wanted to go."

Glancing at the clock, Nicole saw it was almost four thirty. "That's great. Leave now so you can get a jump on the evening."

"I couldn't do that."

"Sure you can. I'm the boss and it makes me feel good to tell you to go home early once in a while."

"Okay. Thanks so much."

With a shy smile, Chelsea quickly turned off the computer and was gone. Since a legitimate visitor would ring the doorbell, Nicole locked the front door and went to her office. She wished she'd brought Toby for companionship, though it would have been awkward taking him outside to do his business.

She couldn't deny that she was lonely once in a while. But she'd felt that way sometimes before moving to Seattle and it didn't mean anything. Besides, her partners would be here before long and she was making new friends. Today she should get a stack of files together so she could work at home on the deck, Toby at her side.

As she straightened her shoulders, Nicole's spirits rose. Moments of loneliness aside, she liked how everything was going.

CHAPTER NINE

CHELSEA WATCHED AS they inched forward in the heavy traffic and wondered if they'd be able to get parking. She'd already learned that Seattle had traffic congestion issues, just like LA.

"I'm awfully sorry," she said. "You probably would have preferred leaving even earlier, instead of waiting for me."

Barton's eyebrows rose. "Nonsense. I'm just glad you were able to come."

"What if the parking garage is full?"

"We'll deal with it. There's lots of parking, I just prefer the garage across the street from the stadium entrances. Besides, I doubt this will be a top attendance night, so we should be fine."

"You act as if it's no big deal."

"That's because it isn't."

Chelsea relaxed slightly. It was hard to stop reacting as if she was still with Ron—to him, *everything* had been a huge deal. He would have berated her all the way to the ballpark, despite her getting home sooner than expected.

Barton probably thought she was an idiot for saying anything—after all, he was the one who'd invited her, aware that she had to work until five, and he hadn't known Nicole would let her leave a half hour early. If they were going to be friends, she had to remember Barton was his own man.

Despite the slow traffic, they managed to arrive in time to get the desired parking.

Safeco Field itself was splendid. It had a retractable roof, but Barton explained that even when it was closed for rain, there was plenty of open air on the sides. Today the roof was retracted and she was delighted to see seagulls go sailing through.

"These are good seats," she said as the first inning ended.

"Better than I normally get." Barton suddenly appeared uptight. "On a teacher's salary, I'm usually in the family section."

"Same here. There's nothing wrong with economy—and the family section is nice because of the rules about alcohol—but it's fun to enjoy treats like this when they come our way."

He grinned and seemed less tense. "Absolutely."

During the third inning they hurried out and got food. There were several cuisines to choose from, but they both opted for traditional ballpark fare. Barton seemed amazed when she squirted a huge blob of mustard beside her garlic fries.

"Mustard and fries?" he asked.

"It sounds strange to some people, but I like it."

He tried it himself and added a large serving of mustard to his French fry container. "It's terrific. I've been missing out."

Ron had done the same thing on an early date, later saying he'd "endured" it so she wouldn't feel uncomfortable with her weird choice. Once again she reminded herself that she couldn't keep seeing Barton or anyone else through the lens of the past. It wasn't fair and could mess up a friendship.

Returning to their seats, they saw that the score hadn't changed. There weren't any significant plays during the next inning as they ate their fries and hot dogs. The people around them grumbled at the lack of runs for the Mariners, but Chelsea was having too much fun to care.

It was a great stadium, with the feel of an old-time ballpark. Not that she knew much about old-time ballparks, but it was what Barton claimed and she was willing to take his word. One thing was sure, he consumed his mustard-laden fries with every sign of liking them that way.

"Do you think you're going to enjoy your job at the agency?" he asked.

"It's different because I worked for a large company in the past, but it's easier at Moonlight Ventures to see how much difference I can make."

"Nice. That turns it into more than a job."

"I guess it does."

Just then a Mariners player hit a long ball and Barton leaned forward as he cheered. Chelsea shifted in her seat. It was a good hit, but it was his arm brushing against her that consumed her attention. He was dressed in a short-sleeved cotton shirt and the muscles flexing in his bare forearm showed he was in good shape. Barton was awfully attractive, something she didn't want to keep noticing.

Friends, she reminded herself.

"You know, I like the way the Mariners play," she said a little later, when he returned from buying lemonade for them both.

"Ah, my plan is working," he said with satisfaction. "I figure if I get someone into the stadium, the Mariners will do the rest."

"I'm already a fan of Safeco Field, but I can't claim to be a *Mariners* fan just yet. I just like the way they play, that's all."

"Then we'll have to keep coming back until you're hooked."

Tingles went up and down her spine. As much as she didn't want to think of Barton as anything except a friend, there was something exciting about getting acquainted with a guy who was already talking about future…baseball games.

It had been a long time since she'd gotten excited about much of anything.

JORDAN SPENT TUESDAY morning trying to write his column, but his mind kept wandering to how Nicole had looked—earnest and energized—as she'd dealt with her clients on the winter wear photo shoot. They had responded to her, too, obviously trusting that she had their welfare at heart.

Perhaps it would help if he studied her file rather than keep on denying how much thoughts of her were distracting him. Except that made things worse since the file included numerous photos. And the pictures that hadn't previously interested him now served as a reminder of the effect she was having on his body.

Finally he went for a run, then came back and forced himself into finishing a couple of columns. He liked having a stockpile ready—it helped to avoid submitting something that didn't meet his standards.

He ate dinner at a favorite restaurant, but became concerned when he noticed a man berating his companion for something inconsequential. Jordan saw evidence of bruises on her arms.

His stomach churned.

As in his sister's case after the car accident, there could be legitimate reasons for the injuries, but it was hard to interpret the wariness in the woman's eyes as anything but fear. It could have easily gone that direction with Chelsea...and he wasn't entirely convinced it hadn't.

When the woman stood and went toward the restroom, he tried to follow casually and while he waited for her, he pulled a worn card from his wallet. He'd been given it when doing a column on domestic violence.

He cleared his throat as she emerged from the restroom, hoping he wouldn't startle her. "I might be butting in here," he said, "but I have a sister who's gone through a lot and...well, here."

He handed her the card and she looked at it, then nodded silently before tucking it deep in her purse.

"Thanks."

Jordan felt helpless, but knew that to push any further might put the woman at greater risk.

A cold shower, some work on a possible second column about domestic violence, and three BBC documentary films later, Jordan finally fell asleep.

CHELSEA SEEMED CAUTIOUSLY cheerful as Jordan came through the agency door on Wednesday afternoon.

"You look good," he said, "the job must be going well."

"Oh, yes," she agreed with obvious sincerity. "I also got to see the Mariners game on Monday night at Safeco. It was loads of fun."

"How did that happen?"

"Barton was given two tickets by someone at the school and he said it was a chance to draft a new fan for his team."

"That's nice, but is it wise to get involved with someone so soon?"

A soft noise drew his attention to Nicole, who stood a few feet down the hallway, her eyes narrowed. But it was nothing compared to the mulish set of Chelsea's mouth.

"Jordan, whether I do or don't get involved with anyone is my decision," she said. "By the way, I buzzed Nicole when I saw you coming toward the door."

"Here I am," Nicole added pleasantly. "We'd better get going."

Outside in the parking lot, Jordan walked deliberately toward his car. "I'll drive."

Nicole's face was amused as she gave him the address of their destination. Though she said nothing, Jordan felt as if *sexist* was emblazoned on his forehead. And not just because of the driving issue. Just how much was a brother supposed to say to a grown-up sister?

"I don't have a problem with women drivers," he said, programming the address into his GPS.

"I never said you did."

"Did you think it…that I'm a sexist who has to stay behind the wheel?"

"I believe it's possible you're a sexist about a great many things. Most men I've known are, even my closest male friends, though they don't like admitting it any more than you apparently do."

"The problem is, the target keeps changing,"

he said, feeling annoyed despite having no reason for it.

"How do you mean?"

"I'm talking about the way an enlightened man is supposed to think and act."

"Ah, but enlightenment is a continual process and every time there's a setback for women, I think some of us respond by doubling down on our expectations."

"That doesn't make sense."

"I'll put it this way: the space program would have never reached the moon if they'd only aimed at the top of a mountain."

It still didn't make sense, yet in a way he understood.

"You might be right, about the moonshot, anyhow. But I still say that it's uncomfortable not knowing how a man is supposed to respond on various issues."

"Does that include brotherly advice versus unwelcome interference?"

Nicole's face was expressionless as she fastened her seat belt, but Jordan remembered the look in her eyes when he'd been talking to Chelsea.

"I'm not interfering," he insisted. "Look, you don't understand the circumstances. Chelsea just left a really bad relationship and—"

Nicole held up a hand. "I told you it's none of

my business. If Chelsea wants me to know, she will tell me."

"Then isn't how I talk with her about it also none of your business?"

"You're right," Nicole conceded unexpectedly. "Besides, she seems capable of telling you herself when you've gone too far."

"You think I went too far?"

"I thought we just agreed that it isn't my business."

Jordan laughed ruefully. "True, but I'm still worried about her." He didn't even know why he was pushing the subject. He'd already realized he should let Chelsea be an adult, the way Nicole was doing.

"In that case," Nicole said, "what I think is that it's nice you care so much about your sister."

Curiously pleased, Jordan started his car. Yet, he realized, he could have made better use of time. He'd been talking with Nicole for several minutes about nothing to do with the article. Not that they could have gotten into anything very much since they had agreed to suspend the interviews while driving. But he needed to keep on track; the sooner he finished the *PostModern* articles, the sooner he might get a better night's sleep.

NICOLE STEPPED FROM the small sports car, barely touching the polite hand Jordan had offered. She didn't want to appear as if she was avoiding his touch, even if that was the case.

"Why a gym?" he asked as they walked into the building.

"They're shooting sports gear ads for a local company that is poised to go national."

"Are the models new? That is, why come to this particular photo shoot? Or is it the potential for national exposure?"

"The exposure has nothing to do with it. There are seven locations that I'm *not* visiting today, including two with clients on their first jobs. Four of the six models at this shoot have experience, but I've had mixed reports on the photographic studio."

"I see."

His eyes were enigmatic and she didn't know what he was making of her explanation. Truthfully, while she would have come regardless, she wanted Jordan to observe this particular photo shoot. After the comments he'd made, she'd decided he should see some of the realities of modeling and suspected this would be one of the more challenging jobs.

Inside the gym she forgot her speculations and focused on the models being given the outfits they were supposed to wear. Then they were directed to the locker rooms to dress.

Jordan was speaking with the photography

crew, asking them to sign releases for the pictures he wanted to take himself.

"I'm nervous," Crystal Draper said as she came outside, looking cute in a trim biking outfit.

"You'll be fine."

She *was* fine in the end, though she had to work for it. The photographer wanted "honest perspiration," by which he meant Crystal riding an exercise bike until moisture gathered on her forehead.

Periodically Nicole was aware of Jordan snapping his own pictures.

"What's his thing about?" another model, Martin Carter, asked during a break, gesturing toward Jordan. Martin was a college student trying to earn money toward graduate school, though he was still deciding between architecture and engineering.

"That's Jordan Masters. He's writing a series of articles for *PostModern* magazine," Nicole explained. "There won't be anything printed about you without your permission. He's going to ask for a release, and if you don't want to sign it, that's entirely your decision."

"But it might help our careers, right?" Crystal asked. "It's good exposure to get into a big magazine like *PostModern*, even if we aren't paid."

"True," Nicole confirmed.

"Then he can take as many pictures of me as

he wants." She gazed at Jordan appreciatively. "He's sure good-looking, isn't he?"

"Say it a little louder," Martin drawled, "I don't think he heard you the first time."

Crystal giggled.

There was no question that Jordan had heard. The half smile on his lips reminded Nicole of the teenaged boy she'd known long ago. Did any man completely lose the boy inside…and wasn't that one of the things women found both appealing and irritating?

Pushing the thought away, she focused on the work. An hour later, her attention was caught by a commotion across the gym with the second photographer. He was shouting and the model was obviously at the point of tears.

Nicole hurried over. "Hey, how is it going?"

The photographer looked disgusted. "The blasted girl doesn't know how to climb."

Nicole raised an eyebrow. "Climbing wasn't one of the skills you specified in your contract with Moonlight Ventures. Jackie fits everything your studio stated you were looking for when you chose her and the others at the go-see."

"I guess, but I need someone who can scale a climbing wall," he declared. Loudly.

"Apparently *you* don't know how to fill out paperwork and fill in the right boxes and blanks, but I'm not yelling at you for it. Let me work with

Jackie and we'll see what can be done. What shot are you trying to get?"

He described what he wanted, the model in full climb, right hand reaching upward, coyly glancing over her left shoulder.

"That sounds familiar." Nicole remembered it was the exact pose she'd done for a major sportswear ad a few years earlier.

"Maybe you could take over the shot, since you already know what I want." His voice was eager, his eyes sharp and speculative.

Jackie's expression fell.

"That isn't possible," Nicole said coolly. "I'm here as the agent for my client, not to take her place. Aside from that, copying another company's advertising campaign would be unethical. It's possible you might even get sued." He couldn't afford her modeling services, either, but that was beside the point.

"It isn't going to be exactly the same. For one, that was outdoors, this is in a gym. Anyhow, you just…we didn't *have* to use your agency and we don't have to use it again."

"That's absolutely correct," she agreed smoothly. "And we aren't required to do business with anyone who doesn't behave appropriately. This is a two-way street, Mr. Stanton."

Jordan was approaching, a belligerent glint in his eyes, and Nicole got the strangest idea he was prepared to battle the photographer on her behalf.

He halted when she fixed him with a sharp look and shook her head.

But as she started working with Jackie, the stray thought crossed her mind that Jordan might have latent knight-in-shining-armor instincts. It would be an interesting aspect to his self-defined skeptic persona.

A rather endearing one.

JORDAN WAS CAUGHT between a primitive desire to see the photographer knocked on his ass and admiration at Nicole's skilled handling of the situation. Stanton had tried to threaten and manipulate her and she hadn't even flinched. And it had obviously given her client confidence. Jackie listened carefully to Nicole's instructions and was able to make her way up the climbing wall a few feet.

"I want her toward the top," the photographer complained once Nicole had Jackie settled in place.

"Then you aren't as skilled as the woman who shot the ads you claim you *aren't* trying to reproduce," Nicole shot back smoothly. "This is the exact height and position I was in when the original photos were taken."

Jordan nearly choked, trying to restrain his glee. The photographer was a petulant fool who was too dumb to know he was outclassed and had been beaten at his own game.

"Who does that bimbo think she is?" the guy

stalked closer and grumbled to Jordan. He didn't seem to mind that Nicole was close enough to overhear. "I hope you're getting all of this down for those articles you're writing."

"Absolutely," Jordan assured him. "It's always interesting to readers when a man is incompetent and gets rescued by a smart woman. They'll probably grind their teeth over your pathetic attempt to manipulate her, but what's a story without drama to give it spice?"

"You... I, that isn't..." the man sputtered. "You can't say something like that about me."

"Don't worry, you aren't important enough to mention by name."

Nicole's shoulders were shaking, her eyes merry, and Jordan's body tightened with desire at the sight.

The photographer stared with a horrified expression, then rushed to finish his shots. After another thirty minutes he packed his equipment and went over to the other photographer, who listened, then shook his head and said something that made Stanton shout a curse and stomp from the gym.

It wasn't long before the rest of the photos were completed and the models had gone to the locker rooms to change into their street clothes.

The remaining photographer walked over to Nicole. He looked tense. "Ms. George, I understand there was a problem with Bob Stanton."

"Yes. He berated my client for not being a climbing expert and then tried to manipulate me into taking her place. That kind of behavior is problematic, at best."

"I can't apologize enough. He told me he had a plan to get you into the ads and I told him to forget it, that isn't how my studio does business. He wants to rescind his release for *PostModern*. Even though Bob is my employee, I don't think I can ignore his request. I should say I *did* employ him. He's fired, as of this afternoon."

"I didn't ask for that."

"Today was just the last straw. I've given him several chances and while he's a decent photographer, he won't follow directions." He turned to Jordan. "Mr. Masters, pictures of Bob should be excluded. In any case, I'd prefer not having him associated with my studio. It's tough enough making it in this business without me getting a bad rep."

The man's face seemed open and straightforward and Jordan sorted through the releases. He handed over the one for Bob Stanton.

"Stanton isn't very bright, is he?" Jordan said to Nicole once they were alone. "If he'd been warned not to pull that game, why did he complain to his boss about how it turned out?"

"He was probably trying to tell his side first. I hadn't planned to say anything, but he must have assumed I would. People like that generally seem to think you'll behave even worse than they do."

"But you also wouldn't have sent any of your clients to work with him again, right?" Jordan hazarded a guess.

"We have a few tigers at the agency who'd chew him up and spit him out, but I wouldn't inflict him on rookies. His name goes on my watch list for the future."

"Is it a long list?"

"Nope. I rate studios and photographers for how well they handle various aspects of the work, but there's only one other name on the list. Now he'll have Stanton for company. By the way, we can leave now, if you like."

"Do you mind if I have a private chat with your clients?" Jordan asked. "I need to get releases and ask a few questions."

"If it's all right with them, it's fine with me."

Jordan found the models were pleased to sign releases that might get their pictures or names into a national publication. Jackie had obviously told everyone the story about the photographer and they were filled with admiration for Nicole.

"I almost didn't apply to Moonlight Ventures because I thought she wouldn't be interested in representing someone who wasn't already famous," Jackie said. "But I decided to take a chance and she was so nice."

Martin laughed. "I applied in case I got a

chance to meet her. She was awesome and now I'm making money as a model. Who'd have thought?"

"I was really nervous when Nicole and her partners bought Moonlight Ventures," Cara Williams confessed. "Mr. McClaskey took such good care of everybody and I thought they'd dump most of us since we hadn't become superstars. They didn't and I was so grateful. Then I got worried whether they'd know how to run a talent agency, but I'm getting more calls than ever."

The general consensus was the same—they were glad Nicole was their agent. Jordan jotted down several potential quotes, then said goodbye and went to join Nicole, who sat on a bench near the door, reading something on an e-reader. As he approached she turned off the device and stood.

"All set?"

"Sure."

It was a bad time to be leaving the gym, with afternoon commuter traffic at its worst.

"Traffic is one of the reasons I'm especially grateful I don't have a regular nine-to-five job," Jordan said as he inched his car out onto the road.

"True, and I've been glad that my job is flexible enough that I can usually avoid it as well. I feel for people who don't have options."

"I have a friend who actually likes commuting. Dan keeps a supply of lecture CDs and audio books and says it's *his* time," Jordan explained.

"When he gets home, it's all about mowing the lawn and taking out the garbage, washing the windows and completing other jobs his wife finds for him. Dori keeps him really busy."

"Too bad he has such a demanding wife."

"I didn't say that."

"Except that you made it sound as if anything he does around the house is because his wife requires him to do it. Did they buy the house together, or move into her place?"

He shifted uncomfortably. "Dan bought it a couple of years before they met."

"Then is it his belief that Dori keeps him busy, or yours?"

"Mine," Jordan conceded. "I guess I simply don't get the suburbs and white picket fence routine."

"Yes," Nicole mused, "I was surprised to find myself buying a house as well. Perhaps I was looking for something." Her voice almost sounded wistful.

"Something you can find in real estate?" he asked.

"More the illusion, I suppose."

"And what was that?" he pressed, thinking her answer might help explain her decision to leave modeling and move to Seattle.

"Never mind. It's personal."

"You're the one who wanted to avoid interview subjects while we're on the road."

Nicole let out a derisive sound. "I'm not stupid—your questions have more to do with the magazine article than casual conversation."

She was right and Jordan sighed. No wonder she seemed to have trouble regarding him as a responsible, ethical journalist. "Okay, what are your hobbies?" he asked the first thing that came to mind.

"I like reading, especially biographies."

"What are you reading now?"

"Alexander Hamilton. I'm behind. I saw the musical in New York and am finally getting around to the book it's based on."

Jordan nodded. "What else do you enjoy?"

"Why does this still sound like an interview?"

"Sorry. Should we sit in silence?"

"That would be awkward as well. Why don't you tell me about some of *your* special interests?"

He thought about it, not wanting to reveal too much. "As you already know, traveling is one of the big ones. And before you ask, I've enjoyed all the countries I've visited, but for different reasons."

"I know what you mean. It's hard to say that a single place is a favorite, because it's like comparing papayas with grapes. I was always frustrated when my schedule meant I had to leave a country and all I'd seen was the hotel and the photo location. The one time I was in Moscow, I only saw the Hermitage from a distance."

Once before, when she'd alluded to something similar, he couldn't deny that he'd been dismissive, even derisive, implying she felt sorry for herself without a valid reason. Now he considered what it would be like to be in Athens and not be able to visit the Acropolis, or in Paris and miss seeing Notre Dame. Or not being able to just laze a few days away in Hawaii. He would feel extremely deprived.

"That's like being invited to a feast," he said, "and only getting to sniff the scent rising from the table."

"Yes. I'd like to try road trips. You know, driving cross-country, maybe following the old Route 66. Or it would be interesting to visit all the Civil War sites. Then there are the national parks. It feels strange when I talk to someone from Australia who raves about the Petrified Forest in Arizona and I have to admit that I haven't been there."

Jordan thought back to his childhood and the times they'd been in the car, his parents arguing while he and his sisters poked each other in the back seat.

"Road trips might be over-romanticized," he said. "We did a few when I was a kid."

"Where did you go?"

"There was a trip to the Grand Canyon."

"That's an amazing place. Did you ride the mules down to the canyon floor?"

"Yes." He snickered. "Terri picked out the most cantankerous mule she could find, one that's usually left in the corral or ridden by the mule driver. They got along great. The driver couldn't believe it."

"That sounds like Terri."

"You bet. Mom and Dad joked about taking the mule back to California and keeping him in our backyard."

Nicole's voice was soft. "That must be a good memory."

It *was* good. Now that he thought about it, the arguing hadn't been on road trips, but around town. Vacations were the times when the Masterses had been a family. Jordan's standby position was to forget his childhood or only recall the bad parts, but that didn't provide a complete picture.

"When was your family at its best?" he asked curiously. "On vacation?"

"We didn't take that many, since we were on the go so much, partly for my parents' work as fashion buyers, and partly when I was on assignment." Her lips curved. "But there was one time we flew up to my aunt's funky little cabin on the Northern California coast. It verged on primitive and definitely wasn't something my parents usually liked."

"Which is…?" Jordan prompted.

"Luxury hotels with room service. Anyhow,

Mom went there often when she was a kid and Dad had visited a few times, too, so I guess nostalgia helped. We all collected shells and sea glass, along with so much driftwood, we couldn't get it into our suitcases and had to ship it home. I remember being supremely happy, and I think everyone else was, too. The greatest part was being able to walk on the beach with Emily and just be sisters."

It wasn't quite the answer Jordan had expected, but maybe that was par for the course when it came to childhood memories. What he couldn't explain was his sudden wish that he could have been there with Nicole, picking up shells on the beach.

CHAPTER TEN

NICOLE WONDERED WHAT Jordan was thinking about; there was a relaxed smile on his face, as if he was contemplating something pleasant. Probably her imagination.

The traffic was stop-and-go, even on surface streets.

"I'm sorry," he said after a particularly long wait on the freeway. "My talk with the other models probably put us in even worse traffic than if we'd left immediately."

"I doubt it made much difference and you're the one paying the price, if there is one. All I have to do is sit back and relax while you drive."

"How about avoiding this mess by getting a bite to eat? Or do you have plans?"

"No plans, so I guess it's all right."

A freeway exit was ahead and Jordan went off with a string of other vehicles. He seemed to know where he was headed and soon turned into a restaurant parking lot.

"I eat here often," he said.

Nicole made sure to get out before he had a chance to walk around to the passenger side. She had a feeling the restaurant was a place where he normally took a date. If they were observed, she wanted this to appear to be what it was, a simple business dinner.

"Mr. Masters," the maître d' greeted him, "how nice to see you. Did you have a pleasant trip to Fiji?"

"Excellent. I didn't make a reservation, but we were stuck in traffic and stopping for dinner made more sense than sitting in gridlock. Is there any possibility of getting a table?"

"It's before the rush and there's always room for you." The man's gaze shifted to Nicole and he bowed slightly. "Ms. George, isn't it? I read that you had moved to Seattle. Welcome."

"Thank you," Nicole acknowledged. The restaurant was the sort of high-class establishment where the staff expected to see people from the news. As time passed, she'd be recognized less often and become more anonymous. Agents simply didn't have the same public profile.

With Jordan there to interview and probe her transition to a behind-the-scenes agent, she was asking herself the kind of questions he might have asked, such as...how would she feel about becoming a face in the crowd?

Being human, the answer was complicated. Part of her would miss the attention. She recalled reruns of an old television series she'd seen as a kid. The theme song had said something about being in a place where everyone knew your name. Undoubtedly it *was* nice to be recognized in certain situations.

"What are you thinking about?" Jordan asked as they were seated at a discreetly secluded table.

"Honestly? About what it will be like when waiters don't recognize me any longer. It isn't as if I'm known everywhere I go, but for a while there will be restaurants like this one, where I've never eaten and I'm still greeted by name."

"Will it bother you if people forget?"

"It's inevitable they'll forget, so there's no 'if' about it. I bet even the most famous actors and actresses walk into places where people don't recognize them. And once they move out of the public eye, they're naturally recognized less often."

"You sound pragmatic about it."

"There isn't much point in being anything else."

His intense brown eyes studied her. Jordan had the same rugged good looks as a man like Matt Damon, only his coloring was dark. No doubt Jordan had sat in this restaurant many times with a woman who'd felt fortunate to enjoy his attention for the evening. *She* might have felt the same... if she didn't know every word from her mouth could end up in print.

"You still haven't said whether it will bother you to be unknown," he prompted.

"I don't think it will, but no one can say for sure how they'll react as time goes on."

"You aren't a diva."

"And you sound surprised by that."

"I'm always surprised when I look in the rear-view mirror and see my preconceptions lying in pieces on the road."

Grinning, Nicole sipped from the goblet of ice water the waiter had brought. Jordan wasn't the only one whose beliefs had been run over by current experience.

"It's odd," she said, "when you realize how many alternate realities are possible in life."

"How do you mean?"

"If certain things had been different, we might have become friends, the way you and Emily were. I know you and Em are the same age, but you were only two years older than me and we lived close to each other."

"So what would have had to be different?"

"I'm sure it would have helped if I hadn't seen you as an arrogant egotist and you hadn't seen me as a brain-dead puppet."

He grimaced. "You knew I called you that?"

Nicole rolled her eyes. "Of course I did. There were kids who couldn't wait to tell me whatever names you or someone else devised for me. High school was the worst. You were the star, whether it was in soccer or one of the other sports, while most kids either resented me or tried to suck up in hopes of getting something."

"You were invited to parties, but you mostly didn't go. The other kids thought you were too stuck-up."

"I was embarrassed to explain my parents wouldn't let me because they were afraid I'd mess up my clean teen image."

He looked rueful. "Our fellow students probably would have resented that as well."

"Probably. Lissa Anderson was furious when I sneaked out to her birthday bash and my parents showed up to rescue me from the wild crowd, then called the police after we were safely away. It caused quite a ruckus. Lissa said she'd been humiliated in front of everyone who mattered and would never forgive me. I didn't get many invitations after that. She made sure of it."

His brow creased. "Did I go to Lissa's party?"

"Yes, but you were drunk by nine. Lissa's parents weren't there and they hadn't locked up their liquor. Most of the kids were drinking."

"I'm impressed you remember."

"Well…" Nicole hesitated, wondering if she should tell him what had happened, but it wasn't important enough to keep secret. "Mostly I remember because when I went out to the patio for air, you grabbed me and gave me a very hot kiss."

JORDAN'S MOUTH WENT DRY. In his high school years he would have been mortified to know he'd kissed "the brain-dead puppet." Now he'd give a lot to remember it—which made him a fool, since he was already having a difficult enough time controlling his response to her.

"Should I apologize?" he asked finally.

Nicole chuckled with easy humor. "If it *mattered*, I wouldn't have mentioned it. We were kids. You were a typical teenage boy, into sports and cars. I was a weird teenage girl with one foot in high school and the other in the bizarre world of modeling."

At the moment, trying to wrap his brain around the image of them pressed closed together was too much of a challenge, so he focused on her choice of words.

"Do you tell your clients that modeling is a bizarre world?"

"I'm honest with them."

"Does your family appreciate the description? You mentioned that they made the decisions about your career until you were nineteen."

Her gaze dropped to the menu. "I don't say it to them, since they'd consider it a criticism. As fashion buyers they love the culture surrounding haute couture and advertising. Having a daughter they could promote as a model involved them even deeper in the international fashion scene and gave them even more influence."

"*Is* it a criticism?"

She lifted her eyes again and stared at him frankly. "Every life, every career, every choice we make is full of pros and cons. When I was a kid, the only reason I knew my parents' life in the fashion industry was bizarre was when I saw how other people lived. Maybe the hardest part was knowing my sister was getting left out. It kept us from being as close as we should have been. I love Emily, but we don't have much in common and I don't know how to bridge the gap, especially now that she's married and starting a family in another state."

"Why especially?"

"Because I don't expect marriage and children will be a part of my life."

His start of surprise must have been obvious, for her brow rose and she regarded him with a bland expression.

"That's unusual. Why don't you think your life will include those things?" he asked.

"You think it's perfectly all right for a cynical columnist to be happy with his bachelor life, but a woman can't make the same choice without it being questionable?" she countered.

Jordan felt the walls closing in him again... cave walls and he was a Neanderthal. Only a man mired in old-fashioned stereotypes assumed all women wanted marriage and children. Still, his gut told him that Nicole wasn't being entirely truthful. But the article he was writing wasn't about her love life and asking out of personal interest was too, well, *personal*.

He'd be wise to keep his distance from anything approaching intimacy. Yet his job as a reporter was to get at the real Nicole. It was a quandary he didn't know how to resolve.

BARTON DROVE TOWARD his house, whistling happily. He was tired—short nights could do that to a guy—but some things were worth a few after-the-fact yawns. Monday's game had gone into extra innings and he was still catching up on sleep. He'd offered to leave at ten and, to his delight, Chelsea had made a face at him.

"Leave?" she'd asked. "With the score tied and the home team needing support? What kind of fan are you?"

The Mariners had won the game at midnight. Chelsea had cheered and clapped along with the faithful diehards in the stadium, and then they'd made their way to the parking garage. With the late hour, the traffic wasn't bad and getting home hadn't taken long.

Part of him had wanted to kiss Chelsea goodnight, but she'd stopped him from even going up the stairs to her apartment door. Instead he'd watched until she was safely inside, then strode home to slide into bed and think about what a great evening it had been.

Now as Barton came down the street, he saw Chelsea walking up the sidewalk in shorts and a light sweatshirt. The air felt hot to him, but it wasn't unusual for newcomers to find Seattle weather cooler than people who'd lived there for a while. He braked and rolled down his window.

"Hi, Chelsea. There's a great walking trail at the park. If you're interested, we could go together."

He liked the quick, shy smile she gave him.

"Okay."

"Do you want to ride back to the house with me?"

"No, I'll meet you there."

Once home, he hurriedly changed into casual clothing and was ready when she came up the driveway. He knew he might be rushing things with Chelsea, but he wasn't thinking completely straight around her, despite the voice of caution in his head.

"How was your day?" she asked as they headed for the park.

"Mostly right now it's riding herd on kids who can't wait for summer break to get here. The unseasonable weather is making them stir-crazy."

"I remember how it felt to be anxious for summer, though I could also be sad if I really liked my teacher."

"Did you enjoy school?"

"Um...sometimes. When I didn't, it wasn't because of school. My home life was messed up."

Barton saw a fleeting sadness on her face. "That's too bad."

"It's just the way it was. My folks had problems. I think we were all relieved when they finally got a divorce."

He winced.

"Did I say something wrong?" Chelsea asked.

"No, I was thinking. I got divorced two years ago and I was grateful that we didn't have kids to be hurt by our failure. Odd, because I'd really love to have children."

"I've heard that teachers sometimes change their minds about having a family."

He shook his head. "Not me. There are days when I pray I won't make the blunders that produced a few of the students in my class, but I've never stopped wanting kids of my own."

"I know what you mean. I swear that I won't make my parents' mistakes, then humility forces me to admit that I'll probably screw up my own way."

Barton glanced at Chelsea. Essentially she'd told him she hoped to have family someday, which was nice. Looking back he couldn't honestly say that his ex-wife had ever expected them to have children. Maybe if he'd listened closely enough when he and Ellyn were dating, he would have realized they were in completely different places about what they wanted.

"Reality knocks us all down to size," he murmured. "But we have to hope that love will make up for some of the inevitable errors."

"Yeah, and that they'll forgive us for the rest."

He grinned. "You bet."

They reached the park and Barton veered toward the hiking trail. "Runners are discouraged from using this one," he explained, "and bicycles aren't allowed."

"That's good. I'm uncomfortable sharing a trail with bikes. One knocked me down a while back and just kept going."

"That's awful. At least they're reasonably courteous in this neighborhood."

Chelsea nodded, but despite his reassurance, she seemed uncertain and Barton wondered what made her so tentative at times. During the excitement of the game, she'd come out of herself; now she was more guarded. Perhaps that was to be expected, especially when making a new acquaintance.

Something Terri had said in passing made him think Chelsea had recently gone through a bad breakup. Maybe she was still picking up the pieces. He could definitely sympathize.

In the meantime, he would to do his best to get to know her better. He was sure she was worth the effort.

NICOLE ENJOYED THE perfectly prepared shrimp scampi she'd ordered, trying to ignore the raw tension inside of her. Perhaps she shouldn't have told Jordan about that long-ago kiss, but it had seemed silly not to mention it. The same with the time Jordan had knocked her down when she was trying to skate. The events had been meaningless kid stuff, yet his eyes had flared in a very un-kidlike way when she'd explained about them kissing.

It didn't help that the restaurant's atmosphere made the meal feel like part of a romantic tryst... low lights, flowers and candles on the linen-covered table topped by fine china and crystal. But she and Jordan didn't want anything together, despite whatever physical attraction existed between them.

"Would you care for dessert?" he asked as the waiter cleared their dishes.

"Not for me, but go ahead."

"I'm fine. With luck, the traffic has eased up by now."

"I hope your meal was adequate, Ms. George," the maître d' said in calm understatement as they neared the door.

"Everything was delicious," Nicole assured him.

"As always," Jordan added.

She breathed a sigh of relief when they stepped outside and the aura of romance vanished. As they walked toward the car she drew a calming breath and glanced around, appreciating the evening light. "Seattle is a beautiful city. I'm looking forward to the long days during summer."

"Short winter days are the downside."

"True," she conceded. "But while it may not be your idea of a great evening, I love curling up with a good book by the fire. And this year I'll have Toby lying near the hearth. I suppose you pop off to Hawaii or the southern hemisphere when the worst of winter approaches."

"I spend a fair amount of time away," he conceded. "As I've mentioned, I can work from anywhere, even in a hammock under a palm tree."

"A rare and pleasant circumstance."

"But you chose a second career that keeps you tied to the same place most of the time. I know we've talked about this a little already, but weren't you tempted to retire and enjoy a leisurely life style?"

Nicole shrugged. If they were two other people, someone might think they were innocently chatting, getting to know one another as friends or potential lovers. Instead, anything she said would have a good chance of finding its way into a *Post-Modern* article.

"I was tempted," she acknowledged, "but it didn't seem like much of a life goal. I wanted to accomplish something."

"So you don't anticipate any regrets?"

"I'm not saying it wouldn't be nice to fly off to Paris or Rome whenever the urge strikes, but I'm putting something else first. And as I've indicated, once my partners are all here, I'll have more time for other things."

Jordan inclined his head and she could practically see the wheels turning in his journalistic brain. "Aside from reading, what other hobbies do you enjoy?" he asked.

"I'm still figuring that out. I'm curious about many things and would love a pastime that I could be excited about." She grinned. "You know that movie, *Indiana Jones and the Last Crusade*? I love the diary Indy's father kept for years, filled with arcane details and lore about the Grail. It might be fun to get totally absorbed by something. Does that sound silly to you?"

They'd gotten into the car while talking and there was a funny smile playing on Jordan's lips.

"I have to confess," he finally said, "I have a book like that. Actually, more than one. I've collected every single bit of information and speculation about Sasquatch that I can find. Go ahead and poke fun at me."

"Not *at* you," she assured. "You live in the Northwest and Bigfoot is a big thing here...if you'll forgive the sort-of pun."

"In my case I'm fascinated that modern people still persist in believing without real scientific evidence."

"So you don't actually believe in Sasquatch yourself, it's more about his followers?"

"I'm keeping an open mind. They discover new species every day, so anything is possible."

Like Nicole's earlier suspicion that Jordan had latent knightly impulses, his interest in Sasquatch gave her an unusual glimpse into his psyche. On the other hand, she wasn't entirely certain he was telling the truth; he might be teasing her.

"Do you include the yeti in your research?" she inquired.

He started the car. "I've concentrated on local legends."

"But the yeti could be Bigfoot's cousin. You might be ignoring a branch of the family."

"There's a thought. If the Bigfoot info runs dry, perhaps I'll head to the Himalayas and check on yeti references. Or maybe you could do that for me."

"Hey, I'm not your leg man. I'll find my own obsession."

"I'm not obsessed," he complained in a light tone. "I just enjoy being well-informed on the subject."

"Do you have a Bigfoot lamp hidden in your closet?" she inquired, hoping to keep up the relaxed conversation until they ended the evening. Anything was better than the yearning to invite him home to spend the night.

"Nope, I'm an information man. But I confess to having *Harry and the Hendersons* on Blu-ray."

His embarrassed smile convinced her he was telling the truth about his hobby. The film, however sweet, was hardly in the top ten best-known flicks.

"I like that movie, too, especially Harry's distress when he sees the husband helping his wife into a hot tub."

"Be careful," Jordan warned, "it's only a small leap from where you are to tracking down old folk tales and newspapers on microfilm."

Nicole turned toward him. "That sounds cool."

"It's amazing to tread through the old reports, quite apart from anything related to Sasquatch."

The skeptical mask that Jordan habitually wore seemed absent, but it dropped back into place as he parked next to her sedan in the agency parking lot.

"Thank you. This was an informative afternoon for the *PostModern* article," he said politely.

"How so?"

"I shouldn't say. I'm still putting my impressions together."

He was definitely back to his normal, closed-in self. Illogically, she was annoyed.

"The afternoon was quite informative for me, as well," she told him crisply.

"In what way?"

"I'm still putting my impressions together."

"How amusing, to throw my words back at me."

"Turnabout is fair play. In a nanosecond you went from pleasantly discussing hobbies to being an aloof interviewer."

"You're the one who didn't want to answer interview questions while we were driving. This wasn't a date."

Nicole stared in astonishment. "Thank you so much for the information. Just think, if you hadn't said anything I would have gone home to my little diary with the heart-shaped lock and written about the journalist who wined and dined me this evening. A journalist who claims he isn't cynical or biased, but keeps going out of his way to show that he is."

Jordan had the grace to look abashed. "I'm sorry."

She wasn't in the mood to be forgiving. "I'm not interested in getting involved with anyone. I've learned my lesson when it comes to romance and if I ever change my mind, I certainly won't want a guy who's pursuing a tidy, controlled bachelor life. So, whatever is going on inside your suspicious brain, it's your problem, not mine."

Getting out, she slammed the door and got into her own car, fuming. Apparently Jordan was the sort of person who only recognized a line that shouldn't be crossed when he was looking back at it. Everyone made mistakes and she wasn't immune to them herself, but he'd leaped over boundaries more than once, including the other night when he'd kissed her. She might have given him a friendly hug, but it hadn't been an invitation for more. And she was quite certain he knew that.

The challenge, of course, was wondering if her hug really had been as innocent as it could have been. There was no question she had felt attraction from the start. It had only grown in the days since, so she felt as if she was walking on shaky ground when trying to evaluate Jordan's actions. But what she was feeling was only physical...wasn't it?

CHAPTER ELEVEN

CHELSEA WAS A little scared. She liked Barton far more than she should after such a short acquaintance. It wasn't as if she wanted to get involved with anyone. For months she'd gathered the courage to get Ron out of her life, so leaping into a relationship right away wasn't smart. She reminded herself, once again, that Barton didn't necessarily want to do that, either. He had been divorced for two years, but everyone moved on at a different pace. Maybe he wanted to play the field for a while...though that didn't seem his style.

"This is a nice park," she said. "I mostly see families here."

"That's one of the things that sold me on the neighborhood. It didn't hurt that the house was in my price range since it was basically a wreck."

"You're kidding, your place looks terrific. On the outside, at least," she added.

"Now it does. I poured myself into restoring both the interior and exterior for the last year and a half. It helped to focus on a specific task instead of on my life, if you know what I mean."

"I've never been divorced, but I can imagine. Was it bad, what happened with you and your wife?"

"Yes. She wanted money and success and simply couldn't adjust to being married to a teacher who was never going to set the world on fire. I guess I was too selfish to compromise."

Chelsea wanted to ask what he could have done, given up the work he loved? "It's nice that you don't lambaste her," she said hesitantly.

"What would be the point? I screwed up. When we got married, I was a stockbroker. But more and more it just seemed meaningless, so I decided to become a teacher. Now I'm never bored. But Ellyn thought she was marrying a guy who'd make a splash in the world and be able to provide a certain lifestyle. There's no denying teachers don't make a lot of money."

"You just developed different priorities after you got married. That happens. It isn't as if you set out to hurt her."

"I suppose. She hung in for a while, but couldn't adjust."

"I'm sure your students are glad you became a teacher."

He grinned. "Some of the time. Tests and homework are rarely popular."

"I guess no teacher is loved *all* of the time, but I had several who made a difference in my life. And I wish I'd applied more of what one of them used to say."

"What was that?" Barton asked.

"She would quote Eleanor Roosevelt about no one being able to make you feel inferior without your consent. I didn't really get it at the time, but I do now." If she'd remembered that bit of wisdom when Ron had been picking her confidence apart, she might not have wasted so much time being miserable.

"That's one of Eleanor's best. From what I've read, she learned that after experiencing a lot of pain."

"But doesn't it also mean that some things are partly our own fault?"

"In a way, I suppose," Barton said. "I don't think it's something to beat ourselves up about, though. The trick is to learn and move on."

"Right." That was what she needed to remember—not to let it happen again. "So, is it okay for someone to make us feel *better* without our consent?" she asked.

Barton winked. "That's a serious problem, but it might be forgivable, as long as we don't let it happen too often. Say, no more than several times a day."

"Sounds about right." She was glad that he'd taken the cue on lightening the conversation.

They were passing behind the dugouts at the baseball field and the players inside started waving.

"Hey, Barton," one kid called, "you wanna play?"

"Sorry, not tonight," Barton told him.

Another boy rolled his eyes. "I told you he wouldn't, not when he's with a *girl*."

"She might be his sister."

"Sisters aren't *pretty*."

"Hah," said a girl stomping out to the plate with a bat in her hands. "And brothers are, like, total jerks."

Barton's shoulders were shaking and Chelsea was afraid to catch his eye for fear he'd lose it. Out of sight of the kids, though, they shared a laugh.

"Were they your students?" she finally asked.

"Nah, this isn't my school district. But they play here several nights a week. Kitty is the girl. She can pitch the stitches off a ball. As she says, that just *slays* her brother."

"I'll bet it does."

"But Cory was right, you know."

"About what?"

"When he implied that you're pretty."

Chelsea felt the warmth rising in her cheeks at the compliment. Being with Barton made her feel good. Maybe she shouldn't worry so much and just enjoy it without taking everything seriously.

JORDAN DIDN'T SLEEP again that night. At six in the morning, he gave up trying, showered and dressed. At his desk, he loaded the pictures from his SD card into the computer and clicked through the shots he'd gotten the day before.

There were over a hundred, a few of the models as they worked, but mostly of Nicole. He'd told himself that she was, after all, the subject of the article, but he had mostly been fascinated with how the camera seemed to love her face. No wonder she'd hit the top echelon as a model. It almost seemed as if a bad picture couldn't be taken of Nicole George.

Years ago he'd toyed with the idea of photojournalism, before deciding he preferred writing. That was another aspect Syd had liked about him doing the article; she wouldn't have to send a photographer since he could handle it.

His body grew tight and hard as he viewed the picture of Nicole showing Jackie how to perch on the climbing wall. Her muscles were contracted and her lithe curves were more than evident under her classy business attire.

He understood why the photographer had wanted Nicole, rather than Jackie; she had the name and an allure that would help sell the product. But the guy was an idiot to use those sorts of tactics; she'd seen through him as if he were an empty aquarium. Come to think of it, she had done something similar to him in the car afterward. While someone might occasionally find a stealthy way around her, she was too bright for it to happen often. The problem was, he *liked* intelligent women. It only increased their appeal.

Jordan couldn't entirely blame his wakefulness on Nicole. In childhood he'd been a chronic insomniac and he hadn't been able to break the pattern as an adult. Maybe he didn't *want* to break it. Something about the night touched on the mysterious, as if doors to the unknown were waiting in the darkness—not that he'd tell anyone how he felt. That sort of belief was too fanciful to confess.

He yawned. The few times he'd come close to dropping off, his imagination had drifted to a long-ago patio and the image of holding Nicole close in a kiss. Yet it wasn't a teenage girl he saw in his mind, but the woman she'd become—pure fantasy, but enough to disrupt his already elusive sleep.

Turning off the computer, he went for a run, then showered, worked on his column, and at 10:00 a.m., headed out to the talent agency. The interview process was taking more time than originally anticipated, but he still hadn't gotten that special something needed for the articles. Nicole *was* right about Syd maneuvering to push his skills; he was sure of it. He was enjoying the challenge, but would enjoy it more if he wasn't wrestling with desire at the same time.

What was it that Nicole had said about not wanting romance, especially with a guy who'd chosen control along with his bachelor existence? Or something like that. Well, fine. He enjoyed his life and didn't want the messiness that came from romance and commitment. His reasons might be different from Nicole's, but they apparently both wanted to stay unattached.

At the agency by ten thirty, he bought two cups of coffee from the Crystal Connection. The shop had a side entrance opening onto the atrium. The building was interesting and very attractive for converted industrial space. He went outside to the Moonlight Ventures door. His sister smiled as he entered.

"Hi, Jordan. Do you have an appointment with Nicole?"

"She's meeting with prospective clients this morning and was going to see if they minded me observing the process. I forgot to ask if it was okay yesterday, so came on the off-chance they've agreed. Could you let her know I'm here?"

"I texted her when I saw you coming."

"Great." He handed Chelsea a cup of coffee. "This is for you, in case you want it."

"Thanks."

He eyed a chunk of amethyst crystals sitting next to her work area. "That looks new. Are you getting swept into the crystal craze next door?"

"It was so pretty, I couldn't resist when I went by earlier this morning. Anyhow, when I got up today I decided to do something special for myself, and this turned out to be it."

Her face was brighter and happier than she'd looked for years. Jordan wanted to ask if the reason was the job, the new city, the guy next door or simply Ron's absence. But his sister had been very direct in saying that most of those subjects were out-of-bounds.

It was a new experience, having Chelsea set boundaries. But he couldn't bemoan the development.

A thought struck him that she could do well to take Nicole as a role model, as least in regards to her strength of mind. Of course, Chelsea had also spent time with Terri and Terri was strong as well, except that her strength seemed to be grounded in defiant belligerence. Nicole's example might be healthier, which was a startling conclusion—he would have given an entirely different answer if asked about it a few weeks ago.

Jordan frowned.

He couldn't afford too much of a rah-rah attitude about Nicole. He had to maintain objectivity and not let the articles he was writing become her public relations pipeline.

"Good morning, Jordan." There wasn't any hint in Nicole's face that they'd parted the previous evening on poor terms. "I emailed the family I'm meeting with and they just sent back a message saying it's fine for you to be there, provided you don't take any pictures or use their names."

"Family?"

"The daughter is underage, so her legal guardians are part of the process."

For the next hour, he sat in the background as

Nicole talked with the parents and their daughter. The eight-year-old girl appeared shy and Nicole had to coax her out of her shell. It seemed to him that one of the things she was trying to learn was whether the kid really *wanted* to be a model. She also seemed to be checking on the parents and how reasonable they were about expectations.

"Didn't *you* become an internationally known model when you weren't much older than Amber?" the father asked at one point.

Nicole's face became guarded. "Yes, my parents were in the clothing business, which gave them extensive connections. It meant a lot of doors were opened early for me. So luck was a—"

"But wouldn't you have the same connections to use for Amber?" he demanded.

"It doesn't work that way," she said smoothly. "In the meantime, please read the materials I've given you and perhaps we'll talk again."

With that she graciously ended the interview. She sighed and dropped into her office chair once they were gone.

"Is it tough to deal with families like that?" Jordan asked.

She jerked as if she'd forgotten he was there. "To an extent."

"When it comes to a minor child, is part of your decision based upon how well the parents may fit into the process?"

"For me, yes."

Jordan rubbed his face. "Look, I know I've been a bulldog on this issue and I know you want your parents to be off-limits, but as you already pointed out, there are gray areas where it's hard to know the dividing line. Is there any way to separate the experience of how your parents handled things, with how you view any child models you might decide to represent?"

Nicole tossed her pen onto the desk. "Probably not. I asked before, and I'll ask again, how much do your mom and dad influence *your* view of the world?"

She was good at throwing questions back at him, but he wanted to stop that game. For good or ill, his parents had influenced him the way any parents influenced their children. But at his age, he was responsible for his own thoughts and feelings, he didn't need to blame his childhood. Of course, Nicole was probably trying to say the same thing about herself.

As for the uncomfortable secret he held about his mother throwing herself at Nicole's father? For years he'd thought Mr. George had told his wife, explaining the sharp rift in friendship between the families. But Nicole had been clear about not knowing the reason, so what purpose would it serve to tell her now? And if he did, would she feel he was obligated to treat her especially well in the *PostModern* articles because of what his mother had done?

Nicole cocked her head in challenge at Jordan's silence.

She was torn between not wanting to deal with him and an odd anticipation of it. There was something compelling about Jordan that she couldn't ignore. Originally she'd thought the interviews would simply entail a few hours of sitting and talking. Yet the elongated process was partly her own fault since she resisted revealing too much about herself to Jordan. The odd thing was that she didn't think she'd have felt the same with a true stranger and it scared her to realize her emotions might be at risk around him.

"Do you realize how often you don't answer questions, instead turning them around to me?" Jordan asked.

She kept her expression neutral with an effort…it was almost as if he'd read her mind. "Sorry, it's an old reflex with reporters."

"Frankly, avoiding your parents as a topic gives the appearance of a dark mystery."

"No mystery, just a hint of guilt and mixed feelings."

"Why would you feel guilty?"

Nicole drew in a deep breath. "Okay, *off the record*, my parents poured a lot of their lives into making a great career for me. It was a good career and I enjoyed it. But as I've told you, I feel bad because my sister got left out. Emily was called the smart George sister and that hurt her. It also hurt me because the implication was that I just got by on my looks."

"Did your parents foster the smart versus pretty comparison?"

"They would rave about how smart she was, as if it made up for not paying that much attention to her. It didn't, which I think they knew, but they just couldn't break the pattern."

Jordan frowned. "So Emily's unique attractiveness didn't get appreciated and neither did your brains."

"Yes. They were proud when Emily built a hugely successful clothing boutique in LA. It was something they understood and now they had two daughters making waves in the fashion world. Imagine their shock when Emily put a manager in charge of her business and moved to Schuyler, Montana. They would have approved of Paris or New York, not a tiny town in the middle of ranching country."

"Then you retired to become a talent agent. I imagine that didn't go down well."

"You're telling me." Nicole stirred restlessly. "Shall we take a walk? I've been here since 6:00 a.m. and I'm getting cabin fever."

He nodded and they went outside.

"Did you start early this morning because of

me?" Jordan asked as she led him toward the back of the parking lot.

"Not specifically because of you. But setting time aside for interviews means I need to get work done at another hour."

"Nice of you not to make it personal."

"That's because it *isn't* personal. I would have to do the same for any reporter writing the *Post-Modern* articles."

Moonlight Ventures wasn't far from Lake Washington and Nicole already knew the best route to the shoreline. Her nerves eased once they were at the water's edge, though not as much as they would have if she'd been alone.

"Are your folks adjusting to your decision?" Jordan asked.

"You bet. They're even offering me advice on running the agency," Nicole said wryly.

"From what I've seen, it doesn't look as if you need it."

She smiled. "Their focus is different, but I'll take wisdom from whatever direction it arrives."

"I don't want to put words in your mouth," Jordan said carefully, "but is part of becoming an agent because you want to claim an accomplishment in your own right?"

He was a bulldog on *that* issue, too. The question was whether he wanted something intimate, or just confirmation of his assumptions that she was trying to break away from a parental choice in her life.

Nicole wrinkled her nose. "It's never that simple, is it? I'm benefiting from the experience and contacts I made while modeling, so it isn't as if I started at Moonlight Ventures and had to learn everything from the ground up. Mostly I was ready to pass on what I know to other people and help them succeed. But in a larger sense, I've been genuinely fortunate. I think I have an obligation to pay some of that back."

She sank onto a bench and gazed across the lake. There was a light breeze and the sun was shining. It was the kind of day that almost made her regret choosing a working life.

"Some of that is remarkably similar to something you said before," he pointed out. "Are you still claiming that becoming an agent is based on altruism?"

His voice held a slight edge of sarcasm and her jaw clenched. Why had she wasted time wondering whether Jordan had hidden finer qualities? Even if he did, they were obviously repressed by his jaded outlook. It bothered her. There was enough negativity, and it was sad to think Jordan might be part of it.

"You said you weren't going to put words in my mouth, yet you keep doing it," she returned sharply, her frustration rising. "Obviously you think I'm putting on an act to look good. I believe 'noble' is the description you used before. Now you're calling it altruism."

"It just seems there must be more to it."

"Your note of sarcasm implies much more than that."

Nicole reminded herself that it didn't matter if he thought she wasn't being genuine. They weren't friends. It was messy because of their shared past, but ultimately he was just the reporter doing an article on her. Any disappointment on her part was illogical.

"I'm sorry you don't like my answers," she continued. "Will it help for me to say I *also* wanted to succeed in a new way, or do you want to pick that apart as well?" Jumping to her feet, she gave him a polished smile. "I need to get back and finish a few things. I promised to attend a career fair between two and four, so my afternoon is occupied."

"May I go to observe?"

"Suit yourself. You can get the address and contact information from Chelsea." This time she didn't intend to expedite his participation the way she had with the performance at the high school. He was on his own.

"Wait," Jordan said as she started back in the direction of the agency.

"Yes?"

"You don't need to get in a snit because I was honest about my doubts. I'm trying to be objective."

"First of all, I question whether you'd claim a man was getting in a 'snit' over something. Beyond that, you're free to doubt anything you want. I wouldn't expect anything else from a cynic. However, I'd like to point out that *objective* means being free of bias and personal feelings. Despite your claim that you'd try to control your biases, your preconceived opinions seem to be more rampant than ever."

Nicole saw red creeping up Jordan's neck.

"Believe what you want, you will anyway," she continued. "But in actuality, you keep straying off topic. These articles are supposed to be about my transition from model to businesswoman. Instead, you mostly want to talk about the past and try to show my motives are all *based* on the past. Of course the past influences me, but I'm not a puppet. Yet when I try to express my thoughts and feelings, you slap them back in my face."

Jordan looked shocked. "I didn't intend to do that."

"And yet that's what you did. By the way, don't forget that talking about my family is off the record, so they're still off limits for the article. Oh, and be sure to call ahead for permission to attend the career fair. School officials are very cautious about who they allow on campus these days."

JORDAN MENTALLY KICKED himself as he watched Nicole moving swiftly away. He'd come closer to achieving the kind of rapport needed for his articles, only to blow it.

He definitely wasn't himself these days.

Her comments about her family had roused sympathy and he'd promptly reminded himself that he was a skeptic. Then the sunlight had glinted across her hair like a golden fire. If he'd been a poet he might have said something metaphorical about her intensely azure eyes that looked like the Mediterranean on a clear day or that her complexion rivaled the finest silk. Then there was her personality, which sparkled like champagne. He'd been fighting the impulse to leap in that direction, which resulted in his graceless response.

It wasn't that he'd lied. He questioned and doubted everything, and that was as neutral as he could get. It might not be the most illustrious claim a guy could make, but he would never pretend to agree with something and then write something else. Still, he *was* guilty of clinging to his biases. And the way he'd responded had also shut down any budding trust.

When I try to express my thoughts and feelings, you slap them back in my face.

Jordan flinched at the memory. Getting Nicole to open up might be impossible now. As for saying she'd gotten into a snit? Blast it all, she was right. He would never have said that to a man, and probably not to another woman. Instead he'd reverted to sophomoric behavior. Given Nicole's sex appeal and the average man's libido, he was likely just the latest in a long line of idiots she'd encountered. As consolations went, that wasn't much, but it was all he had.

Well, no point in whining over his mistakes. He glanced at his watch; it was past twelve. He'd get the information from Chelsea about the career fair and make the necessary call, then grab lunch and wait for Nicole. When she headed for her car, he'd ask her to let him ride along. He could attend the career fair on his own, but it seemed diplomatic to go with her.

She might agree, though considering how angry she'd been, it was a good thing she didn't have an ejector seat.

A WHILE LATER Jordan opened his eyes and glanced out of his car window, which he'd left down to catch the breeze off Lake Washington.

What? Nicole's car was gone. He fumbled for his phone to check the time and saw that he'd slept through the afternoon.

He frowned. There was a sticky note on his side-view mirror.

Jordan,
Lack of sleep interferes with cognitive function and/or social ability. Good to see you're catching up.
Nicole

Groaning, Jordan rubbed his face. He gulped what was left of the coffee in his cup, even though it would probably inhibit him getting to sleep that night.

When Nicole got back to the agency he'd have to eat crow, or something equally hard to stomach. As he sat ruminating on the forthcoming recipe, his sister came out and locked the agency door, then headed in his direction; she carried an express box from the post office, her handbag laid over it.

"Hey, Jordan," she said, peering through the window. "I've been watching you out here all afternoon. At first I was going to check to see if you were okay. But Nicole said you were taking your kindergarten nap, whatever that means."

"She has an unusual sense of humor. When does she expect to be back?"

"Not tonight. She has plans for the evening."

Despite having no reason to think Nicole had arranged a romantic interlude, his mind immediately went in that direction.

"So," he said to Chelsea, "would you like to eat dinner with your brother?"

"That would be nice, but I'm busy, too."

Great. He was supposedly a carefree bachelor with an active social life, yet *he* was the one without any plans that evening.

"In that case," he said, "have a good time."

"Thank you." Her expression seemed strained,

but he had a feeling she wouldn't admit anything was wrong.

He watched her drive away before starting his car. Nothing about the day had been good. He felt like going home, putting on a hockey game and opening a bottle of beer. And why shouldn't he? Well, maybe not the beer since he avoided drinking alone, but the game might be a way to finish the day on a more neutral note.

It would be nice to watch something for which he had no responsibility. A small break would be even better than having a beer. And perhaps he could briefly forget the way he kept thinking about Nicole. At the oddest times he found himself remembering things she'd said, her smile, her intelligence and gentle humor. He didn't feel the way he was supposed to feel about the subject of an article. That might explain his complete incompetence in dealing with her.

CHAPTER TWELVE

NICOLE HAD DECIDED to join a planned video conference with her partners from home, rather than going back to the agency.

When the conference ended, Nicole sat back in her easy chair. At some point she'd have to create a home office, but right now she kept the computer in the den. It was the only furnished room in the house aside from her bedroom.

Toby scrambled up onto her lap and she sat petting him, thinking over what had happened that day.

She'd probably been reckless. After all, she had invited Jordan to say what she already knew, that he didn't trust her. So why be offended or hurt when he obliged? It was illogical, especially when he clearly questioned everything and everyone.

Most of her anger had passed by the time she'd come out to the parking lot on the way to the career fair. Noticing Jordan's car, she had walked over, intending to mend fences by inviting him to drive with her, since he'd obviously stuck around for that reason. But he'd been deeply asleep.

Unlike some folks who looked slack-jawed

while napping upright, Jordan had simply appeared relaxed—in some ways the happiest she'd ever seen him. It had to be her imagination. She'd hate to think any person was at their happiest while unconscious.

Deciding not to awaken him, Nicole had left a note as a way of ribbing him over their earlier clash. So far, she hadn't seen many signs he had a sense of humor, but she didn't think it was totally absent. And if he was tired enough to fall asleep in his car, that *could* account for some of his stiff-necked attitude.

Her phone rang. "Hello?"

Jordan's deep voice came over the line. "Nicole, I'm glad I caught you. I apologize for missing this afternoon's event."

"It was mostly teenage girls hoping for their big break. You probably would have been bored."

"Yeah, well, I also called because I wasn't at my best earlier and I'm sorry."

"That's water under the bridge," she said lightly.

"Can we discuss it?"

"Is there any point? Jordan, you don't seem to like or believe in anyone or anything. Trying to convince you that I'm an exception is a waste of energy. Besides, I'm *not* an exception. I've traveled all over the world and worked with good and bad and found that most people tend to be decent. I'm sure that doesn't suit your skeptical outlook."

Nicole intentionally didn't use the word *cynical* since he'd objected to the description.

Silence.

"There's nothing wrong with skepticism," he finally said. "It keeps you from being disappointed."

"When it's your ironclad fallback position, it also keeps you from getting close to anybody because you're always looking for their faults instead of being with them. I'm guessing that also has something to do with why you decided to stay single."

"That's ridiculous."

Toby had been looking up at her and seemed distressed at the tone in her voice. He snuggled closer and sighed as she rubbed his neck.

"Perhaps," she acknowledged, "and for your sake I hope I'm wrong because nobody is perfect and control is an illusion. But it doesn't really matter, does it? After the articles are written, you'll go your way and I'll go mine. We won't see each other again unless we happen to pass each other on the running trail or you come to visit Chelsea."

Another silence, longer this time, before he answered. "Right. I'll get off now so you can get ready for your date."

"What do you mean?"

"Don't think that Chelsea was speaking out

of turn. I asked her if you were returning to the agency and she explained you had other plans."

Nicole's eyebrows rose. Jordan assumed that "plans" meant a date? Perhaps that was best.

"Fine. Have a nice evening, Jordan," she said.

"Thanks. I'll call or come by in the morning to arrange another time for us to get together."

"Okay. Good night."

"'Night."

Nicole smiled wryly as she hit the off button on her phone handset. For a moment she stepped into the downstairs powder room and looked in the mirror; her hair was mussed and her lip gloss had worn off hours earlier. Hardly the image of a supermodel. One thing was certain: she was even more convinced that Jordan was the last man to develop romantic ideas about. He *would* want the fantasy, the perfection that only existed in a photograph. Someone who was flawless in every way.

Maybe he knew it wasn't possible for any woman to be like that, or any relationship to be without its difficulties. So he'd decided to go it alone, to be content with being single and able to do as he liked.

She wrinkled her nose at her reflection, then went to fetch Toby's leash.

Now that the Skype conference was done, her plans for the evening were simple—take Toby for a walk, eat leftovers from the fridge, read more of her book, go to bed early...

And try not to think about Jordan Masters.

BARTON WALKED ACROSS the driveway and waved at Nicole as she came down her front walk. Toby yipped and tugged the leash in Barton's direction.

"Hello, pal." He crouched to greet the friendly animal. "You'd never guess that someone abandoned the little guy," he said, standing upright again.

"Toby was young when it happened, so I keep hoping he doesn't remember what it meant to be set adrift. But he gets anxious sometimes about being left behind."

"Hard to believe anyone could be that uncaring."

"Yeah, but all you have to do is spend a few minutes online and you see one story after another about abandoned animals. I know the system tracks what you've looked at and feeds you similar stories, but it's depressing to see how many animals are neglected or abandoned."

"You sound like an activist."

"No, though it's something to think about. One of my partners at Moonlight Ventures is involved in environmental causes and wildlife conservation. And I've been looking for a hobby."

Nicole had an odd twist to her lips, but Barton decided it might be intrusive to ask why.

"Have a good time on your walk," he urged instead.

"Thanks. See you," she said with another odd smile. He wondered if she was upset about something. If so, it was a shame. Nicole George had turned out to be a nice person.

Turning, he trotted up the stairs to Chelsea's apartment. She was fixing him dinner as a thank-you for taking her to the Mariners game. It wasn't necessary, but he would enjoy spending more time with her. Since he'd initiated contact the last two times, he hoped the invitation was more than mere courtesy.

"Hi, Barton!" She greeted him in a friendly way, though she was pale and looked nervous.

"Is everything all right?"

"Yes, of course." Her answer came too quickly to be reassuring. "Would you like something to drink? Since I'm just living here temporarily, there isn't much on hand, but I've got soda water and regular soda. Also there's a bottle of wine and some juice."

"A soda sounds good."

"Help yourself. It's in the fridge."

She was setting a small table, so he went into the kitchen and got a cola from the refrigerator. After doing so much work on his house, he couldn't help evaluating the apartment. It had plenty of light from the windows and seemed very pleasant.

He was interested to see a utility cupboard; the door stood open and contained a garbage can, broom and similar items, which was a nice way to keep things out of sight in the limited space.

Then he saw an express mailing box on a shelf, with bold letters saying: RETURN TO SENDER! The name on the return address was Ron Swanson. The former boyfriend? He wanted to ask about it, since sending the box back unopened was a definite sign that something was wrong, but he wasn't much more than an acquaintance at this point. And the fact that Chelsea might want to keep it private was highlighted by her hurriedly closing the utility door when she came into the kitchen.

"This is a well-designed space," he said as she checked a pan on the stove.

"I like it."

"I've thought of expanding over my garage to create a guesthouse. Either that or a genuine master bedroom suite."

"Both would be nice."

"If you were buying a house, which would you think was most important?"

"A master suite, maybe. Especially if I had a family. It would be nice to have private space."

He chuckled. "Good point. Hey, is there something I can do to help? I'm handy around the kitchen."

"Everything is ready. If you don't mind, let's serve from the stove. The table is too small for family-style meals."

"No problem." He got a serving of pilaf and vegetables and looked into another pot. "What's that?"

"You said you liked chicken, so I made it with lemon and garlic. I… I hope it's all right."

He spooned the fragrant mixture over his pilaf. "It sure smells tasty." When they were both seated he tasted the chicken first. "Wow, that's terrific."

"I took a chance."

"You're a good cook."

"No, I'm not. I mean…it's nice of you to say that."

Whatever had happened, he had a feeling she'd been spooked, or reminded of something unpleasant.

"Is everything all right?" he asked finally. "You seem edgy, as if something upsetting happened."

Chelsea stared at her plate, moving the food around, separating the rice and veggies, then moving it back again. "It's just something I'd rather forget," she said at length. "Sorry if I'm bad company."

He laid his hand over hers. "I think you're fine company."

The corners of her lips curved upward. Lord,

she was pretty. For a man who knew it was best to move slowly, he was experiencing the temptation to make a headlong rush. Caution, he reminded himself. Caution. Besides, Chelsea didn't need some guy bearing down on her.

He drew a deep breath. "If you ever just need to talk, remember you've got a friend next door."

Her beautiful dark eyes rose toward his and she seemed to relax. "Thanks, Barton."

Forcing himself to focus on his plate, he continued eating. It was one of the best meals he'd had in a long time.

CHELSEA'S SPIRITS ROSE as she and Barton began discussing cooking. Her lemon chicken recipe had come from a Spanish woman she'd known in college and they debated whether it was Spanish food, or simply a dish someone from Spain happened to make.

"She could have gotten the recipe from someone in the United States," Chelsea pointed out.

"True. Or France, or the Middle East or Canada. Good food comes from all over."

He truly seemed to enjoy the chicken, going back for seconds and eating every bite. Ron had been so critical of her culinary skills that she hadn't known how to respond when Barton had complimented her.

Should she explain? Or would discussing it fall into the category of "she won't shut up about her ex?" Some guys hated hearing about a former boyfriend. Barton had offered to listen, but she didn't think she could face telling him what had happened.

The truth was, she felt horribly embarrassed about letting Ron manipulate her for so long. Each day that passed made her more aware that she should have walked out on him a long time ago. It wasn't as if she'd still loved him; that had been over longer than she could remember.

Then a package had arrived late that afternoon at the agency. The postman, a genial middle-aged man who came by the agency each day, had grinned as he'd made a special stop to give it to her, joking that it must be from an admirer.

Hardly.

She didn't know what was inside and had decided to return it unopened. That would send a clear message to Ron that she wasn't interested in anything he did or had to say. If they'd been sharing an apartment she might have opened the box, in case it was something of hers. But she had resisted his attempts to move in and hadn't even given him a key. Luckily her lease was up at the end of next month and Terri was putting everything in storage.

Chelsea knew she'd have to move the rest of her things up to Seattle once she had her own place. After all, she couldn't stay in Nicole's guesthouse forever.

Yet a different kind of anxiety nibbled at her when she thought of finding a new apartment. She liked living next door to Barton.

JORDAN FOUND HE couldn't concentrate on the hockey game. He couldn't even sit back and simply let it be a background to the evening. Instead he kept wondering where Nicole was having dinner and whether she'd invite her date back to spend the night at her house.

It was as if he'd regressed to being a jealous teenager.

And who wouldn't be jealous? What red-blooded man wouldn't appreciate the thought of spending the night with Nicole George?

Grunting, Jordan switched off the TV and lunged to his feet. There was no way he was going to reason his way out of the mental quagmire. So either he needed to take a cold shower, or to run until he was too exhausted to allow his imagination take over.

Thirty minutes later he found himself turning up Nicole's street, having driven toward the running trail near her house without thinking.

What was it that someone had said? There aren't any accidents?

That was almost a comforting thought, to think there was a plan or purpose in everything. Maybe he should kick it around in a column. It wasn't a place to wax philosophical too often, but his readers liked being surprised.

He ran for an hour, finally slowing and heading by the baseball field so he could get a drink at the water fountain. Besides, it could be fun to stop and watch the kids at their game for a while.

His hair was dripping and his T-shirt stuck to his skin. The endorphins coursed through his veins and he felt much better than when he'd started…until he saw Nicole crouching in front of the backstop in the place where an umpire was usually situated.

She wore a protective mask so he couldn't actually see her face. But gold hair rippled in a light breeze, and those long, shapely legs couldn't belong to anyone else.

Swallowing, he moved closer, hoping he was wrong. But there was Toby sitting in the dugout as if waiting his turn in the batting lineup, his tail wagging as he watched the game.

"Strike," the woman called.

"Aw, Nicole, not really."

"Yeah, really, Danny. I calls 'em like I sees 'em."

The boy giggled and, even when he finally struck out, didn't seem too upset. Jordan wondered if he was old enough to be wowed by a beautiful woman, or if he just liked her. There were a few men in the bleachers and they were clearly enjoying the sight of Nicole's sexy figure shifting side to side as she sought a good view of the ball. Could one of them be her date for the evening? Or had the guy been crazy enough to stand her up? If so, she seemed to be taking it well.

Fascinated, Jordan kept enough distance that Nicole was unlikely to notice him, but close enough to see and hear what was happening.

"Which one is yours?" a voice inquired.

He turned and saw a burly man with a military-style haircut standing nearby.

"I don't have kids," Jordan said. "I just stopped to watch the game for a while. My name's Jordan."

"Rick. The girl at second base is my daughter."

"I know your umpire," Jordan said. No doubt the man had a legitimate concern about a strange guy lurking around a group of children, so while Jordan would have preferred complete anonymity, it seemed best to indicate where his interest lay.

"Nicole?"

"Right. I didn't expect to see her here tonight, though. How did that happen?" he asked, wondering whether umpiring a baseball game might be the plans Nicole had made. It would be the last thing he'd expect, but he was getting the feeling his expectations were screwed up when it came to her.

"The kids wanted someone neutral to call the game," the man said. "It blew my mind when she accepted, but she's good and exceptionally nice. You know her long?"

"Back when we were kids. We recently reconnected."

"Brilliant, as my kid—the Harry Potter fan—would say." A jingle sounded through the air and he pulled out his cell phone. "Hey, hon, everything is fine...no, we got a game going, and you know who's umpiring it? Nicole George...yeah, the model...no, I'm not ogling her...it may be a while before we get home... Jess is doing great, hit a homer in the second. She's a chip off the old block...yeah, I'm talking about you, not me." He shoved the phone back into his pocket and nodded at Jordan. "Have a nice evening."

Rick strolled back to talk with the rest of the parents in the bleachers. Several of them glanced at Jordan before focusing on the playing field again. Rick had probably been deputized to make sure the stranger watching their kids was on the level. Smart parents.

The game continued another twenty minutes before a team was declared the winner.

In the melee that followed, Rick spoke to Nicole, who looked at Jordan and bobbed her head. She handed the umpire's gear to Rick before taking Toby's leash and walking in Jordan's direction. Her progress was slow because the kids kept stopping her to talk. They also had to pat Toby, who was licking hands and wagging his tail so hard his entire butt swayed.

"Good evening," Nicole finally greeted him.

"I was here for a run," Jordan said, bending and patting the beagle who remained eager for attention.

"That's what I figured from your running clothes."

"Uh, yeah. Was this your plan for the evening?"

"Not really. I had a teleconference with my partners. After that I expected to spend the evening with a book, but took Toby for a walk first. We ran into this crowd while we were out. I'm flexible."

She certainly was. His body grew taut as he recalled the positions she'd gotten into while she'd called the game. He wished that was the only thing that made her attractive. But there was that look on her face of total involvement. And for the kids at the game, it must have been her kindness and enthusiasm that had won them over. As a kid, he would have loved her for all those reasons and more, and the thought made him distinctly uncomfortable.

"That guy with the military haircut says you do a good job of umpiring," Jordan said.

"How nice. Rick is a Little League coach, so he should know."

"I was impressed, too. Not that my opinion counts."

"Modesty doesn't suit you."

He grinned. "That's because I forgot to get my invisible modesty suit from the dry cleaners, but it's on my to-do list."

Her lips twitched. "Yes, it's hard to get around to all the necessary chores of living." She stirred. "I'll leave you now and go home to scramble something for dinner."

"How about taking pity on a hungry man? I'll order takeout and we can eat together on your deck."

It was a stupid thing to suggest, and the last thing he ought to do.

NICOLE DREW A deep breath. Jordan was gazing at her with an inscrutable expression, but she didn't think it was entirely lacking in sexual energy. Or maybe that was simply what she felt deep in her abdomen.

"If you're hungry for company," she said, "it would be better to go to a restaurant. You know, neutral territory."

A rueful nod. "It would be even wiser for us each to go home and check out our respective refrigerators."

"Probably."

They were headed toward the parking lot when Nicole noticed Toby was lagging on his leash. It had been a long, exciting evening with the walk and the game and all the kids paying attention to him. She bent and gathered him into her arms. He sighed and settled his head on her shoulder.

"Are you going to carry him home?" Jordan asked.

"It's only half a mile. In some ways he's still a puppy and this was fun but tiring for him."

"I'll give you a ride."

"That's okay."

"It's only a few blocks out of my way. He may not be huge, but he'll get heavier the farther you go."

"Well, all right. Thanks."

He politely opened the passenger door of his silver sports car and supported her elbow as she lowered herself into it with Toby in her arms. With the prospect of something new happening, the beagle lifted his head and started sniffing. She patted him and fastened the seat belt.

It didn't take long to reach her house. While she was releasing the belt and reaching around Toby's wriggling movements to find the latch, Jordan went around and opened the door. The gesture was old-fashioned, but nice.

Toby jumped to the ground and trotted to the front door as she got out.

"Uh, thanks," she told Jordan.

Stepping away, he nodded formally. "Good night."

Walking swiftly toward the porch where Toby was waiting, Nicole unlocked the door and glanced back to see Jordan in his car, still looking in her direction, so she gave him a casual wave and slipped inside.

After taking care of the alarm, she fed Toby and drank a glass of milk before going upstairs, too tired to get anything else for dinner. Umpiring the impromptu baseball game had been fun but dusty, so she took a long shower before sinking onto her bed.

If she'd taken Jordan up on his suggestion to eat takeout, there was a chance they would have ended up between the sheets together. Of course, she'd never gone in for casual sex, so perhaps she would have resisted. And he might have remembered that sleeping with the subject of his interviews would seriously compromise his pretense of objectivity...except he already knew he wasn't objective, so he might have decided to hang the consequences.

The other side of it was the rumor mill. She was no longer as much in the public eye, but if it got out, some people might assume she was using sex to get the kind of article she wanted from Jordan.

Toby had jumped up next to Nicole on the bed and his chin was contentedly planted on her ankle. Everything about him suggested he'd achieved nirvana that evening. How lovely to have the ability to simply exist in the moment, with no yesterdays or tomorrows to think about.

"Hey, little guy," she murmured, but he was fast asleep. While she'd heard people debate whether letting your dog sleep with you was a good idea, she didn't mind. And it wasn't as if she expected to have someone in her life who'd complain about it, not anytime soon, at any rate.

An image of Jordan floated through her mind and she ground her teeth. For a woman whose face and body had been used in marketing for sex appeal, she actually understood very little about the opposite sex. What had Rita Hayworth said…men went to sleep with Gilda, her most famous film role, and were disappointed when they woke up with her? Nicole had heard that line in the movie *Notting Hill*. It had struck an instant chord with her and she'd quickly added that film to her secret collection of romantic movies.

Nicole yawned. The evening had been fun until she'd seen Jordan. While walking past the baseball field she'd stopped and said hi to some of the kids and the next thing she knew she was umpiring a game. It had been wholesome and genuine, uncomplicated and…she yawned again.

Sleep was a good idea. Hopefully, her dreams would be of baseball, ice cream cones, puppies and pizza. Not Jordan, she told herself. Definitely not Jordan.

CHAPTER THIRTEEN

NICOLE WOKE IN the early morning, unable to remember what she'd dreamed, or if she had dreamed at all.

For the moment she was relatively current on her paperwork, so she sat on her deck, enjoying a cup of tea and reading a book, before heading to the office.

Once there, she arranged several go-sees and bookings and reviewed the folder of pictures collected at the career fair. The girls had been eager and hopeful; it really *was* the worst part of her job to tell dreamers that she couldn't be the one to help them. Yet it would be cruel to take someone on as a client, making them believe they could succeed, when she didn't think it was going to happen. Not that she ever told them the last part. She wasn't going to be the one to kill a dream, and there was always the chance she was wrong. More than one star had succeeded where the experts had said it wasn't possible.

Jordan arrived shortly before she planned to leave and check on modeling jobs in progress.

"Really?" he asked. "Do you get time for anything else?"

"I'm probably doing more of them than most agents because I'm new," she explained. "I was hoping you'd get here before I left to see if you would like to tag along. Today I'm mostly doing spot checks."

"That sounds interesting."

Nicole smothered a smile since he obviously found the entire process a bore. But maybe he was also getting the picture that modeling wasn't a cakewalk. Of course, some people saw only what they wanted.

At the reception area, she handed a stack of folders to Chelsea to record the bookings, then headed to her car, wondering if Jordan would want to take his vehicle. Instead he settled without protest into her passenger seat. She'd planned the visits carefully by location to minimize driving time. It went smoothly, with Jordan observing, taking notes and occasionally speaking with the models.

The last stop was at a carpet store where the model—dressed in a Cleopatra-type costume—was being unrolled over and over from a length of carpet for a local television ad. The director looked as if he planned to keep doing it the rest of the day.

"How about lunch?" Jordan asked as the young woman's hair and makeup were refreshed.

"Oh, sure. Let's just pick up a sandwich or something."

"Fine with me."

She wasn't as oblivious to him as she was trying to appear. While sitting and making notes, Jordan in the seat next to her, she'd tried not to take in his clean male scent, or notice the dark waves of his hair and remember how it had felt under her fingers.

Had *that* been in a dream? She was pretty sure she hadn't actually touched his hair since they were teens.

JORDAN WAS GLAD Nicole had finished her last site check. It was clear she was intentionally showing him the less-than-glamorous side of the business. Wearing coats on hot sets, trying to look presentable and sexy while running on a treadmill... getting rolled out of a carpet over and over again. None of those were jobs he'd relish.

He didn't blame Nicole. He'd taken the assignment with a number of biases, and he had been unable to conceal them from her. So she'd flung the truth in his face. Modeling could be difficult— why had he assumed anything different?

And in Nicole he was observing an intelligent, deliberate woman at work. That was another blow to his underlying assumption that she'd probably skated by on her looks. What had it been like to spend years being told to smile for the camera as if her beauty was the *only* thing she had to offer?

He tried to imagine how it would feel if people constantly praised his height or his hair, his eyes, or something else over which he felt little sense of achievement, and never mentioned his actual accomplishments or abilities. True, a model had to know how to enhance his or her appearance, keep in shape and follow instructions. And unless they left everything to their agent, they had to have business sense and be savvy about the public. They also had to know how to protect themselves against anyone who might be less than scrupulous. It must be hard to have those abilities and so many others ignored.

Or was he getting taken in again?

Abruptly Jordan recalled what Nicole had claimed the night before—that he believed in nothing and no one. That he only wanted an illusion. It had almost seemed as if she felt sorry for him. No need, he was fine. The assurance had a hollow sound, but he was used to that since he regarded himself with the same skepticism as he viewed everything else.

He looked at his watch. It was after one.

"Do you have time to talk?" he asked. "Or would you rather wait for another day?"

"Now is fine, or rather when we get back to the office."

"It's a nice afternoon, and I'd hate spending it indoors. I have a boat moored at a dock that isn't too far away. How about sitting on the deck and enjoying the lake and sunshine while we talk? We're actually closer to my boat than your office. We could even take her for a sail afterward, or do you have plans for tonight?"

"No, nothing. But maybe we shouldn't…" Her voice trailed off as she looked toward Lake Washington. "Okay. People keep telling me this is an unusual spring for the Northwest and to enjoy the warm weather while it lasts."

"The weather is changeable up here," Jordan acknowledged. "One year we had a string of hot days in May, then it turned cold and didn't get above fifty degrees until late June."

He parked at the dock, and as they were climbing aboard *The Spirit*, Nicole appeared surprised. "I thought it would be smaller."

"Originally I got her for ocean sailing, and even lived aboard for a few months. When I have time, I still take her out through the various canals and locks to face the waves."

Nicole settled into one of the low-slung deck chairs with her usual grace. Perhaps he was being fanciful, but it seemed as if she couldn't get into an awkward position.

"Excuse me?" she said.

"Uh, what?"

"You said something about awkward positions."

"It's nothing," he answered, amazed that he'd spoken the words aloud. Talking to himself wasn't unusual, but he generally didn't do it in anyone else's company.

"Okay."

The breeze off the lake cooled the air and he wondered why he hadn't thought of coming here the last few nights. He might have gotten a decent night's rest.

Now that they were settled, he felt disinclined to leap into official interview mode. Yet that was the reason for spending time with Nicole in the first place.

"You're obviously educating me on the challenges of modeling," he said. "What if I hadn't shown up to see Cleopatra being rolled out of her carpet over and over again?"

Nicole shrugged. "There are ample opportunities to demonstrate how demanding the job can be."

"And demeaning?" he found himself asking.

"Sometimes. Of course, models who feel the work is beneath them usually don't last since they can be hard to work with."

"So in modeling it's important to work and play well with others."

She grinned. "Sure, the same as everywhere.

Lessons learned in kindergarten. A lot of the things they taught apply throughout our lives."

"Be a team player. Clean up after yourself. Say please and thank you."

"No name-calling," she added. "Hold someone's hand when you cross the street. Don't take things that don't belong to you. Share and play fair. Strange how some people forget those lessons."

"Yeah." He yawned.

"You don't look seriously engaged with this interview," Nicole said with a smile.

"Suggesting the boat probably wasn't the best idea. All I can think of is taking *The Spirit* out for a sail."

Her nose wrinkled. "That sounds wonderful, but I'm not dressed for it. Especially in my heels." She lifted one of her legs, displaying a pair of stylish pumps.

Jordan leaned forward. "If you're serious, Terri keeps fresh clothing on the boat. She hates my condo and doesn't like hotels, so she usually stays here. I'm sure her stash includes casual outfits and boat shoes. If the shoes don't fit, you could go barefoot."

"Won't she mind if I borrow something? We just repeated the lesson about not taking things that don't belong to you."

"It isn't one of her hang-ups."

Nicole got up from the deck chair. "In that

case, I'm ready to play hooky for a while. Just not for too long, I don't want to be late getting home to Toby. He has the dog door so he can go outside, but I think he gets lonely."

"Gotcha. Check in the cabin. I'm sure you can find something more comfortable."

Jordan was pleased. Sailing might help them loosen up so he could get the kind of interview he needed. Of course, as he watched Nicole carefully descend the steps into the cabin, he also wondered if it was smart on other levels, but he was tired of second-guessing everything. In fact, he was tired of trying to be smart and careful in the first place.

NICOLE ADMIRED THE well-designed cabin, which had a cooking and eating area, along with a sleeping compartment and a full lavatory. It wouldn't be a bad place to spend a few nights, though she wouldn't be comfortable staying there alone. Terri was clearly bolder than she was on several levels.

After a short hunt, she located some women's clothing. If they'd belonged to a girlfriend of Jordan's, she wouldn't have touched them, but she didn't mind wearing his sister's clothes. A pair shorts and a T-shirt didn't take long to don, along with a pair of boat shoes. They were a little large, but not too bad.

The Spirit was already moving out of its mooring as Nicole made her way to the deck. Not being an experienced sailor, she sat and watched as Jordan managed the boat; it was obviously a task he loved. His face grew relaxed and he looked happy as they sailed away from the shore.

They talked little as the boat skimmed across the water, and it was a surprisingly easy silence. Nicole reminded herself not to make too much of it. This was an unusual situation, as if they'd agreed to take a break from reality. Desire still simmered beneath the surface, but it was possible to pretend it wasn't there…which probably wasn't realistic. Wisdom suggested this time with Jordan was a bad idea, but wisdom hadn't gazed at the lake recently and wished she could go sailing.

"Have you ever steered a sailboat?" Jordan asked after a while.

"Not with a tiller."

He grinned. "Come on, give it a shot."

Nicole jumped up from her seat. "I'm game."

Taking the tiller in her hands, she felt the energy of the wind and the water. Jordan placed his hand over hers and it seemed as if they swayed together with the boat as she experimented with how their movements changed their direction. It was almost like dancing.

"I can't believe how much better this is," she finally said. "A wheel is easier but not as…connected, if you get what I mean."

"I know what you're talking about. With a tiller, you can feel the movement of the rudder in the water. I'd never have a sailboat without one, even if it does take more space."

Nicole nodded. Sailing this way could be addictive. Or was part of the attraction doing it with Jordan? On the water, separated from reality, they'd seemed in almost perfect sync, which should have scared her, but for the moment it was simply wonderful.

IT WAS PAST five when Jordan tied up the boat.

Nicole stood. "I'd better collect my things."

"Not yet." Jordan pointed at someone walking toward them carrying a bag. "You said you didn't have anything planned for tonight, so I phoned and ordered dinner for us."

She'd seen him on his cell, but hadn't listened to the conversation. If he had asked if she wanted to eat together, she would have said no, which was probably why he'd ordered and told her after the fact.

"Nice timing for them to get here as we arrived."

"I know the place and how long it takes them to deliver to the marina." Jordan gave money to the delivery man and took the bag. "Keep the change."

"Thanks. Enjoy your meal."

Jordan pulled a container from the bag and handed it to her along with a plastic fork and a napkin.

"Hope you like surprises, though I should have asked whether you had any allergies."

"None, and I enjoy most foods." It was the kind of thing she might have thought was romantic if this had been a date.

She opened the lid and found eggplant parmesan with grilled vegetables on the side. It smelled wonderful, reminding her that the lunch she'd barely touched had been hours earlier. The only problem was that the silence was no longer comfortable.

Jordan went down to the cabin and returned with bottles of seltzer. "This is all I have and it isn't chilled," he said. "I should have ordered something to go with the food."

"It's fine," she said, accepting the bottle. Their fingers brushed and energy traveled up her arm, reminding her of all the reasons she hadn't invited him home for dinner the night before.

No restaurant had a view better than the one from the boat. The sun was dropping below the horizon, and across the water, city lights began barely glimmering.

"It's beautiful," Nicole said, pausing between bites to soak in the scene.

"Absolutely. Because I travel often, I have arrangements for a guy to check on *The Spirit* occasionally. But there is a downside to not being required to visit the boat regularly. Sometimes I let weeks or months pass without going for a sail."

"That's too bad."

The conversation was prosaic, but he kept looking at her instead of the vista.

"The temperature has dropped," he said, "you must be getting chilly in those shorts."

"I'm all right." She swallowed. There was nothing odd in his comment, except that she suddenly remembered how her bare legs had brushed against his during their time at the tiller.

Finishing her meal, she placed the plastic fork inside and closed the container.

"I think I'll go change into my own clothing, though."

There was a long moment as his gaze locked with hers. He stood and offered her a hand, and as she came to her feet, she swayed closer, knowing what she was inviting.

Nicole held her breath as he bent low to lay a trail of kisses alone her jaw line until reaching her lips.

"Mmmm," he murmured. "Better than dessert."

But the words had the opposite effect than he'd probably intended, reminding her of another man who'd said the same thing. It wasn't a positive memory.

She broke the contact and moved aside.

He frowned. "Did I say something wrong?"

"Not your fault. It's just that someone else used to say the same thing to me. It was my last attempt to form a relationship, the one that finally convinced me wedding bells and happily-ever-after weren't in the cards. I've found I can count on friendship and a useful career, not love and romance."

"Now you're the one who sounds as if you've given up on believing in things."

"Not really. Marriage and romance are terrific for some people. You should have seen Em's wedding. She and Trent are so much in love, and they've made such a difference to each other's lives. I've seen plenty of couples in Schuyler and other places who seemed equally happy, so I'm all for the institution in general, even if I've decided it isn't something I want personally."

"Maybe you'll find someone equally well suited."

She lifted an eyebrow at him. "Has anyone tried that sort of argument on you? 'Hey, Jordan, you'll joyfully give up that happy carefree bachelor life once you find your soul mate.' 'Don't be ridiculous, once you find the right person, all your doubts will vanish.' Or how about, 'You've got to be kidding, marriage and family are the most important things in life and you'll realize that when the right woman comes along.'"

A wry smile twisted his lips. "You're right. I've heard those arguments and more to push me toward an altar. But your decision still seems based in a negative experience."

"The people we are today come from everything we've experienced. All that has to be taken into account in our decisions, doesn't it?"

"Sure. Isn't that a justification for asking about your past for the article?"

"Perhaps if it didn't feel as though you're steering everything in that direction. Are your parents' problems the only reason *you're* a bachelor?"

"No, I'm just happy that way."

"Then it's partly based on the fact you've had happy experiences as a bachelor, right?" she asked. "And also because your logic says it works for you."

Jordan groaned. "You really enjoy making rational arguments, don't you?"

"I like to understand a situation. It's part of how I solve problems, or at least it affects how I feel about them. I don't know if that's true for everyone, but it helps me. All I can say is that I understand my past and I've learned from it, which I believe is the mature approach. But it isn't controlling me."

"Except it made you react against something I said."

Nicole pursed her lips. "I could say something brutal, such as the jerk who used that line taught me that cheesy lines are a dime a dozen. But I didn't assume you're a jerk because of him. It simply broke the mood."

The wind blew tendrils of hair against her

cheek and he raised his hand to brush them away. Despite her words, her breathing quickened. How was she supposed to think her way through something that was primarily instinct?

JORDAN HADN'T PLANNED to kiss Nicole when he'd suggested the sail or ordered dinner. Nor had he planned on getting into a debate about how life decisions should be made. The golden light of early evening had felt like a sensual painting, perhaps leading to the kind of moment he'd cherish as an old man and mention in his memoirs. Well, something of the sort. And how cheesy would *that* sound to her?

He was also struck with another realization. Nicole had talked about him just observing life, keeping his distance. The last thing he wanted to turn into was one of those pseudo-intellectuals he'd sometimes met, the ones who discussed everything with a pretentious air of detachment.

Lord, he remembered one columnist he'd known when he was a reporter. Ken hadn't been syndicated in many newspapers, but he'd acted as if he was sending his wisdom down from Mount Olympus. Jordan had just gotten back from the Middle East with Syd; he'd had bruises all over, cracked ribs and a nasty cut on his leg, and Ken had pontificated on the sociological history of the conflict...without even getting it right.

That was definitely not the sort of person he wanted to become.

"You know something?" Jordan asked. "I have this sudden urge to go skinny-dipping, but I'm too grown-up and have too much of a false sense of dignity to do it. Besides, we'd probably get arrested."

"We could inaugurate my hot tub." She seemed surprised by her own suggestion, but straightened her shoulders with an air of not backing down.

"It's in a private part of your backyard," he said, trying to make sure he hadn't misunderstood her.

A long pause. "True," she finally agreed.

"Will it bother you if Chelsea sees me arriving?" he asked.

She lifted her chin. "We're both taking risks, here, Jordan. You know that, don't you?"

"Yes."

The word hung between them.

"No regrets or recriminations?" she challenged.

"I'll do my best."

He stepped back and she hurried down into the cabin, coming out a few minutes later with her arms full.

"I'll leave you to do whatever is needed on the boat."

Jordan watched in the golden light as she walked swiftly along the dock. With any other woman, he might fear that she'd change her mind, jump in her car and speed away, leaving him to find a taxi to get home. But that wasn't Nicole's style. If she changed her mind, she'd tell him to his face.

Shaking the thoughts aside, he made sure *The Spirit* was secure and followed Nicole to her sedan.

"I'll drop you at the agency to get your car," she said. "I'm not sure how good that lot is for overnight parking."

"You want me to park up the street and sneak through the side gate?"

"Or we can be open about the fact you're spending social time with me that has nothing to do with any magazine articles. Objectivity has been shot to smithereens already. I'd just as soon the *public* didn't know you'd spent time in my... er...hot tub, but that's one of the risks here, isn't it?"

"I don't like the idea of hiding or sneaking. I'll park in front of the house and not pretend there's a reason to do anything else."

"That's fine with me."

He was fairly sure his head was going to explode, that is if another part of his anatomy didn't beat him to it.

CHAPTER FOURTEEN

NICOLE WAS GLAD Jordan didn't seem interested in conversation as she drove them back to the agency parking lot. What was there to say? They found each other attractive. The hormonal energy had been turned up to high since the day he'd charged into her living room. She knew what the signs were; no one had to hit her on the head or paint a picture. He'd likely recognized it in her as well. And no matter how many times she'd tried to ignore or manage it, some things couldn't be controlled.

"See you in a bit," he said, sliding from the passenger seat.

"Right."

Deciding not to wait for him to follow her home, she headed straight for her place. That way she could turn on the hot tub before he arrived and take a few deep breaths.

One thing she was sure about: there were things you did that you regretted, but there were bucketloads of other things that you regretted *not* doing because you were too cowardly to take the leap. Of course, she couldn't be sure this was one of them, but it would be hard to know until after the fact.

It wasn't as if she'd been fantasizing about Jordan her whole life. Aside from reading a handful of his columns, she had barely thought of him in the years since high school.

Now things had changed.

The mature man was far more dynamic. He was an insightful writer, albeit too cynical, and sexier than any guy had a right to be. The thought that had struck her on the deck of his boat was that she could well look back and regret not taking the opportunity to be with him. It didn't mean she'd changed one iota of her plans for the future; this was just a small holiday.

At the house she turned on the hot tub, changed into her own clothing and put Terri's things in the washer.

Nicole had carefully planned the hot tub location along with its protective features. It wasn't that she'd planned to have nights like this, but because she valued privacy after so many years of living a very public life.

The minutes passed and she began wondering if Jordan had changed his mind or gotten a phone call that was detouring him to another task or destination. She laughed to herself. That would certainly take any decision-making out of the picture and at least she wouldn't have to agonize over whether she'd have something to regret, one way or the other.

Then the doorbell rang. Taking a deep breath, she opened it.

"Sorry I took so long," Jordan said. "I stopped to pick up strawberries and champagne."

"Sounds...good."

He walked inside and glanced around the living room. "Still no furniture?"

"I haven't had a chance to go shopping, so there's just furniture in my den and the bed... room."

There was a glint in his eyes, which she ignored. "This way," she said, turning and walking toward the back of the house, trying not to think too much.

JORDAN BARELY BREATHED as he followed Nicole to a part of the house he hadn't seen. There was a separate exterior door off a hallway leading to the spacious spa area. The water bubbled and tiny twinkling lights lit the space from above. Sliding louvered doors made it private and intimate.

To the side was a small refreshment area and he carried his purchases there.

After opening the champagne, he took a large strawberry and splashed the sparkling wine over it so the excess fell in the sink.

"I remembered you said that you didn't drink

much, so I thought this might be a unique way of washing the berries. I didn't know this area would be so well-equipped."

He came closer and held the berry to her lips. Nicole hiked an eyebrow and he grimaced ruefully.

"Don't tell me that's cheesy, too."

"Not exactly, but I have experience. While it sounds pretty in theory, it's a messy way to eat a strawberry."

Her slender fingers took the dripping berry and she bit into the juicy red fruit while he prepared one for himself.

"I think I should mention," she said after they'd finished the basket, "that unlike you with female guests on the boat, I don't come prepared with men's clothing or swim trunks."

Heat surged into his groin. "I thought this was a skinny-dipping exercise."

"I didn't know whether you might be all talk, but modest in action."

"If I recall correctly, you told me that modesty doesn't fit me very well."

Nicole sat on the edge of the hot tub. "But you might have gotten your invisible modesty suit from the dry cleaner after all."

"Not since last night."

"So what you're saying is that modesty will be lacking this evening."

Jordan started unbuttoning his shirt. The repartee between them had only made him hotter. "Judge for yourself," he managed to say and shrugged off the shirt. It left his chest bare while her gaze lingered over him.

"Where did the scar come from?" she asked, pointing at the jagged white streak that sliced across his ribs.

"It was during my time as a reporter. I got too close to the action during a police standoff."

"Looks painful."

"Didn't hurt as much as the way my editor ripped me up one wall and down the other for being stupid."

Smiling, she loosened the sash on her wraparound dress and eased it off her shoulders. Underneath was a bikini...barely.

"I thought tonight was about skinny-dipping," he choked out of a tight throat.

"I invited you to indulge, never promised I'd do the same."

She stepped down into the gently steaming water and leaned back, closing her eyes, which was a good thing. If she'd kept watching him, Jordan feared he might have been in danger of the same sort of accident he'd had in his youth, when the hormones raged and he hadn't learned control. At the moment, any of the control he *had* learned seemed utterly absent. He hurriedly stripped and sank into the bubbling cauldron, trying to chuckle as he did so.

"Three guesses about what I'm picturing at the moment."

"Harry and the Hendersons," Nicole said promptly.

"Right."

Despite the silly image, it did nothing to slow the euphoria that was spreading through him. A private spa was rare in his experience, though he'd spent time on a few nude beaches. The advantages of privacy were extreme.

Half floating, Jordan nudged himself closer, his legs brushing against Nicole's. She opened her vibrant blue eyes again and stared into his as he pulled her close. Even in the warm water he could feel her shuddering response.

NICOLE BARELY BREATHED as Jordan pulled her into his arms, giving her one teasing kiss after another. He hadn't waited for any pretense of enjoying the water first. Twining her arms around him, she returned his kisses fully. He quickly disposed of her swimsuit and it was only skin against skin. It felt like a moment outside of time.

Suddenly his caresses slowed and he drew back a few inches, his eyes wide and glazed. "Sorry," he said in a strangled voice. "It just occurred to me...stupid not to have considered it before, but are you on birth control?"

She drew in a shaking breath. "No."

"Condoms are risky in water. They can lose effectiveness."

"Right."

Releasing her, he edged back to the other side of the hot tub.

"We could consider drying off and heading upstairs," she managed to say.

"You *did* mention it was one of the few furnished rooms in the house."

Slowly she stood and waited as he looked his fill. But the tension in her body grew almost unbearable. "Then what are we waiting for?"

"Nothing." But when he also stood, like Poseidon rising from the waves, Nicole didn't mind spending a few extra seconds enjoying the view.

She was uncertain whether she was making the best decision, but it was easy to ignore her nagging doubts.

IT WAS 6:00 A.M. and Chelsea tried to ignore the fact that her brother's car was parked in front of the house in the same position as when she'd driven back from an evening trip to the grocery store. Where he spent the night was his business—his and Nicole's if he'd spent it with her.

Terri might tease, even poke Jordan about finding ways not to be objective, but Chelsea wouldn't dare, even if Nicole wasn't her boss.

It would be great if they ended up together, but

as much as Chelsea loved her brother, she knew he wasn't interested in marriage or commitment. For that matter, she didn't know if Nicole was interested, either, but she clearly had a soft heart beneath her polished exterior.

Chelsea also wasn't sure if Jordan realized how easily a guy could hurt a woman, even if he didn't hit her. Ron would probably be appalled to be described as abusive or hurtful, but he'd controlled her and made her feel as if she couldn't do anything right. Jordan would never physically abuse a woman, but he liked to keep his life orderly, or maybe he'd call it managed. More than that, he kept a distance between himself and other people. To a woman in love, craving tenderness and connection, that could be deeply painful.

Her brain buzzed. None of this was her business, but she loved her brother and she cared about Nicole and hoped neither of them would end up with a broken heart.

She got dressed and looked out the window again, wondering when she should leave for work. It would be awkward to run into Jordan. Maybe she should get an early start—there was plenty to do and she wanted to make up the time Nicole had given her for the baseball game. Or would Jordan leave early himself, to try to keep them from crossing paths in case she found it awkward? He was a cynic, but she knew that when it came to her and Terri, he tried to watch out for them, even if the way he did it could be overbearing.

Oddly, she wished she could ask Barton's opinion—except that would just underscore Jordan's overnight presence in the neighborhood. Besides, she needed to make her own decisions.

Grabbing a box of protein bars on the way out of the apartment, Chelsea hurried downstairs and into her car, breathing easier once she'd left the neighborhood behind.

This way she'd have two full hours of phone silence at the agency. Well…two hours when she wasn't obligated to answer the phone, giving her time to concentrate on the various forms Nicole had shown her. Nicole wasn't crazy about paperwork, but Chelsea enjoyed the precision of seeing a task accomplished and was looking forward to taking full responsibility.

Two hours later a hard rapping on the door drew her attention. Swiftly she unlocked the door and Ashley Vanders rushed inside.

"Why is this door locked during work hours?" she demanded.

Trying to quell the quaking in her stomach, Chelsea glanced at the clock. It was only five after nine and she could see Nicole coming in from the parking lot. Surely opening a few minutes late wasn't a firing offense.

"Can I help you, Miss Vanders?"

"I'd like to know why the door was locked when the agency is supposed to be open."

Nicole had stepped inside, but the model paid no attention to the chime.

"I apologize. I was concentrating on paperwork and didn't realize it was past nine," Chelsea said.

"In any case, Ashley," Nicole said briskly, "Chelsea isn't your employee, she's mine. If you're interested in leaving modeling and becoming an agent, that's your decision, but first you need to serve out the contract I negotiated for you at the car dealership. Plus you should know we won't be able to consider taking you on as a junior agent at Moonlight Ventures."

Tory's face turned flustered, though still belligerent. "No. I mean, I wasn't saying that. I was just upset because she was here and the door was locked."

"So that's why you dropped by today, to find out if *my* office manager was doing things to *your* liking?"

The arrogance in the model's face faded and she blushed. "No. I'm sorry, Nicole and, uh, Chelsea. I'm here because I need to talk."

"Then come back to my office."

After giving Chelsea the barest of winks, Nicole conducted Ashley down the hallway. Chelsea tried not to giggle. If only she could be so poised and quick-witted when someone was being difficult. But she *was* getting better at it.

Settling back in her chair, she returned to the form she'd been studying, certain she could begin taking care of this part of the paperwork for the agency right away.

The phone started ringing and she launched into the more challenging aspect of her job, dealing with people.

Much as she loved working for Moonlight Ventures, the people part took a lot of energy. She was looking forward to this weekend when she was going hiking with Barton.

A shiver of anticipation went through Chelsea. Doing something with Barton was another challenge because of the way he made her feel, but she was looking forward to it. He'd promised they wouldn't do anything too strenuous—he just wanted to show her the Smith family's favorite huckleberry picking sites.

Her lips curved. Things in Seattle were good, even if Ron had sent another package and called again. Surely he'd give up soon and she could focus on her new life.

NICOLE FORCED HERSELF to listen as Ashley complained about how the car dealership commercials were being made. Then she explained, *again*, that it was normal. Ashley needed to remember that the product being sold was the car, not the actress.

"But they want me to do the same thing over

and over as if I hadn't done it right and I know I did," Ashley protested.

"Ashley, you've modeled before and know that repetition is to be expected."

"Not like this."

"Live action commercials often require even more repetition. The photographer and the director are the ones who get to decide if something is right, not the models or actors. Are they asking you to do anything dangerous or treating you inappropriately?"

"Uh, no."

"So you need to do it as many times as *they* decide are necessary unless you want them to try and break the contract. Trust me, the last thing you want is a reputation for being difficult. It can kill a career."

Ashley gulped and left, looking both alarmed and chastened. Nicole sighed. Dealing with her most annoying client wouldn't have been her first choice to start the morning.

The night before had been pleasurable in the extreme, and it had gone on until after midnight. She would have preferred Jordan to leave at that point, but they'd fallen asleep before any discussion could take place. In the morning she had woken up and managed to dress and slip out without disturbing him.

Jordan's life seemed so polished and planned. Maybe she should have made sure he saw her with mussed hair and creased skin from wrinkles on the pillow case. Instead, she'd simply left written instructions on how to leave the house without setting off the security system and then headed for the office.

She checked back with Chelsea and realized she must have come in early. Chelsea waved it off, pointing out that she'd left before closing on Monday to attend the ballgame. While they were still discussing paperwork, Nicole saw Jordan pull into the parking lot.

She groaned to herself.

So she hadn't totally avoided the "morning after." Knowing Chelsea might realize where her brother spent the night made it even more awkward.

Nicole straightened. She had made a decision; she hadn't been coerced or seduced into something she didn't want. Now she simply had to deal with the fallout.

"Good morning," she said as Jordan came through the door. "I didn't expect to see you today."

"I wondered if you have time for more interview questions." His face and tone were admirably casual. Perhaps he didn't feel any awkwardness since he must have plenty of experience with morning-after encounters. Though maybe not…he might be the type to get dressed and be out the door as soon as the fireworks ended. Besides, he'd spent the night with someone he was interviewing for an article. That put a whole new, uncomfortable twist on it.

No recriminations or regrets. That was what she'd proposed, so it was time to practice it.

"If you can wait an hour, I'll give you about ninety minutes."

"Sure."

Turning, he walked out the door.

"I'd better get busy," she said to Chelsea and went to her office where she dealt with several requests and returned a number of phone calls. The hour passed swiftly, too swiftly, without a chance to think ahead.

"Nicole?" Chelsea stuck her head through the door. "I saw Jordan coming from the far end of the parking lot. Just thought I'd alert you."

"Thanks. I've got one more call to make, so keep him in the waiting area until you see the light on my phone blink off."

She called the director who'd been working with Ashley and caught an earful about sulky models who'd gotten too bigheaded. After she promised she had already discussed the reality of making television ads with her client, he calmed down and agreed to give it another shot.

Hanging up the phone in relief, she settled back in her desk chair and waited. It didn't take more than a minute for Jordan to tap politely and come inside.

"Is everything good with you?" he asked. He

wasn't hesitant or uncertain—something like that would be out of character—but he was intently focused.

"Absolutely. What are your questions?" Nicole kept her voice and expression brisk and neutral. Nothing had changed provided they didn't make a big deal out of it, though she couldn't help wondering if Jordan's cynicism would make him decide she'd slept with him to influence the article. If he said something, he'd find out just how forthright a former model could be.

JORDAN HADN'T KNOWN what to expect from Nicole since her reactions generally didn't fit what he expected from women. The obvious and rather embarrassing explanation was that he usually sought out a certain kind of feminine company, so naturally Nicole didn't fit his preconceptions.

"Should we talk about last night first?"

She shook her head. "It isn't necessary to talk about it at all. We didn't unexpectedly lose control, so we aren't faced with any 'oh no, what have we done,' questions. Or is there something *you* need to discuss?"

"I suppose not."

"Then let's get to the interview."

Jordan couldn't decide which seemed most unreal, the night before, or Nicole's calm dismissal of it.

"I was thinking about your popularity as a

model," he began. "Are you frequently asked to return to modeling? I don't mean in the way that photographer tried to manipulate you, but on legit jobs."

"My former agent has sent me a number of offers and I occasionally get them directly."

Jordan wrote something in his neat little notebook. "How do you feel about that?"

"It's flattering. Who doesn't enjoy being in demand?"

"But does it make you regret changing careers?"

"Wouldn't that be normal?" she said casually.

"There you go, answering a question with a question."

"Sorry. I warned your editor that I wasn't a good interviewee." Nicole leaned forward. "But I keep wondering something…why did *you* agree to do these articles? Was it just the loyalty to Sydnie Winslow that you mentioned? While you seem on board now, you didn't seem in favor of it when you first started."

"I wasn't," he admitted. "The only reason I agreed was because Syd asked. I had no interest in a supermodel's decision to change careers and I didn't want to interview you because I knew I wasn't objective, not with our history and, er, other things."

She cocked her head. "I keep getting the impression there's something you aren't telling me."

"It isn't relevant," he said. What good would it do at this late date for Nicole to learn his mother had tried to seduce her father and how it had poisoned the relationship between the two families? Or that he'd witnessed the hideous event.

"I'd like to know," Nicole said firmly.

"Later, maybe. For now, I'd like to hear about when you first considered leaving modeling."

As they talked, he could see she was making a genuine effort to answer his questions. It was probably better than he deserved. At the same time he kept wondering why he'd been determined to speak with her. Less than twelve hours earlier they'd been entwined in her bed. Under ordinary circumstances, he would have avoided seeing her in the immediate future. Of course, he'd never been in this kind of situation, either.

If he was any judge, spending the night with a man wasn't something Nicole did often. He'd found it thoroughly pleasurable, but something in her responses had made him think she wasn't highly experienced.

According to the research notes, at one point she'd been engaged to a man she'd met in Italy. Her engagement had ended without an explanation to the press and Jordan couldn't help questioning whether her ex-fiancé, Paulo Gianetti, was the man who'd compared kissing her to dessert. If the breakup had been painful, that might explain her reaction to someone else saying it.

He made notes as Nicole talked, yet his brain kept circling the subject of their intimacy.

She'd worked with men considered to be among the most handsome in the world. Adam Wilding was just one example, a guy his sister had described as dreamy. While there had been endless speculation, Nicole had been adamant there was only friendship between her and her business partners. So why had she chosen to become intimate with him last night?

All too soon the ninety minutes she'd agreed to were over and he was no closer to understanding.

"That's great," Jordan said, closing his notebook without any prompting. "I want to respect your time limitations."

"Thanks. When do I get to hear the great mystery you keep avoiding?"

"It isn't something I want to discuss here." He sighed. "How about getting together for dinner tonight?"

Nicole's eyes narrowed and she studied him carefully. "That's hardly a promise to give over with the facts."

He was highly uncomfortable at the thought of telling the whole story. Years ago he'd decided it was something no one else needed to hear about, at least from him. The problem was that things had changed with Nicole. How could two people really know each other if one of them was keeping a secret? And he couldn't even explain to himself the desire to know her on a deeper level.

Jordan shrugged. "At the very least I'll tell you some of the story. I'll get food and come to your place so we can talk in private. Do you like chicken pad Thai?"

"Yes, but don't plan on spending the night."

"I would never assume that."

Deep down he expected Nicole to kick him out once she heard the story he had to tell, so he definitely didn't think he'd be sharing her bed again.

School wasn't in session that Friday, so Barton was spending most of the day with Girard and Sylvia, helping his old college friend with the addition they were putting on their house. With a second baby on the way, the two-bedroom starter home they'd picked up wasn't enough. Sylvia wasn't due for almost six weeks, so they were trying to add on a nursery before she delivered.

As much as he loved teaching, Barton looked forward to summer break and couldn't help considering the other things he'd like to do…such as taking Chelsea camping or riding the ferry over to Bainbridge Island for lunch.

He'd have to be careful; his plans seemed to include a lot of time with his new neighbor. Almost without thinking, he drove past Moonlight Ventures and had to resist stopping to say hello.

He mustn't forget they were simply friends and this was a new job for Chelsea.

He frowned, recalling the uncertainty he often glimpsed in her. There were serious cracks in her confidence that he found hard to understand. Chelsea was a gentle, beautiful woman who was intelligent and competent, yet also unsure of herself. Perhaps it wouldn't be as striking if her siblings weren't the opposite. Terri and Jordan exuded so much self-assurance that it seemed to emphasize their sister's lack of it.

Perhaps it was due to the bad breakup with her boyfriend, but he suspected there was more to the story. Maybe she would eventually tell him if he proved a good enough friend.

Yet Barton made a face, knowing he felt more attraction to Chelsea than he should for a strictly platonic relationship.

Was it possible they could be more someday?

No, he shouldn't be speculating in that direction. If nothing else, he didn't want to be a rebound guy for her. The sanest approach was to enjoy her company without anticipating romance. Otherwise, he could be inviting another emotional crash.

Perhaps he should stop thinking so much and go to the store and pick up the supplies needed for tomorrow's hike. After all, he wanted to show Chelsea how terrific it was to live in the Pacific Northwest.

As a friend.

NICOLE WORKED FURIOUSLY hard the rest of the day. Even what she called a break—sitting with Chelsea and having coffee together—was about seeing how things were going with the office manager.

Chelsea had already mentioned a recent end to a relationship, and, during their talk in the afternoon, referred to it again.

"Uh, my ex-boyfriend has called here a few times," she said apologetically. "I don't answer when I see Ron's number on the caller ID, so please don't think I'm ignoring the phone."

"I don't know if it's possible to block his incoming calls on a business line, but contact the phone company to see what's available. In the meantime, if anyone questions you, just say it's a private matter and you've been authorized to deal with the situation at your own discretion."

"Thanks."

On her way home from the office Nicole decided how to prepare for Jordan's visit.

Dining inside the house at the breakfast bar was an option, but the table and chairs she'd gotten for the deck were more comfortable. Besides, enjoying the wholesome evening sunlight was better than them being alone in the house with the bedroom upstairs.

Because they'd be on the deck, she securely close the louvered doors around the hot tub, latching them so they couldn't be accessed from outside. It was a feature she'd insisted upon so she could feel safe using the hot tub alone in the evening. It hadn't occurred to her that it could also provide protection against impulse.

Honesty compelled her to admit that she *wanted* to spend another night with Jordan. But while one slip in her resolve was all right, another might send her in a direction that could only lead to heartache.

CHAPTER FIFTEEN

JORDAN DIDN'T BELIEVE the evening would end with pleasure, but people sometimes changed their minds. It was improbable, to say the least, considering what Nicole had said, and he would be wise to resist temptation regardless. One option that could help was not restocking his wallet with condoms. Would having no protection available help him resist?

He pictured Nicole in the hot tub, her skin flushed and eyes filled with allure.

Maybe not.

He'd never been reckless and was always prepared, no matter what. There were several things he was genuinely old-fashioned about—especially that a man didn't make a baby without taking responsibility for it. So if he wanted to maintain his carefree bachelor life, protection was the route.

Yet a voice inside Jordan's head had begun teasing him, asking if the single life was as great as he believed. And what if one of the reasons he'd rejected fatherhood was because he was sure he'd be rotten at it? Maybe he wouldn't be. And was the reason he wanted to be honest with Nicole about the past because he couldn't see them building a trusting relationship if he kept that kind of secret?

The cold shock of his soul-searching brought him up short. He'd never doubted that being single and free of encumbrance was what he wanted. It stunned him to know that Nicole, of all women, was tempting him to consider alternatives. Could he actually contemplate taking the proverbial plunge?

The chilling irony of it struck Jordan. Since Nicole appeared genuine when saying she wasn't interested in marriage, he'd better *not* fall for her.

It was probably stupid to tell her about their parents. Personally he'd put the matter aside, having had fourteen years to deal with it, but it might upset her. Then it struck him that he still wasn't giving Nicole enough credit to assume she'd react like a teenage girl.

He drove to her house after picking up food from his favorite Thai restaurant. As he got out, Chelsea came down the stairs from her apartment.

"Hi, Jordan." She smiled at him cautiously.

"Hey, Chelsea." Jordan wished his sister didn't seem so uncertain, but she appeared to be getting more confident. When he'd gone through the Moonlight Ventures reception area earlier in the day she'd been dealing with a man who was insisting on an immediate meeting with Nicole. Chelsea had handled it so competently he had realized that she'd finally gotten what she most needed, a fresh start.

Blast it all. That was another thing in Nicole's favor. She had hired Chelsea and was obviously giving her the support needed to make the transition to Seattle. And while Chelsea wouldn't say anything about the agency, it was obvious that she was filled with admiration for her new boss.

"I'm, uh, going for a walk," she said. "Have a nice evening."

"You, too." Jordan continued up the walkway.

"Is something wrong?" Nicole queried when she opened the door. "You look grim."

"Not wrong, exactly." It was hard to break the habit of keeping everything to himself, but she seemed to understand people in a way that he obviously didn't. "I just wish I knew how to connect with my sister better."

He wasn't sure what more he should say. Chelsea was the one who had taken their childhood the hardest. Sweet and gentle, she had been frightened by their parents' relentless fighting—arguments that had often gotten physical.

"Oh?" Nicole said, and he was sure she was trying to sound noncommittal.

"What is it?" he asked. "I can tell you have an opinion."

"I have an opinion about practically everything."

She closed the door behind him and started toward the back of the house. On the deck, he put the food on the table and looked at her with a fixed expression he'd once found useful as a reporter in getting someone to give him an answer.

"Well?"

"I think that your intense personality could be daunting for someone like Chelsea."

"That's ridiculous. I'm a very laid-back guy."

Nicole laughed and the sweet sound and movement of her body almost made him forget his affront at the suggestion he somehow intimidated his own sister.

NICOLE SAW JORDAN'S eyes darken with desire and held herself together with a firm grip—not easy since her first impulse was to suggest they forget dinner and head upstairs.

So much for resolutions.

She put her hands on her hips. "Jordan, you're the last guy I'd call laid-back. As a kid you were ambitious and charged ahead to get anything you wanted and you don't seem to have changed. Even when you relax, you do it with a fierce determination. All of that could leave a sibling feeling overwhelmed, especially a sensitive younger sister. I'm not saying you did anything wrong or that you intended to make her feel that way. It's just family dynamics."

The lines on his face smoothed from annoyed

to thoughtful, and she dropped her gaze. She didn't need to see how expressive his face was or remember the way his lips had kissed practically every inch of her body.

"Okay," he said slowly, "how do I stop overwhelming her?"

"I'm not a relationship guru."

"I'd still like your opinion."

That was new.

"I don't think you should try to change who you are, but you could listen to her more without making judgments."

He frowned. "You think that's what I do?"

"Come on, Jordan, I've heard you tell her how to live or do things at least twice since you started the interviews with me. So I suspect you do it other times as well."

He muttered an expletive under his breath, then shrugged. "I've been trying, but shouldn't a brother or sister try to help if they see someone they love making a terrible mistake?"

"I suspect you're talking about the guy Chelsea was dating down south."

"You know about Ron?"

"She's mentioned him."

"Terri and I both tried to get her away from that manipulative creep. Was that wrong of us?"

"Probably not, but you may also be in the habit of assuming she can't handle *anything* for herself."

"You might be right," Jordan admitted with obvious reluctance.

Nicole released a gasp of mock surprise. "You think I could be right about something? I may die of heart failure."

"Amusing. Okay, enough of that. I picked up the pad Thai and chicken curry. I see you have plates and silver ready, so let's eat."

"Nothing to say concerning the mystery first?"

"If it's all right with you, I'd rather talk afterward."

"Sure." Nicole didn't know what to think. His manner was subtly different and she didn't believe it was merely because they'd spent the previous night in bed together. Asking her opinion about Chelsea could be another example. Were some cracks forming in his cynical surface, or was she just imagining things?

The deck had been the right choice for dinner. The spacious backyard, tall trees and early evening sky fostered a comfortable atmosphere. While it wasn't possible to relax and completely forget the desire tugging at her, at the very least she was able to suppress it.

"I was wondering something," he said partway through the meal.

"What's that?"

"Why did you leave before I woke up this morning?"

"I needed to get to the office."

"I think it's more than that. Were you embarrassed? It isn't as if I believe those salacious scandal papers and the party-girl stories they wrote about you, especially now that we've gotten reacquainted. Hopping from bed to bed doesn't fit the person I've gotten to know. Why *did* you leave so quickly?"

She sighed. "It's nothing mysterious. I just don't enjoy the way a guy stares at me when I fail to look like an airbrushed magazine layout, and it's impossible to look that way first thing in the morning."

His brow creased, but Nicole launched into asking him about the history of Fiji. Considering his aggressive curiosity about everything, it wasn't surprising that he knew quite a bit.

After they'd eaten and cleared the table, Nicole poured cups of coffee and sat back to listen.

Jordan didn't seem primed for immediate disclosures, so she waited patiently. A variety of emotions crossed his face—pain, embarrassment, anger, even sadness. What could evoke all that?

"It's about our parents," he finally started, absently stroking Toby, who'd been begging for attention.

"That's what I figured."

"Aside from them, I may be the only one who knows what happened. Did you ever wonder why our mothers started hating each other?" he asked.

"Sure, but to be honest, I was mostly grateful I

didn't have to see you as much, though you acted even worse at school."

He let out a short, hard chuckle. "I wanted to believe it was partly your family's fault. I'm sorry I behaved badly."

"I already told you it isn't a big deal any longer."

"So you did. Well, in a nutshell, my mom tried to seduce your father. He rejected her and said he would tell his wife, which ended the friendship."

"Wow. That explains a lot. How did you find out?"

"They didn't know, but I was in the hammock around the side of the house and overheard the whole nasty mess."

Nicole winced. "That's a terrible thing for a teenager to deal with."

Jordan gazed at her, surprise in his eyes. "You aren't upset?"

"I wouldn't be thrilled to find out my dad had an affair after believing he was faithful to Mom all these years, but about your..." She stopped and focused on her coffee cup. No matter what else she might be, Delia Masters was still Jordan's mother.

"Go ahead and tell me what you were going to say."

"It isn't necessary."

"Let's be honest with each other about this."

She took a breath. "Okay. The revelation about your mother isn't shocking. She had a reputation."

"My father did, too," Jordan added harshly. "And they both deserved it. As long as I can remember, they fought constantly and blamed each other for their serial infidelities."

A part of Nicole ached for the boy she'd known. Underneath his bravado he must have been hurting deeply. It was ironic that he'd taken his teenage angst out on her since the George family had been the wounded party, but kids that age weren't always rational.

"Do you hate your parents for your childhood?"

His eyebrows lifted. "No, and life got decidedly better after they finally split. The thing with your family was the last straw." He paused. "On second thought, I probably hated them for a while. What teenager doesn't hate their folks occasionally? In the end, I still love them."

"That's nice, and I've got to say that while they made a lot of mistakes, they couldn't have been total disasters at parenting."

"How do you mean?"

She lifted her shoulders. "All three of you turned out to be productive adults. You and Terri have edges, but you're still decent people, and Chelsea is a love. That doesn't happen in every dysfunctional family. I'm sure you've all got scars and issues you've had to wrestle with, but your mom and dad were either amazingly lucky or they did *something* right."

Jordan stared at her with eyes wide and inscrutable. Then, after a long moment, he lifted her hand from the table and kissed it gently.

"Thank you for saying that."

NICOLE HELD IT together for the short time Jordan remained at the house. When she walked him to the door, he turned and kissed her again. But it was a gentle caress with none of the teasing or passion he sometimes displayed, and it was also so brief she didn't have time to respond.

"Thanks for the evening," he said gruffly.

"You're the one who brought dinner."

Then he was gone.

It was best this way, though if she was any judge of the matter, he felt as much attraction as ever. But in addition to the revelations he'd felt necessary to share, Jordan may have discovered some regrets after all. She wasn't the one who was supposed to be objective—he was. Bad enough to have had a one-night stand. Anything ongoing would only compound the situation.

Still, his restraint was probably due to her warning that he wouldn't be staying. Not all men respected "no," but she suspected Jordan did. He might test the waters occasionally, but he'd never drag a woman into them.

She smiled wryly as she recalled him describing himself as laid-back. Hardly. It might be how he saw himself—an easygoing guy swinging in a hammock by the beach—but it wasn't him. On the other hand, he might simply feel he was laid-back in contrast to his intense parents.

As for Jordan's revelations? Delia Masters had been a strikingly attractive woman, but Nicole's father had chosen fidelity. It was nice to know. Sadly, Jordan had something less pleasant to remember.

After cleaning up the few dinner dishes, Nicole decided to spend time in the hot tub. Sensual memories swirled along with the curls of steam gently rising in the cool air. But she didn't want that to be the only connection in her mind.

Opening up the cover, she saw her bathing suit floating lazily in the water. Her immediate impulse was to slam the cover back down again and put the house on the market. Instead she rescued the bikini, hung it up to dry, and forced herself to sit in the bubbling water while she considered her past and future.

Had she given up on the idea of love and family too quickly? The end of her engagement had felt like the last straw; she'd grown so tired of getting hurt. Now she wondered. While her well-known face—and undeserved notoriety, thanks to the paparazzi—would complicate a relationship, the right man might be able to handle it. Even Jordan might be able to do it…except for all the reasons he wouldn't want to.

Angry, she slapped the water and got out. How could she consider the possibility that Jordan was the right man for anything? He'd spent his life determined to be a bachelor, traveling the world. His idea of commitment was spending the weekend with a temporary companion in a hammock built for two.

CHELSEA TURNED AND gazed in awe at Mount Rainier rising through a gap in the trees. It was the second Saturday she and Barton had hiked and she was getting the feeling he wouldn't mind making it a tradition. To think that she'd spent her whole life in a city and had never thought of taking a day off to do something so wonderful. When she was a kid they'd gone on a few vacations to national parks, but spending a Saturday or Sunday in nature had generally meant visiting a crowded beach.

"You doing okay?" Barton asked, looking back at her.

"Great. I'm sure going up the stairs to my apartment several times a day has helped my climbing muscles."

"You appear to be in good shape."

She wasn't sure whether it was a compliment in the usual sense, but his eyes seemed to show approval.

On both hikes they had chatted occasionally, other times just concentrated on their surroundings. She was glad he was okay with them not constantly talking. Ron had…she promptly cut off the thought. It was getting easier to stop looking at the world through Ron-colored lenses.

Even though he didn't know it, Barton had been a huge help. He was sane, sensible and nice, and could tell the goofiest jokes. No wonder kids seemed to think he was the greatest guy on earth.

The previous Saturday, they'd come back early because Barton had gotten a call from his closest college friend. His friend's wife had gone into early labor, so Barton had gone to the hospital to bring his godson back to his house. Barton hadn't expected her to stay, but she'd wanted to. Charlie was a cute five-year-old who had begged her to eat dinner with them and play, declaring that "you need at least three people for a real game."

The evening had been loads of fun, although it had also made her sad. She'd expected to have kids by this point in her life, and spending time with Charlie was a reminder that so many of her hopes and dreams hadn't come true yet. Still, other things were great and her job was one of them. Another of the Moonlight Ventures partners had been there the past several days. Rachel was as nice as Nicole.

They rounded a curve in the trail and Seattle's distant skyline broke into view. Amazingly, her cell phone rang, though she couldn't imagine a cell tower being anywhere nearby. Pulling the phone out, intending to turn it off, she saw the call was from Ron. Somehow he'd gotten her new number.

Suddenly angry, she hit the button to answer. "Hello," she said crisply. Barton had moved a few feet further along the trail, perhaps to give her privacy.

"Honey, you haven't been answering my calls or getting back to me," Ron said in his most reproachful I'm-hurt-but-I'll-forgive-you voice.

"That's because I don't want to talk."

"I know you don't mean that."

"Ron, we're through and we've been through since the day of the accident. Long before that, if I'm going to be honest. I should have broken things off months ago. So stop calling. Stop sending things that I'm going to send back or dump in the garbage can. I never want to see you or hear your voice again. Is that clear?"

"How can you treat someone who loves you this way?"

"You don't love me. You love yourself and how you can try to change me into something you want."

He clicked off after a brief silence. Chelsea sighed.

Ron wasn't even her first lousy relationship that had held the same creepy dynamics. She'd heard that men like that could zero in on the kind of woman they could control. It was a sobering thought to wonder if she was putting out the wrong kind of signal and attracting the wrong sort of man.

Well, she didn't have any intention of being a doormat for the rest of her life. Or even for another day.

"You look determined," Barton said, bringing her attention back to the present. "Did you convince him to leave you alone?"

No doubt he'd picked up on the clues and had guessed what was happening.

"I hope so," she said.

Before meeting Barton, she hadn't even realized a man could be so decent.

"Did you want to talk?" he offered, but not in a pushy way.

"That's all right. We're having too much fun to drag Ron into it," she answered lightly. How could she tell Barton about the garbage in her past? Maybe if he *was* truly just a friend, she'd be more open. But she was drawn to Barton in ways that went well beyond friendship.

Still, while he was extraordinarily nice and attractive, that didn't mean they were leaping into a relationship. If they ever moved in that direction, she'd have to tell him more...*if* she felt he'd understand, which he probably would. Barton was a good person and actually discussed things with her, rather than trying to tell her what to think.

BARTON WISHED HE knew the right words. He hadn't figured on falling in love until he was good and ready, nor was he certain he'd fallen for Chelsea. But he cared about her, even if only as a neighbor and a friend.

"I know it's probably easier to let down your hair, as my sister says, with another woman," he finally ventured, "but I should tell you, in the interest of full disclosure, that I couldn't keep from overhearing part of your conversation."

Her pretty face scrunched up and then relaxed. "Sorry, that sort of garbage doesn't belong on a hike in the mountains."

"It's as good a place as any."

She was chewing the side of her lip, something he had begun recognizing as one of the signs she was feeling uncertain.

"The thing is… I kind of let my old boyfriend push me around a lot," Chelsea admitted.

Barton frowned. "You mean he hit you?"

"Not that," she said quickly. "He just had a way of making me feel as if everything was wrong and that it was my fault, so I'd try and try to do things to make him happier, but it was never enough."

"So he's trying to use guilt to get you back."

"Yes. When I was with him, it often seemed as if I wasn't quite sure where the ground was, if that makes any sense."

"Like nothing was firm and there was nothing you could count on?"

"Yeah."

"He probably wanted you to have to hang on to him to keep from falling. What a jerk."

She smiled in what seemed to be a determined way. "Look, I don't want to think about Ron any more. I'd rather look at trees and squirrels and mountains. Do you ever see bears or mountain lions around here?"

"Uh, that isn't likely," he reassured her.

Her nose wrinkled. "That's too bad. I'd be a *little* nervous since they're wild animals, but from what I've read, they aren't too dangerous unless they feel threatened or you get between a mama and her babies or their prey."

"That's the general wisdom," Barton agreed.

The shift to a casual subject was disappointing, and he reminded himself that he was supposed to be taking things slow.

CHAPTER SIXTEEN

"I'LL MISS YOU," Rachel said as Nicole drove her to the airport Saturday evening. It had been good having her in Seattle, but Rachel was due in Rome on Monday.

Nicole nodded. "Me, too. It'll be great once you're all in Seattle. Then we can expand even more rapidly."

"I'm impressed by the difference having a decent office manager makes. It was the right decision to give her a pay raise, retroactive to the day she started." Chelsea's salary was one of the things they'd discussed on a call with Logan and Adam the night before.

"And since you've been here," Nicole told her, "I've had time to show Chelsea more of what we need done, though she's picked up a lot on her own."

They hugged goodbye at the passenger unloading zone and Nicole drove back to her house.

The week had gone smoothly.

She hadn't seen Jordan since the night they'd eaten dinner together on her deck. He *had* emailed saying that since the articles weren't due for a while, he thought a break would help them catch up on their mutual responsibilities. She'd replied that it was a good idea.

Nicole just wished she could have focused better during Rachel's visit…particularly on sorting out her thoughts about Jordan. The time had given her distance and a small measure of perspective but no great wisdom. Too often she'd found herself daydreaming about the hours on his boat, watching as he handled the sails, his muscles flexing beneath tanned skin. He'd been relaxed that day, the calm on his face making her think of how he must have looked on the beach in Fiji.

But it would be a mistake to think Jordan was just a relaxed sailor. He seemed to care intensely about a great many things. He also worked hard on his columns and from what he'd said, usually had them written weeks in advance. So she didn't know what he'd been catching up on.

Perhaps he had remembered she'd been going into the office early to keep up with her work at the agency and had backed off to help out. On the other hand, maybe he just needed distance from her in order to come up with more questions and ways to be annoying.

Of course, he might be looking for a new challenge, either personal or professional. He was hardly the type to be content with sitting on his laurels. Success had come to him early and he wouldn't want to write an opinion column for the rest of his life without ever trying something new. While he hadn't wanted to write the *Post-Modern* articles, now he was fully engaged and he wasn't a man to do anything halfway. Considering the night they'd spent together, she could vouch for his determination. He was a generous lover and had made certain they were both thoroughly satisfied.

Nicole breathed carefully. Sex with Jordan wasn't something she should think about. It would be easier if it had just been about physical pleasure, but more was involved. She didn't discount the power of biology—there were few things more explosive—yet she was convinced it wasn't sex, or the lack of it, that left a person aching the most. Instead, it was the near misses on genuine love that haunted someone's soul.

The problem with love was the lack of power. You couldn't make someone love you, and you couldn't make yourself stop loving someone who didn't return your feelings. The result was heartache and endless regrets.

"Shut *up*," she ordered her brain.

She shouldn't be losing sleep over an impossible situation; after all, she was at the beginning of the adventure that she and her friends had been planning for over two years. They were building something solid, something which would allow them to take on new challenges.

When she got home, Nicole went inside to try a new recipe. But she only ate a small amount and stuck the leftovers in the refrigerator. Her appetite had also suffered during the past week.

The phone rang shortly before nine and the caller ID showed it was Jordan.

"Good evening," he said. "What are your plans for tomorrow afternoon?"

She drew a deep breath. "I have stuff to do in the yard that I've been putting off."

"No yard service?"

"I want to take care of this section of the garden myself."

"Mind if I come over and lend a hand? We could talk while working."

"More interview questions, I suppose."

"Right. If tomorrow isn't good, I'm happy to wait."

His voice was casually friendly, with no hint of anything except professional courtesy.

"Tomorrow afternoon is fine," Nicole answered, resigned. After all, she couldn't refuse to finish the interviews; she was a business professional, not a histrionic teenager. She'd just have to suck it up and do her job.

JORDAN DISCONNECTED, PLEASED that Nicole had agreed. He'd never done yard work. When he'd been a kid, his mother had insisted upon having a yard service, and he'd lived in apartments or

condos once he was on his own. But how complicated could it be? Moreover, gardening seemed to
fit what he'd learned about Nicole. She wanted to
grow flowers, not have it done for her. She also
wanted to earn a living and help people succeed
along the way. Meeting a challenge was part of it,
along with being able to do something that used
her abilities, not just her appearance.

Resignation went through him. He had definitely surrendered his suspicions about Nicole's
motives.

What had Nicole said…that she had an obligation to share her good fortune? At the time he'd
filed it in his mental skepticism drawer. Not that
he objected to the idea, but when other people had
said something similar, he'd figured there was a
better than even chance they were just putting on
an act. Perhaps some of them were just pretending to be altruistic; perhaps others felt the same
way about *his* character. Skepticism could give
birth to skepticism.

It was a sobering thought.

He received a fair amount of mail about his
column, and a percentage of the letters were
from annoyed readers asking what gave him the
right to comment on other people's choices. He'd
dismissed them, knowing if he started second-
guessing his work he would crash and burn as
an op-ed writer. Besides, he figured his job was
to both entertain people and make them think.

Yet the authors of those angry letters didn't see it that way. They called him a judgmental jackass, often using much stronger language. Now Jordan wondered if he'd bought too far into the concept that being controversial increased readership. It *did*, of course. If he said something outrageous about marriage or politics, body image, or even about a movie, it got attention. After all, however outraged some of those people might be, they were still reading his column.

But if he wanted people to think, maybe he shouldn't make them so angry that they barricaded themselves inside their ideological positions without questioning why they held those beliefs in the first place.

It was something to consider.

ON TUESDAY EVENING Barton knocked on Chelsea's door and gripped the package he held harder than necessary. The delivery person had asked him to sign for the parcel and Barton had instantly begun steaming about the implications. It was from Ron Swanson, postmarked *after* Chelsea had ordered the guy to leave her alone.

The door opened and he saw Chelsea still in her work clothes. "Hi, Barton."

"I signed for this and told the delivery guy I'd bring it over," he explained.

"Oh." She looked at the return address and frowned. "My neighbor down south thought Ron was wonderful. Turns out she gave him all my contact info."

"Give me the creep's phone number and *I'll* call him." The words came out more forcefully than they should have. Chelsea bit her lip and Barton kicked himself. "I shouldn't have said that," he added quickly. "I just hate that he's still bothering you."

"Ron is my problem. I need to be the one who deals with him."

"There's nothing wrong with someone helping out."

Her lips trembled then firmed. "No, Barton. This is something I have to handle. It isn't your problem."

"Except that you're my neighbor and my friend. Surely it's okay for me to lend a hand."

"No."

"Why not?" he asked.

"Because it isn't the first time I've screwed up this way," Chelsea hissed, "and I have to find a way to finish it, for my own self-respect."

Barton stirred restlessly. To him it was natural to want to protect someone he cared about, so when she'd refused his help, it had felt as if she was rejecting him. Obviously it had nothing to do with that.

"Can we talk about it?" he asked finally.

Shrugging tiredly, she stood aside to let him into the apartment. When she sank onto the couch, he wanted to sit and hold her close. Instead he chose a nearby chair. She clearly wasn't thrilled to discuss the matter, and he felt a moment's uncertainty whether he should be pushing. Still, they had to talk if they were ever to get anywhere.

With the thought, a wry recognition went through Barton. Once again he was considering the possibilities of a relationship.

"I'd like to understand," he said.

Chelsea drew a deep breath and let it out again. "I told you my childhood was rotten before my folks got divorced. What I didn't say was that they abused each other. They argued constantly and sometimes their fights got violent. As if that wasn't enough, they both cheated constantly and it seemed as if they couldn't wait to boast about it during their battles."

Nausea twisted Barton's stomach.

"That must have been rough on you," he said, trying not to sound as appalled as he felt.

"It might have been better if I'd been more like Terri and Jordan. They got angry and defiant. Instead I was scared all the time. And it seems as if I attract guys who continue to make me feel that way."

Barton shook his head. "The wrong guys look for someone too sweet and kind to see what creeps they are. Don't blame yourself for their inadequacies."

A smile flashed like sunshine on her face.

Then she sobered again. "But do you understand? I mean, that I really need to stand up for myself?"

He *did* understand and respected the effort she was making to reclaim authority over her life. "Yes, but it won't be easy for me," he admitted. "My instincts are to help and protect the people I care about."

She blinked. "I... I care about you, too, but that doesn't change what I need to do for myself."

Barton took her hand. "I don't know where we're headed," he said in a low voice. He could feel her trembling.

"Do you want to head somewhere?"

"I think it would be nice, though I haven't been sure either one of us are ready."

"It hasn't been that long since I broke up with Ron, so it seems too soon. Only the thing is, I... I really like you." Her chin firmed. "But that doesn't change anything about me needing to be able to stand on my own two feet." She frowned. "And no matter where we end up, shouldn't there be a balance between caring and independence?"

Balance.

Not going overboard.

Keeping a perspective.

Great qualities if someone could manage them.

"I wonder if balance is something we may have to help each other with, or at least you might need to nudge me," Barton admitted. "It could even rouse a few arguments. But that's okay, isn't it?"

he rushed to ask when he saw alarm in her eyes. "I know disagreements must seem totally negative to you, but I don't want us to be afraid to say what we think. Isn't it more about *how* two people disagree?"

Chelsea's face turned thoughtful. "That's a good point. It isn't realistic to think people will agree about everything. I've been telling myself not to be a doormat, but I wouldn't want anyone else to be one, either."

"Right."

Her smile blossomed again. "You know, I've got the ingredients in the fridge to make spaghetti. Shall I cook dinner?"

"Let's make it together," he suggested.

"That sounds great."

JORDAN DROVE TO Nicole's house on Thursday afternoon. It would be the first time they'd seen each other since he'd gone over to help with her yard the previous weekend.

Not the best memory.

Upon his arrival he'd discovered she wasn't plucking a few errant weeds from her flowerbeds or planting flowers—she was prepping soil for a vegetable garden on the back end of her double lot. She'd even shown him a hand-drawn map of where she was going to plant more fruit trees—her favorite varieties of apple, plum, apricot and cherry.

So he'd blown it yet again by retreating to his old prejudices about the things that tied someone down. A landscaped yard that could be maintained by a gardening service was one thing, but a giant vegetable patch needing personal attention was an entirely different prospect.

Since then he'd been thinking over what Nicole had said about being able to pick your own cherry tomatoes for a salad or gather fresh basil for a batch of pesto. She'd even pointed out that gardening was similar to writing—you started with a seed of an idea and encouraged it to grow.

Yet ultimately, the real problem was the way she scared the hell out of him.

On one side of the equation, Jordan had everything he'd ever wanted. Nicole was on the other side…a side that was starting to make his single, carefree life look empty. But she'd clearly stated that she didn't expect to get married, and even if she did, why would she consider *him*? Jordan had spent so many years shunning commitment that he'd never wondered whether he would, in fact, be a desirable husband.

Too restless to do anything else, he'd finally gone to Moonlight Ventures to apologize, only to learn she wasn't there. Apparently Adam Wilding had flown in unexpectedly and encouraged Nicole to take the day for herself.

Ringing the bell at the house didn't get an answer, so Jordan dialed Nicole's cell.

"Yes?" Her voice was breathless.

"It's Jordan. Are you home? I'm at your front door."

"I'm still digging, getting ready to start more planting."

"I hoped that was what you'd be doing. You've gotten me interested in seeing how everything will grow."

"Really? I seem to remember you claiming it was pointless to raise my own veggies when I could easily buy them."

Jordan winced.

"I've come around to your way of thinking," he said firmly. "I even brought a peace offering."

The door opened and Nicole stood there wearing shorts and a T-shirt, her forehead damp with perspiration. The day abruptly got much warmer. He turned off his cell phone and dropped it in a pocket, trying to keep his body from reacting.

She cocked her head. "What's the peace offering?"

"You mentioned wanting to plant another apple tree, so I got one." Jordan pointed to his small sports car. The top was down and the vehicle seemed dwarfed by the tree slanting over the passenger area. The root ball, a term he'd learned at the nursery, was on the floor of the car, while the top branches extended past the miniscule trunk.

"What kind of apple?" Nicole asked.

"Fuji. You said you needed a second one for pollination."

"Okay, bring it out."

Turning, she walked toward the back of the house, Toby tagging along, and Jordan was treated to another delicious view of her curves.

Putting a firm grip on his libido, he got the tree and went around by the side gate. It was awkward and heavy and he was breathing hard by the time he'd reached the large section of the property fenced off for a vegetable plot. Nicole eyed the space along the side, then grabbed a shovel and started digging.

"I'll do that," he offered.

"You came to work? I thought you were just bringing a peace offering."

"As it turns out, I enjoyed myself the other day."

Nicole's expression was skeptical. "I also thought you avoided hearth and home activities."

"It may take me a while to admit it, but I'm capable of, uh, appreciating new experiences."

He'd almost said he could change and had made a fast substitution.

"Anyhow," he said to distract himself, "the manager at the nursery said to dig a hole twice as wide and deep as the root ball. The idea is to loosen up the soil so the roots can expand quickly and provide stability for the tree. That's a whole lot of digging. At the very least we can take turns." He fished out the sheet of paper he'd been given with instructions on proper planting. Nicole took the paper to read, while he snagged the shovel.

Toby wisely stayed several feet away, but he seemed fascinated by the activity.

"Why did you get such a big tree?" Nicole asked at length. "I was just thinking about getting a little one."

"This one might start producing fruit faster. The nursery says they have a service where they'll come out and plant them, but I figured you'd want to do it instead."

It took a while, but once the hole was deep and wide enough, Jordan lifted the tree out of the container, shook it to loosen the roots, and held it straight while Nicole pushed the dirt in.

"There, that's good," she said finally.

Jordan wiped his forehead. "You mentioned plums, apricots and cherries. Are there any special varieties you want?"

"I have to research which ones grow best up here. I'd also love citrus, but I don't think they'd work in the Northwest without a greenhouse."

He mentally measured the area. "You have room for one with this huge lot. You know, most people who buy something this large are thinking about family space," he said, picking his words carefully.

Nicole raised an eyebrow. "I suppose it seems strange to a guy with a one-bedroom condo."

"How do you know the size of my place?"

"Chelsea mentioned it."

"Well, it doesn't make sense to have something larger with all the traveling I do."

It was true, but Jordan had also seen his condo as a message to the women he dated—evidence of his disinterest in starting a family. It was the same with his two-seater sports car—definitely *not* a family vehicle. Now both seemed a hollow gesture.

"I suppose."

Nicole turned on the hose and gave Toby a drink before watering the new tree. It gave Jordan a strange sensation to watch her. Nurturing wasn't a word he would have associated with a supermodel famous for wearing the hottest clothes in high fashion. Yet despite Nicole's ability to look sensational in the simplest of outfits, she was a caring person.

Jordan sighed, thinking about all the stupid things he'd said since they day they'd met again. He'd dug a deep hole for himself, and not just in the ground.

Now he'd have to discover if he could climb out—and once he did, what he wanted to do.

CHELSEA SMILED AS Adam Wilding came into the reception area. When she first met him, she'd been dazzled by his good looks. Now she was able to see Adam as a nice boss who fit in well with Nicole and Rachel. The only partner she hadn't met was Logan, but she wasn't nervous about him any longer.

"It was a lucky day for us when you came looking for your brother," Adam said, handing her a stack of paperwork.

"Thanks, I feel lucky to work here."

"In three weeks I'll be at the agency full-time. The Realtor gave me the keys to my new loft this week."

The door chimed and a young man came inside. "I'm Drew Goldstein. I, um, have an appointment."

"Please come to my office," Adam invited. "I know you expected to see Nicole George today, but I'm one of her partners. She's out, so we'll be talking."

To Drew's credit, he didn't look disappointed that he wouldn't be meeting one of the hottest women to ever grace a magazine cover.

Chelsea went through the reports. She'd set up a computer program to track information on clients so they'd have a quick reference. She swiftly entered the data and after a while, realized she was smiling for no special reason.

Being happy was a new experience for her, but she was beginning to think it was a possibility, and not just on the job. Barton actually discussed things with her…significant things like feelings, choices and values. Most important, he was willing to consider how their behavior affected each other. The night before they'd kept talking while fixing dinner, and then long into the night. It amazed her that he was willing to set limits and make adjustments. Maybe it wasn't that unique, but she'd never seen it before in a guy who was interested in her.

The way Barton was acting also made her think a future with him might actually be possible. On the other hand, they'd agreed neither of them were quite ready, even though he'd confessed that his own feelings were becoming more serious.

It worried her to think that by taking her time she could miss out on something special. But Barton insisted he was okay with going slowly, that he wanted them both to be sure.

Poor guy. He'd told her more about his marriage and how he still blamed himself for its failure, since the biggest problem had been Ellyn's inability to adjust to his career change.

But Chelsea didn't know what else Barton could have done. He'd hated being a stockbroker as much as Ellyn had hated being married to a teacher who didn't have a stockbroker's income. And he wanted kids, while she'd been opposed to having a family. Perhaps if they'd spent more time getting to know each other before marriage, they would have discovered how different their interests were.

"I rushed things," Barton had said. "So you see, taking our time works well for me, too."

In a way it remained hard for Chelsea to believe him. She supposed that was another thing she'd have to work on, learning to trust him and her own perceptions about the kind of man he was.

Still, hope kept springing up and making her happier. Maybe she should just be grateful.

NICOLE WAS SURPRISED when Jordan stayed and kept working with her in the garden. If it had been another guy she might have been annoyed, and part of her *was* frustrated. What was he doing, hanging around and making it ever more difficult for her to stop having romantic daydreams?

Seriously, what kind of idiot was she to picture a little girl with Jordan's dark hair trotting alongside the wheelbarrow as he pushed it? Or a boy with golden curls, climbing the apple tree as it grew?

Over and over she reminded herself that Jordan wasn't prime family material to start with. His only preparation for a relationship was arguments, infidelity and domestic violence. His early aversion to marriage was probably based on those negative experiences. Then he'd discovered that being single gave him the life he wanted. So why shouldn't he be happy in it? Why would she want him to change that decision and take the chance of making him *un*happy?

"How many peas are we going to plant?" he asked, crouching along a furrow and poking a seed into the soil.

We.

Why did he have to use words like that?

"The whole row," she answered, amazed her words came out so evenly. "I've got stakes and strings for them to climb up."

He nodded and kept planting, carefully inserting the seeds in the way the seed packet had recommended.

Okay, she needed to be fair. She'd already realized that Jordan didn't do anything halfway. So if he made a real commitment, she found it difficult to believe he'd resort to the lifestyle his parents had practiced.

Yet as she watched him dig up a pea and replant it, she wondered about how badly he needed things to be perfect and orderly. Every marriage had problems. Each relationship hit rocky sections. You woke up in the morning and it wasn't a supermodel or a handsome prince you were married to, but a real person. Because of the rotten example of marriage Jordan had seen as a kid, he might find it harder than the average person to deal with problems. Perhaps he'd always worry that things would slide into chaos.

"You look as if you're carrying the weight of the world on your shoulders," he commented as he helped stretch strings from one stake to another.

"I'm just dwelling on life and decisions."

"Anything that could shed light on the articles?"

She was glad he'd attributed her comment to something less personal than matters of the heart. They'd been talking for hours and he finally seemed satisfied with the material he had for *PostModern*, but he was probably open to new insights.

"Not especially. It isn't that unusual to change careers. Don't statistics show that most people won't retire from the first job they get?" she asked lightly.

"Absolutely. I think that's why articles like this are important to *PostModern*'s readers. Many of them will face similar decisions, so reading how another person did it could be enlightening."

"Are you going to include a comment about that in the articles?" Nicole asked.

"How do you mean?"

"It would be easy for some people to see a feature about a well-known model as just hype to sell more copies."

Jordan nodded. "Good point, especially since I know that isn't why Syd wanted a story about you."

"Then why did she?"

"She thought your transition from being in front of the camera to behind the scenes would be interesting. But she also said that your choice involved giving up the kinds of things that some people badly want—money and fame. It adds a different dimension."

Nicole couldn't help wondering how he planned to characterize her choices. With any other reporter, she wouldn't care, since she'd learned long ago not to base her life on other people's opinions.

If only she hadn't fallen in love…

With a painful pressure in her chest, she acknowledged the truth. She *had* fallen for Jordan. It was stupid and she knew better. There was little chance he would ever want to stay in one place or get married, even if he loved her in return, which seemed unlikely.

Her romantic nature was warring with her good sense and it didn't matter which won the battle, she was going to be left hurting.

Still, when the afternoon drew to a close and Jordan suggested ordering a pizza, she didn't object, even though good sense argued hard for ending the evening.

The pizza that was delivered thirty minutes later included her favorite toppings—mushrooms, zucchini, artichoke hearts and onions. Jordan had obviously paid attention to her preferences, but that didn't necessarily mean anything. He had a good memory and whether it was for the purposes of seduction or getting a good interview, he knew how to create the right atmosphere.

Part of her hoped he might be angling for a night together. With the hard work in the garden, it wasn't unreasonable to consider a trip to the hot tub to ease aching muscles. And from there it was a short journey to her bed.

But he didn't get seductive. While they ate, he chatted in a casual manner.

"You mentioned writing a blog about being interviewed," he said. "Any progress on that?"

"I've made notes, but there hasn't been much time."

"It might have been interesting to do a daily blog. You know, what your thoughts were, how you saw the questions, the challenges, though I'm sure the magazine would have wanted you to wait to post anything until after the article was published."

"You weren't thrilled when I mentioned the blog."

"I'm getting accustomed to the idea. I told Syd about it the other day and she thought it could be an intriguing counterpoint to the article."

"I've been afraid it would come off too much as a 'dear diary' thing."

She'd actually written every day in her journal, but a great deal of it—especially since they'd slept together—wasn't for public consumption.

"Isn't that what blogs are?"

"No need for another one, then," she said lightly.

They were sitting on the deck, the early evening sunlight glinting across the yard. Despite the pull of desire, what tugged on her most was the thought of eating with a man who wanted nothing more out of life than to come home and have dinner with his wife and family. Once that was something she'd dreamed of having. Then she'd given up the idea, so why did she keep thinking about it? How could hope be that persistent, and foolish?

Because while Jordan might find pleasure in planting a garden, it was only the first step. Weeds would come up. Bugs would nibble on the leaves. Sometimes plants didn't yield a crop. That was reality.

She had to stop being an idiot.

CHAPTER SEVENTEEN

JORDAN COULDN'T READ Nicole's mood. She'd worked hard throughout the afternoon, exuding the sexy energy for which she was known. At the same time she had chatted pleasantly, and now sat at the deck table with her customary grace. Toby lay with his head against her ankle, sound asleep.

After dinner she made coffee and Jordan lingered, wishing he could stay. But it wasn't just about sex. Everything felt more vital around Nicole. She had a sharp mind with broad interests that made her a dynamic conversationalist. Yet from various things she'd said, he suspected many men had only been interested in her surface beauty.

His mind drifted back to their high school years…and Lissa Anderson's birthday bash. It had been talked about as the party of the year, which was what Lissa had wanted. Well, party of the year until the police had arrived.

"No matter how hard I try," he said idly, "I can't remember kissing you at Lissa's party. Of course, I really don't remember much from that night, period."

Nicole looked amused. "I'm not surprised. I went to Hawaii the next day for a modeling gig. When I got back, I realized you didn't have a clue."

"Sorry."

"Hardly the crime of the century, though for your sake I'm glad you didn't keep drinking that much."

He shuddered. "Amen to that. Getting so drunk I can't remember what happened? That was the first and last time."

"As far as you know."

Her sly smile made him chuckle. "Let's just say it's a memory I regret not having."

Nicole shook her head, still smiling. "Don't be ridiculous. Even if it hadn't been after our folks ended their friendship, wouldn't you have found it hard to handle the knowledge that you'd kissed someone you disliked so much?"

Okay, she had a point. At the time he would have been upset and angry and probably would have taken his feelings out on her even more. So it was a good thing he hadn't remembered.

"No answer?" she prompted.

"You're absolutely right. I wouldn't have appreciated it at all and likely would have reacted badly, so it's just as well. But having had a similar kiss as an adult, I can look back on my teenage self and know I missed out on pure gold."

"Oh."

"I mean it."

"In that case, thank you."

He stood, taking her hand and drawing her up with him.

"How about letting me catch up on memories, since you're one ahead of me?" Dropping his head, he laid a layer of small kisses down the angle of her cheekbone. "Mmmm."

Her breath was coming raggedly as he pressed his lips against hers. It felt as if the energy from a locomotive was whizzing through his veins. Their mouths opened and he dipped his tongue between her teeth to stroke hers. Her breasts were pressed against his chest, and he wanted to see them again so badly he could believe that it was possible for men to die from pure, unanswered need.

But he could also feel the slight resistance from Nicole, so he forced himself to loosen his grip and step backward.

"Thanks," he murmured. "I was feeling deprived."

"But unless I develop amnesia," she answered breathlessly, "you still finish one behind in the memory department."

He stared a moment before grinning, his chest shaking with a silent laugh.

"You love confounding people, don't you?"

"When it seems appropriate."

The moment was gone and he regretfully

headed for the front door, with her accompanying him through the house. Toby yipped and galloped beside them, pawing at Jordan's jeans in farewell.

"Goodbye, little man," he said, bending to fondle the beagle's silky ears.

"Thanks for the help on the garden," Nicole told him. "Also for the apple tree."

He caught himself from saying the words that occurred to him—that he hoped to share the apples with her someday. Saying that would have implied they would actually be spending time together in the future. Of course, he didn't know how many years it took an apple tree to produce fruit, but it wasn't about a specific number of years. Nicole wasn't the sort of woman who would accept a limited commitment. She deserved someone who saw forever as the only possibility.

The question remained whether he wanted forever with Nicole. Well, that wasn't the whole question, because there was no guarantee she wanted *anything* from him, much less forever.

BARTON WAITED AT the foot of the stairs leading to the garage apartment. After a few minutes, Chelsea's door opened. He watched as she locked it and started down. They'd gotten in the habit of taking a walk together every evening.

"Have a good day?" he asked.

"Great. I'm glad I got the job when I did, though. Once Adam is here full-time, I suspect things will be even busier on my end. This way I can get comfortable at the agency first."

"Will it be possible for one person to keep up once all of the partners are there?"

Chelsea had explained enough of the agency's future plans for him to be familiar with what was happening.

"We'll see," she said with a shrug. "Nicole says I'll have an assistant if the workload gets too heavy and that they'll also hire a receptionist, if needed."

"So they don't expect you to perform miracles."

"No. It's a terrific place to work."

"How are the nerves going when the pushy folks come around?" Barton asked.

"Better, but I'll always dislike that part of the job."

"A few people thrive on confrontation, though I doubt it's something that most of us enjoy. I'm guessing your sister is a fighter, but I'm not sure you'd want to be like her."

That made Chelsea smile. "You're right. Terri is a nice person beneath her aggressive surface, but I've often wondered how happy she is. Still, I'd like a *little* more gumption to keep me from dissolving into melted chocolate when the tough customers come through the door."

If he'd been a suave Casanova kind of guy, Barton would have followed up on the chocolate remark, maybe asking if he could taste it, or something of the sort. But they'd agreed to take things slowly. Chelsea needed space to continue figuring herself out as an individual. Besides, he would never be suave.

"I think you'll keep developing your own brand of strength, without needing someone else's."

She grinned. "That's a nice way of putting it. I'll bet the kids in your class love it when you help them understand that being themselves is best."

"Hey, you're not one of my students," he protested. It was the *last* way he wanted her to see their relationship.

"If I was, then I would have had, like, the *worst* crush on you." She was biting her lip and he wanted to slug the people who had shaken the confidence she should have had in herself.

"Ah, gee," he said, trying for a boyish tone. "That's, like, totally nice of you."

Her face relaxed into a more natural smile. "I was scared to admit it."

"Because you still want to take things slowly?"

"That, too, but I've also worried whether I have lousy judgment about men."

"Hmm. I'd like to say that you've simply had lousy luck until now, but that might sound egotistical of me."

She slipped her arm through his. "I'm sure I'm

right this time. I mean about you being one of the good guys."

"Thank you, and let me return the compliment, except with the gender altered."

As she walked closer in a sweetly intimate way, Barton knew how much things had changed in the past few weeks. Chelsea had helped him look at his marriage in a new way, seeing him and Ellyn as just two people whose goals had changed. It had felt quite freeing to let go of the guilt.

He *was* ready to get married again and was quite certain Chelsea was the right woman. But he was also willing to wait so she could be equally certain of herself and of them as a couple. Patience was something he'd have to work on, but he didn't doubt they'd end up together.

His foot-in-the-mouth cousin had claimed that Nicole moving next door made Barton the luckiest dog in the world. But Greg didn't know the best part had nothing to do with supermodels.

SITTING ON HER reclining deck chair, Nicole wasn't sure she'd made the right decision to send Jordan away. In fact, she wished she'd chosen something to regret in the morning.

He'd been testing the waters that evening, to see if she would be open to further intimacy. She wouldn't have needed to encourage him, just respond. Primal forces would have done the rest.

They could be in bed right now, enjoying what it meant to be male and female.

By some standards it would have been very romantic—lovers destined to never really be together. In college, taking an English literature course, she had been confounded by the medieval concept of great romance—that such lovers were necessarily ill-fated. Why had medieval writers been so addicted to unhappy endings? Maybe, in a strange way, it had been an attempt at realism. The world back then had been hard and difficult to survive. Unhappy or tragic endings may have been the norm, so they accepted it as a necessary component to romance. Maybe she should have remembered that when resisting Jordan earlier.

Though tired, she returned Toby's anxious display of affection. Already he seemed able to tune in to her emotions. As she patted him and rubbed his ears, she remembered her resolution that friendship was more satisfying than love. That was the reality in a world where guys said they loved her but only wanted the glitz and glamor of a supermodel. Their devotion had rapidly diminished, either under the scrutiny of cameras and reporters, or when her hair was tangled or her nose was red from having a cold…something that had particularly bothered her erstwhile fiancé.

Yet in reviewing the past, she knew she hadn't truly loved Paulo. It was fortunate, considering everything, but she wasn't going to be so lucky this time. She'd fallen for a man who wanted to stay single and carefree, both to achieve his ambitions and to safeguard against descending into the kind of hell he knew marriage could be. She could only blame herself for being the fool who'd fallen in love with him.

It was barely dark when she crawled into bed and lay cuddling with Toby.

"Thanks for being here, pal," she murmured into his ear. "You may not be the male I'd like to have with me at the moment, but I appreciate your faithfulness."

Toby gently licked her hand before falling asleep.

In the morning Nicole dressed and headed for the office early, with a determination to embrace the real world.

There was only one more appointment scheduled with Jordan, on Thursday morning. They were going to visit a set where a television ad was being filmed. Ordinarily she wouldn't have gone since it was with seasoned clients and a film crew with whom she was familiar. However, Jordan thought it would provide good photos for the *PostModern* articles. He claimed it would be more interesting to readers if they could identify a Seattle landmark, so she'd agreed to be at the site where the Space Needle could be caught in the background.

"Hi," she said, coming through the door.

"Good morning." Chelsea's voice was bright and relaxed.

"You seem to be in a good mood."

The new office manager's smile was shy, but it made her face glow.

"I am. Things are going really great."

"Terrific."

"And you?"

"Just fine." It was a lie, but she couldn't tell Jordan's sister the truth.

On Thursday Nicole felt like a model again as Jordan took picture after picture. There was little else for her to do, though the models and photographers seemed pleased to have her there.

"Enough?" she finally asked.

"Sure, but how about going up in the Space Needle?"

"Any particular reason?"

"More pictures. And besides, have you ever gone up? It's quite a view."

"No," she had to admit.

"Isn't it time you do? Come on, it won't take all day."

Her objection was less about seeing the sights and more about ending the session with him. There would possibly be a few follow-up visits or phone calls, but she longed to have space for her aching heart to heal, at least on the surface.

The plaza was busy, but when she headed toward a ticket booth, Jordan said he already had them.

"On the off chance you could go, I reserved a launch time, as they call it," he said. "To save time."

Before long they were viewing the Seattle area from the heights. Jordan snapped pictures as she concentrated on the beautiful vistas, trying to figure out where the agency and her house were located.

"Nicole, there's something—"

"He called you Nicole? I wondered... Nicole George," a voice interrupted. "That's who you are, right?"

There was an excited murmuring and a number of people converged around them. Nicole signed several autographs and three people wanted to take selfies with her. Jordan had immediately stepped back and was snapping more pictures. While tourists continued talking, she was aware that he was getting photo releases from the first group who had approached them.

"Thanks for the interest, folks," she finally said, edging away. "I hope you're enjoying yourselves."

Soon they were descending in the elevator.

Jordan said nothing as they walked back to where the car was parked.

"That's the first time we've been in such a public setting," he commented once they were on the road. "Does the excitement and selfie thing happen often?"

"All it takes is one person who recognizes me and then others get interested in someone they think might be a celebrity. But even when I was modeling full-time, it wasn't as if everyone knew who I was. It was more common when I was at a photo shoot. The activity alerted passersby that something might be going on."

"And I was taking lots of pictures up there."

"I suppose."

It was before the start of rush hour traffic, so they arrived back at the agency in good time.

"How about dinner this evening?" Jordan asked. "There's something I want to discuss."

"Sorry, on Thursday I always have a video conference with my colleagues." She would rather have met with him and gotten it done, but it wasn't easy rearranging the schedules of four people located in different corners of the world.

"How about Saturday night?"

She wondered what he was doing on Friday and felt an unreasonable stab of jealousy that it might be a date. Brother, had she lost her mind.

"That would be fine."

"Let's have dinner on the boat with a sail afterward. Would chicken piccata and pasta primavera suit you?"

She wanted to scream "No!" but nodded agreement. "Sure."

"Then I'll pick you up at four on Saturday afternoon. With any luck this great weather will hold out another few days."

Perhaps Jordan thought they could be friends… friends with possible benefits; if so, she'd have to disabuse him of the idea. It might work for some people, but she wasn't built that way.

JORDAN FOLLOWED NICOLE into Moonlight Ventures so he could say hello to his sister.

He waited while Chelsea finished a phone call.

In the short time since she'd come to Seattle, she had grown so much. The move had been good for her and he had Nicole to thank for a lot of that.

Suggesting dinner on the boat had been a spur-of-the-moment idea. It would be a private place to consider how to…uh…make a garden grow. The image made him smile since it held an unusual note of whimsy—nobody had ever called him a whimsical guy. Pragmatic, sardonic and hard-headed were the usual adjectives applied to him.

That night he lay awake until the sun began rising. He finally dropped off and woke after nine. The rest of the day and part of the night, he worked on the pieces for *PostModern*, emailing his first draft on Saturday morning. An hour later, Syd called.

"I knew you could do it," she said sounding smug. "This shows the complexity of modern life when things aren't always clear-cut."

He'd been frank about aspects of his history with Nicole and the challenge of being objective with his sister working for Moonlight Ventures. He hadn't mentioned spending a night with Nicole, and had only alluded to the tension between their families, leaving everyone's privacy intact. At the beginning he'd also planned to interview her partners, but had decided that since Nicole was largely running Moonlight Ventures by herself at the moment, the focus should stay on her.

"Syd, this is just a first draft," he cautioned. "There might be other developments."

"It hardly looks like a draft to me, but I know what a perfectionist you are. Anyhow, congratulations. I'm looking forward to seeing more than your short, snappy columns in the future."

"I've got a few ideas," he admitted.

"Good. Gotta go." Syd ended the call and he tossed the phone onto his couch.

Jordan glanced around his minimalist condo with dissatisfaction. He'd bought it six years ago and if he'd ever felt cramped, he'd just jetted off to another part of the world. When asked, he always said he was living the dream life.

Now the thought of making a garden thrive with Nicole seemed far more attractive.

He *wasn't* good husband material, something Nicole clearly knew. She'd even made a few ironic references to it.

But surely the kind of spouse he'd make was a

choice. He didn't have to repeat his parents' history. They'd been weak and had taken their problems out on each other. In high school he'd done the same thing in a way, making Nicole a target of his frustrations, but since then he'd tried to be a better man.

And Nicole wasn't weak, either. She'd taken responsibility for her life; she didn't whine about it or hold grudges. Instead, she had a generous, loving spirit. It awed him that she had let go of the negative parts of the past so effectively.

Restless, he decided to call his sister and ask if she'd like to have lunch with him.

"Hello?" she said, her voice sounding unusually high.

"Hey, sis, how about having lunch together?"

"I have already made plans. Barton and I are going on a hike."

"That's new, you going hiking."

"Isn't it great? I want to try camping, too, and sleeping under the stars and all sorts of things."

"You sound as if you've got a lot of adrenaline going."

"I just told Ron that if he didn't leave me alone I'd get a restraining order and make sure his boss heard about it. You've never heard a guy backpedal so fast. I think he may have been losing interest anyhow, but I was tired of it and decided this might work."

"It sounds as if you handled him efficiently."

Jordan felt like scum. Chelsea hadn't even told him that Ron was still bothering her.

"I guess so," she agreed. "Oooh, that's Barton at the door. Gotta run." Now she sounded happy and excited.

"Have a good hike."

"We will. Bye."

Jordan stared at the phone in bemusement. How had so many things changed in the past few weeks? Maybe it was just a season for change. If so, he was ready for it.

He glanced at the clock. It was ten, still six hours before he was supposed to arrive at Nicole's house. That felt like a lifetime…to find out if he had a real life ahead of him.

CHELSEA'S HEART WAS light as she opened the door for Barton, so light that she gave in to impulse and threw her arms around him.

"Whoa," he gasped.

She laughed.

"Not that I object," he added with a grin. "Is there a particular reason for so much exuberance?"

"I think I gave the final push to Ron today. If I'd thought of it earlier, you and I wouldn't have had that argument."

"But since that got us really talking, maybe it turned out better this way."

"Possibly." She snuggled against him. "I like the way this feels."

"Me, too."

His lips came closer. Barton's kisses were sweet and Chelsea felt a wild flutter inside. His hands were pretty good, too, as he explored her body. It felt wholesome and sexy and completely exciting.

After a few minutes, he drew back and his blue eyes shone warmly into hers. "In the interests of pacing ourselves, I'm going to suggest we get going on that hike."

"That's a good idea," she agreed. "But someday soon…?"

"That works just fine for me."

She sighed happily as she grabbed the new hiking pack she'd purchased that week. The direction she and Barton were headed was pretty terrific.

CHAPTER EIGHTEEN

NICOLE DRESSED FOR the afternoon in white shorts and a blue T-shirt, but assembled a tote bag with warmer clothes since she already knew evenings could be chilly in the Seattle area, no matter how warm the day had been.

Of course, she could just text Jordan to forget it. Or ask him to say straight out what he wanted without needing to eat dinner and take an evening sail. Logic suggested that he couldn't be expecting his "talk" to be upsetting or he wouldn't have proposed going for a sail after. Then again, some men didn't have a clue what could upset a woman. Not that she had to show it, no matter what he said. There had been plenty of times when she'd acted one way but had felt something completely different.

Through the curtains, she saw his car pull up the driveway. He was also dressed in shorts, his rugged vitality stirring the desire that simmered so close to the surface.

She brought her bag when she answered the door.

"Looks like you're all set."

"Offer me a sail on Lake Washington and I'm good to go."

The traffic cooperated and they got to the marina quickly. Not wanting to accidentally kick her purse overboard, Nicole took it down to the cabin. Her gaze lingered on the bunk. It was wide enough for two, if the two in question didn't mind being friendly with each other. Jordan had said he'd spent a few months living on *The Spirit* and she couldn't imagine anything more symbolic. That was the life he wanted, to sail free on the wings of the wind.

After dropping her purse and tote bag in a corner, Nicole climbed back up to the deck. A familiar figure was approaching along the dock, delivering a large bag and beaming as he saw the size of his tip.

The food was excellent, though she had little appetite. She ate enough to be sociable before sitting back to focus on where the city hugged the lakeshore. Sunlight poured across her legs and the water was an amazing blue.

The conversation remained casual, and after he'd eaten, Jordan tossed a large manila envelope in her direction.

"I wondered if you'd like to read my initial draft of the articles. There's a printout inside."

Slowly she pulled out the neat, double-spaced pages and began reading. The articles had Jordan's quick wit and sometimes sardonic point of view, but they also included a thoughtful examination of the differences between her two careers, the choice to become a talent agent, and the challenges that were part of it. He wrote honestly about his own difficulties in being objective, giving a sanitized version of their history and a brief mention of having a relative employed by Moonlight Ventures.

She kept her gaze on the printout for a while, pretending to be reading while she thought about the contents. Now she knew what Jordan had wanted to discuss with her and it was almost anticlimactic. There were no decisions to make or awkward conversations. This was a proper lead-up to a dignified goodbye. Tears threatened and she blinked them back before they fell. Not for nothing had she been a professional model.

"Finished?" Jordan asked finally. "Tell me what I got wrong."

"Nothing that I can see," Nicole assured. She grinned as if there was little else on her mind except teasing him. "It's possible that you aren't a born reporter after all. Imagine getting the facts straight."

"I'm not sure everything is accurate. In fact, I told Syd that there might be a few corrections or additions."

"Really? It looks complete to me. What part bothers you?"

"The section on being objective."

Thumbing back to that part, she skimmed through it again and shook her head. "You're vague about Chelsea's role, but I assumed it's to protect her privacy and rightfully so."

"No, that isn't the part that's bothering me."

"You don't want to be more explicit about our parents, I hope."

He shuddered visibly. "Not on your life."

"So what's the missing part?"

"The part that hasn't happened yet. It's the moment I suggest we get married and raise peas and cucumbers and kids together."

Blood rushed to Nicole's head while the air grew hard to drag into her lungs.

Finally she forced a smile. "I didn't know you had such a peculiar sense of humor."

"I'm not joking." His face appeared utterly serious.

"That's difficult to believe. An old dog doesn't learn new tricks and a leopard can't change its spots...or something of the sort. You're a confirmed bachelor who loves a carefree life as a columnist. It lets you fly off for as long and as far as you fancy. I'm committed to my home, dog and business in Seattle. We're basically on separate freeways that cross but don't go to the same place."

"That's direct."

"There's no point in being anything else. Look, Jordan, you've got great accomplishments in front of you. I'm sure there's a Pulitzer in your future or something equally splendid. You need to be happy and fulfilled, not tied down and constricted."

JORDAN WATCHED AS Nicole dissected the situation as calmly and rationally as she might evaluate a recipe. There was a time he would have believed she was indifferent to what she was saying, but he saw a hint of emotion in her eyes that suggested something deeper.

Then another realization struck home. She hadn't said she loved him, but all her arguments against marriage had to do with what she believed was best for *him*. Was she being the talent agent now, working to help someone else succeed? Or was she trying to give up something she wanted for someone she loved?

Then it struck Jordan…he'd failed to say the most important part.

"By the way, there are a few words I left out of my earlier pitch. I love you, Nicole."

The emotion in her eyes was now unmistakable, yet she still shrugged casually.

"Most guys lead with that," she agreed.

"So I'm an original. How about you? Do you have any crazy warm feelings going in my direction?"

She moved restlessly. "What I feel isn't important."

"It's important to me."

Jumping up, she went to lean against the mast and gaze across the water. Her face wasn't serene any longer. He stood and slipped his arm around her waist...and felt the trembling in her slender figure.

"I didn't expect to fall in love with you," he said with quiet intensity. "I can't even pretend it's what I wanted. If someone had asked me a month ago if it was possible or desirable, I would have said they were crazy. You're right that I had my life mapped out as a bachelor, free to stay or go as I wish. But then I fell in love and now that seems less and less meaningful."

"That's an odd way of phrasing it."

"It's just the truth. And I imagine many guys have said the same, made lots of fancy speeches. Have you ever loved any of the men who gave them to you?"

"Nothing that turned out to be real."

"Even with your fiancé?"

"I thought it was real at the time. Then I realized it was the glitz he wanted, not to wake up with the real me."

Jordan let out a painful breath, recalling Nicole's explanation about why she'd slipped out the morning after they'd been together.

"I want to wake up with you," he insisted. "I don't want to keep going the way I have. A vacation with my wife looks much more attractive than drifting into the future without being connected to anything genuine."

He tugged her closer.

"But it's nice the way you were trying to give me up for my sake."

Jerking away, Nicole turned to face him. "Excuse me?" she asked in an icy tone.

"Uh, for my writing and my happiness."

"Being snide about my so-called nobility isn't going to win you points."

"I deserve that, except I wasn't being snide. I'm truly grateful you're a generous, caring person, but right now I want you to be selfish. Please grab hold of me and never let go."

Nicole stuck her chin in the air. "I wasn't being unselfish, either. I'm simply aware that no one can be truly happy if they give up their dreams."

Hmmm. She was in an awfully prickly mood. Maybe she needed a distraction.

NICOLE'S HEAD SPUN as Jordan's mouth closed upon hers. Giving up the struggle, she slid her arms around his waist and explored his lean muscles. When his hands surrounded the curve of her buttocks and gently squeezed, the pleasure was intense.

A wolf whistle and shout of "Go, man!" intruded into her consciousness. Jordan must have been aware of it also, because his movements changed and softened. He held her no less snugly, but now his embrace seemed tender and protective.

"You realize," she said, "that someone could have taken a picture of us and be planning to sell it to a newspaper or magazine. Even if they just posted it to their Facebook page, your editor could see it."

"That wouldn't bother me," he answered promptly. "In fact, I'm going to propose another article to Syd about how a man can look at dozens of pictures of a gorgeous woman and never feel attracted to her. Then he finds out that in person, she fires his body and imagination in a way he hadn't believed possible."

"Oh?" Her chest was tight, breaths shallow.

"Right. Then he discovers she's just as beautiful on the inside—smart, logical, caring, hardworking, funny, strong and complex in ways he'll be happy exploring for a lifetime."

Jordan dropped his head for a long, sweet kiss.

"Maybe we…we should sit down," Nicole suggested. "You talked about going for a sail."

"I think we need to talk more first."

Her legs were wobbly, so she pulled free and dropped into her chair. Jordan sat close, his gaze fixed on her.

"I know we've been on separate paths," he said. "I know our lives don't look compatible and we'll have to make compromises. I still want to travel some of the time, but you've talked about wanting to travel more, too, once your partners are on board. We couldn't jet off to the Bahamas or something on a whim, but it's fun to plan ahead as well."

"Studies show anticipation is part of the pleasure," Nicole murmured, shocked that Jordan was talking about compromise.

"Exactly. Now, in some of your old interviews you talked about wanting kids. Do you still want them?"

"I...yes."

"Me, too."

"That's new."

He laughed, though with a sad air. "Since I didn't want to get married, having a family wasn't in the picture, either. But maybe I've also been afraid that I'd be a lousy dad. Now I've decided I don't have to repeat the past. I'm the one who decides what kind of husband and father I'll be. Besides, aren't children an adventure that never ends?"

Nicole grinned. "That's true, though there are dynamics I don't want to repeat from my own family."

"Such as the different ways your parents treated you and Emily?"

She nodded. "That's one of them."

Jordan made a face. "Me, either. We should talk about that as we go along, track each other, help each other be good parents. We can even talk to child psychologists for guidance if it seems advisable, though I'm sure we'll still make mistakes."

Nicole cocked her head. "I wonder if perfect parents make boring kids."

He chuckled. "I don't think we have to worry about boring children. We just have to hope that when we're old and gray they won't publish a memoir about our mistakes and that they'll visit with the grandkids. That's when we'll get really boring, except I'll still be chasing you around, leaning on my walker as you hobble away on your bad knee."

It was a strangely sweet image.

But mostly it was bizarre to be talking about this with Jordan. No matter how much she loved him, it hadn't seemed possible that he'd want any of it. Her abortive engagement had been the final straw, the wound convincing her that when it came to romance, she'd always be nothing more than a shallow cover girl to the men she met.

THE UNCERTAINTY ON Nicole's face made Jordan ache. She had no particular reason to trust him. After all, his plan for permanent bachelorhood was common knowledge; he had only himself to thank for that since he'd put it into his column on a regular basis.

Would she reject him? She'd implied she had

feelings for him but hadn't actually said the words outright.

"You realize that it's okay to show if you're upset or sad, angry or whatever," he said, trying not to sound desperate. "I've seen how you try to keep what you're feeling inside, maybe because you always had to project a certain facade as a model."

"After a lifetime of practice, I'm not sure I can change that much."

"Then I'll have to look for subtle signs and hope you have mercy on me when I guess wrong. But I also need to be clear about something. I fell in love with the real Nicole, not the image on a magazine cover. I fell for the woman digging in her garden with dirt and perspiration on her face. I'm crazy about the person who determinedly painted her living and dining rooms, even though she could have hired someone else to do it for her. I get choked up when I think about how much you hate turning someone down who needs encouragement."

She was silent, staring away from him, across the water. With all his might he wanted to grab her and hold her and never let go. But he couldn't get what he hoped for that way. It had to be a gift.

"So, can you love me back, Nicole? With all *my* faults and missteps? God knows, I'm a long way from perfect."

"Yes," she said softly.

NICOLE FELT AS if she'd thrown everything she had into the pot. If this fell apart, she'd find out if hearts really could break.

"I love you more than life," Jordan promised and she didn't doubt he was telling the truth. "Will you marry me? Will you love me through mistakes and dirty diapers and the kids squabbling? Will you love me when I can't sail this boat any longer because arthritis won't let me hold the tiller? Will you still love me when our hair is gray and we're waiting at the hospital for news that might mean a daunting challenge for us both?"

"Those things don't frighten me. Well, not much." It was mostly the thought of facing them alone that made Nicole shiver.

He smiled. "We'd be idiots if it wasn't scary. And foolish, too, to think it'll be easy. There's a reason that wedding vows include a promise to be there in sickness and in health, for better and for worse."

"As you said, there aren't any guarantees."

"But it helps when two people love each other and share the load."

The evening breeze blew from behind her, as if pushing in Jordan's direction. Silly, since it could also be seen as pushing him away. The thing that would bring and keep bringing them together was what Jordan was offering—love and genuine commitment.

And it was what she'd always wanted.

Nicole put her arms around Jordan's neck. "I'll love you forever," she promised with all her heart.

EPILOGUE

JORDAN DROPPED ONTO the grass next to Nicole and she leaned against him.

Rose, their daughter, grasped a low branch of the larger apple tree as she pulled off a piece of fruit and handed it to her cousin. Then she grabbed one for herself and plonked onto the ground.

"Told you I could do it," she announced smugly, her dark eyes gleaming in triumph.

Scott, who was Barton and Chelsea's oldest *and* a few months older than Rose, was a little disgruntled.

"Mom says boys don't grow as fast as girls," he grumbled. "That isn't fair."

Jordan chuckled and felt Nicole's body shake with suppressed laughter.

Having Chelsea and Barton as next-door neighbors meant less privacy, but their kids were growing up more like siblings than cousins.

Jordan eyed his own son. Blond and determined, even as a toddler, Jeremy was making strides in digging a hole for the new cherry tree he wanted.

Nicole grinned at Jordan. "Never underestimate a kid with the Masters stubbornness."

"Yeah, mix it with George genes for planning and we'll have cherry pie in a few years."

Breathing deeply, he savored the scent from their yard. Chicken was on the grill and fruit was ripening on the tree. They still hadn't caught up with yard work after spending ten days in England, so a few tomatoes had dropped off the vines and split on the ground.

"Getting adjusted to being back in this time zone?" Barton asked. Chelsea lay on a blanket nearby, drowsing next to their baby daughter, Evelyn.

"Slowly," Jordan answered. "It was a great trip, but it's good to be home again."

Chelsea and Barton had kept all the kids while he and Nicole were away, something Nicole claimed was heroic, considering Evelyn was only two months old.

Jordan sometimes wondered why he'd ever thought the single life was so wonderful. Married life had its challenges, but he was happier than he'd ever been. He and Nicole were even discussing the possibility of having a third child.

Toby suddenly dashed through the yard, scrambling over their legs as Spike chased him.

"Spike, how did you get out again?" Barton roared.

Chelsea giggled drowsily. "How do you think?"

Jordan tried to look stern as he eyed his daughter, the usual suspect when it came to Spike getting out. "Rose?"

She smiled back innocently. "But, Daddy, Spike and Toby like playing together."

"I have a feeling we're going to have trouble with her in the future," Nicole murmured.

"You think?" he asked in a dry tone.

Yeah, they were going to have trouble. But they'd face it together and that was as good a future as he could possibly want.

* * * * *

If you enjoyed this story, check out Callie Endicott's earlier books in the MONTANA SKIES miniseries, KAYLA'S COWBOY, AT WILD ROSE COTTAGE and THE RANCHER'S PROSPECT.

And look for more EMERALD CITY STORIES later in 2018!

Get 2 Free Books,

Plus 2 Free Gifts—

just for trying the Reader Service!

♦ HARLEQUIN®
SPECIAL EDITION

Get 2 Free Books,
Plus <u>2</u> Free Gifts—
just for trying the Reader Service!

HRLP17R3

Get 2 Free Books,
Plus 2 Free Gifts—
just for trying the Reader Service!